No One Is Leaving

STEPHEN BARNARD

No One Is Leaving

Copyright © 2023 Stephen Barnard

All rights reserved.

ISBN: 9798865208549

Also by Stephen Barnard (Fiction):

Novels and Novellas
They Let Themselves In
21 Dares
House of Cawdor: The Bewitching of Macbeth
House of Elsinore: The Haunting of Hamlet
Something Close
The Deleted
Portentous 1: Brothers
Portentous 2: Ghosts
Portentous 3: Gods
Corner House

Short Story Collections
Requests From The Dead
Dark Detours
Bitterly
Frightful
Unlucky Numbers
A Very Bad Year

YA Fiction
Leave The Last Page (Stephen Barnard and Aidan Barnard)
Peter's Day
Lucy's Hour

By Stephen Barnard (Non-fiction):
Calamity Cricket: Tales of Ladybridge CC

PROLOGUE

Dining table guest list / invitation, designed by Justin Fisher:

The Post-Covid Ashlands Alumni and Arseholes Weekender
Hosted by Justin and Lucy Fisher @ Kilbride House, Argyll and Bute

Guests:
Justin Fisher
Lucy Fisher
Elliot Tilson
Danielle Tilson
Stephanie Perry
Nicholas Warner
Alicia Gray
Brooke Hughes
Hayley Powell
Benjamin Bălan
Kieran Mooney
Rhea Bennett

CHAPTER ONE

Fat flakes began to fall, causing mini-explosions on the windscreen and prompting the automatic wipers to whoosh. Elliot narrowed his eyes and gripped the wheel of the Dacia more tightly. 'How far away are we?'

Danni, tracking the journey on her phone beside him, checked the details. 'Thirty miles yet. We expected this though.' The forecast had promised snow all weekend.

'I know; I just hoped we'd beat it tonight.' They'd not long gone past Glasgow and were now on the A82, Loch Lomond somewhere on their right in the gloom. He estimated it might be another hour yet to the accommodation just beyond Dunans Castle. There was very little in the way of landmarks, and not so much as a village to aim for. When Justin had said he'd booked somewhere remote, he hadn't been lying. Elliot checked the clock on the dashboard: just after six. It was a Friday in late January and already dark. 'I'm not going to rush.'

'Didn't expect you to. You're doing great.'

'Good, at least.'

She smiled at that. It was a little routine they went through. She played her part and offered the next line. 'Adequate.'

He smirked, but kept his eyes on the road. 'Mediocre.'

'Satisfactory.'

'Average.'

'Stuck in the middle... with you.' It was cheesy, but it was there's. And Gerry Rafferty's.

She reached over and patted Elliot's leg. 'I'll WhatsApp Justin and give him an update.'

Justin Fisher was an old friend to both of them. They'd known him since school, some twenty-five-plus years ago when they all went to Ashlands High. They hadn't seen him since before the pandemic, a garden party during the summer of 2019. In fact, none of them had met up in the three and a half years since. That was why Justin had organised this weekend: the whole gang invited for a celebratory three-night stay at the start of the year in which they all turned forty.

It was just, unfortunately, a little bit out of the way. The wipers moved up to the next speed setting as the snow got a touch heavier.

'Justin says it's just started there. No one else has arrived yet. We're due to be the first ones.'

'Well, I hope they're not too far behind us. This could get treacherous. This road is alright, but…' He didn't have to comment any further: Danni knew how the minor roads and tracks were likely to be. There'd be no gritters or snow-ploughs. They were racing against the weather, albeit cautiously.

Elliot was a safe driver, as he was in most things, and she'd seen them all over the years. Career, money, parenting: Elliot displayed pragmatic caution always, counterbalancing perfectly with Danni's more impulsive nature. They had been childhood sweethearts but not together throughout all the time that followed; they had their difficulties during the university period and just beyond. This was mainly due to Danielle worrying about missing other experiences and wanting different types of relationships. She'd had two other serious boyfriends: one in her late teens and again in her earlier twenties. Men who were perhaps, on paper, more edgy and exciting than Elliot. Christian had been in an unruly rock band and smoked a lot of weed. Ryan worked in a bar and had a motorbike. They might have been thrilling times, but both relationships were done inside six months. And each time she found herself leaning back towards Elliot, first as a friend but then always slipping into his arms. She felt eternally lucky that no one else had snapped him up in that time. They got married at twenty-seven; at that age she was mature enough to know that he was the best thing to ever happen to her.

Stuck in the middle… with you.

'I'll get us there,' he said.

'I know,' she replied.

**

An hour later, with the snow now coating everything, Elliot turned the car carefully through the gates of Kilbride House. There was an extra crunch under the tyres as flattened track turned to packed gravel under the blanket of white. 'It looks quite grand,' Danni remarked. There was still a way to go on a long drive, but lights from the house in the distance gave a sense of its imposing size.

'Justin booked it: what did you expect?' Elliot grinned and the tension left his arms, his grip on the wheel a little less tight. They were virtually there after five hours on the road.

As they continued up the drive, the house came clearer into view through the consistent flurry of white. It didn't seem to be an old house but instead mimicked a style from some golden age of building; Elliot was no expert but he guessed at Georgian. It had three floors and was quite imposing; he imagined high ceilinged rooms within. One aspect at the front of the house had wall-to-wall glass doors – a modern addition that clashed with the overall style – and a couple of the bedrooms he could see had substantial balconies. The front steps and door were set to the left of the structure. It was something of a hybrid building.

Justin had turned a number of the house lights on, perhaps to act as a beacon, but this part of the drive was lit anyway with sturdy glowing orbs on plinths. To the left he saw a car pulled over and headed towards it, assuming it to be Justin's. That's when he noticed another building, flat roofed and one storey, clad in what might be oak or pine although it was hard to tell because the place wasn't lit. It was only the width of a path away from the main house but without light and the snow coming down heavier, it was hard to be accurate about it. It didn't have garage doors though, and it was too big for that anyway. He indicated it to Danni. 'What do you reckon?'

'Pretty sure Lucy told me there was an indoor gym. I'm guessing that's it.'

Elliot pulled over, next to the Bentley SUV. 'Jesus, don't scratch that getting out.'

Danni exercised caution, and when they were both standing, looking at each other over the roof of their considerably cheaper vehicle, they heard their names called.

Justin was on the steps leading up to the property; it was raised above the level of the driveway and had a short, sloping lawn to the right as they looked at it, leading up to the brick and glass. He waved enthusiastically. Lucy was a silhouette in the doorway behind him. 'The first of our intrepid explorers!' Justin called. 'Always a guarantee that the Tilsons will be on time!'

'Hey, Just!' returned Elliot, then aimed his next comment at Danni. 'Go on, you get in: I'll grab the case and supplies.'

She blew him a kiss over the roof and then trotted over to their friend. Elliot popped the boot and pulled out a midsized suitcase and a holdall that had some snacks and booze in. He locked up and followed.

Justin was already ushering Danni inside, out of the snow. She hugged Lucy on the threshold then stepped into the warmth. Then Justin trotted back and took the holdall from Elliot. It clinked in the transfer. 'I said you didn't need to!'

'Who turns up to a party empty handed? Good to see you.'

'And you. Come on: let's get you inside!'

Inside, in the first instance, was a wood panelled entrance hall. Danni was already shaking off the snow; Lucy helped her with her jacket. Elliot took in the two women: his wife a couple of inches taller, broader and a brunette, whereas Lucy Fisher was blonde and of petite build. There were similar contrasts to find between him and Justin. His friend was trim and athletic whereas Elliot had the makings of a middle-aged spread. However, his almost black hair was free from grey. Justin on the other hand had – over the last few years – developed a lightening at the temples which made him look like Reed Richards from the Fantastic Four comics. He was a dashing-looking fellow. Elliot felt under-dressed in his baggy sweater; Justin wore formal trousers and a well-fitted shirt.

'This place looks nice,' Elliot said, opting for that rather than complimenting his friend's appearance.

'Wait until you see the rest of it. Drop the case there; come on through.'

The main room was open plan, and very impressive. There was a huge living space towards the back of the house with four lengths of sofa sunken into a dip in the floor, a formidable looking glass coffee table in the middle of them. To the left of the sofas was a sideboard and a huge wall-mounted TV; to the right were two leather studded armchairs either side of an ornate fireplace. Currently the hearth was cold, the central heating doing the job, but there was chopped wood ready and some ornate irons in a rack; Elliot imagined they'd fire it up at some point over the weekend.

The dining area – nearest to the front of the house – had a long oak table with spectacular high-backed chairs. The kitchen, central, gleamed bright white, completely impractical but stunning nonetheless. A wall of cupboards and appliances and two separate islands. High stools lined one of them which doubled as a breakfast bar.

The floor to ceiling glass was on both aspects of the house; what Elliot had seen from the front had been the dining area, but there was a similarly impressive arrangement at the back near the sofas. He could just see the edges of a grand patio and long garden illuminated by the porch lights dancing off the falling snow.

'Justin,' Danni said, her tone accusatory but also playful. 'There's no way this place is only £200 a couple. Are you paying more than you should for your share?'

'Of course he is,' Lucy replied. 'You know how soft he gets when it comes to you guys.' Lucy had not been a school friend; she'd met Justin through work a dozen or so years ago. It had been more than just their businesses that merged. They'd been married ten years. The wedding was in the Cayman Islands; none of the old friends could afford the trip.

'Who's got Rosalind?' Danni asked. That was the Fishers' seven-year-old.

'The monster-in-law. Yours?'

'Snap,' Danni replied. That wasn't true but it was easier than explaining, and plus she knew that Lucy wouldn't really listen. The fact was the three kids were spread across three friend's houses, and Danni was anxious to get an update from them now they were in. However, Lucy was leading her to the kitchen.

'Come on: a drink is needed.'

'Honey, let them pick a bedroom first!' Justin was grinning. 'Some of the rooms are spectacular.' He held up a hand in apology. 'Forgive us, but we took the best one. Virtually the whole top floor of the house.'

'As you should,' Elliot replied. 'It's great that you've done this for us.'

'You can stop that right now; it was long overdue and I was happy to organise.'

'Who should be arriving next?' Elliot asked.

'A race between Alicia and Steff, I think. So go on: bag a bedroom before they get here!'

The staircase was back in the wood-panelled hall. Danni got her phone out as they went up, Elliot volunteering to grab the case again. 'There's no signal,' she said. 'I wanted to check on the kids.'

'Perhaps when the snow stops it'll be better.' On the wide landing were a number of doors, all slightly ajar, inviting them in. There was another staircase leading to the Fisher's suite. Justin had said there were five bedrooms on this level but only three had adjoining bathrooms. 'I don't mind which room, Danni – just pick one with an ensuite.'

She smiled at him. 'You don't want the second-best room, do you? Even though we got here second.'

She knew him too well. 'Let the others have the choice. Just get us one with a toilet for when I'm emptying my bladder of all the booze Just will make me drink.'

She settled for one that was neat and modern with a fully tiled wet-room, and with one of the balconies overlooking the forest to the side of the house. She left the one with the four-poster bed, the claw-footed tub and the wall mounted TV. She watched Elliot unzip the case. 'Have you checked your phone?'

'Same network as you. We'll ask the other two in a minute.' He pulled out some clothes and laid them in her direction. Together they unpacked, making a his and hers section of the wardrobe.

Back downstairs they asked about the phone reception.

'Oh, it's shocking,' Lucy said, 'but the Wi-Fi code is on the sideboard underneath the TV.' She pointed into the living room area. There was the router, blue light glowing, and a clear plastic stand displaying a sheet of information. 'WhatsApp works fine – as you know from all of Justin's navigational messages.'

'Great.' Danni went across to get the password: she had three children and their friends' parents to message. Carefully orchestrated sleepovers were the only way to secure weekend babysitting.

Justin sidled over to Elliot with a pair of crystal tumblers. Amber liquid swirled in both. 'Be rude not to, seeing as we're in Scotland.'

Elliot took one. They clinked. 'To a great weekend,' he said.

'I'll drink to that,' Justin said, and drained his scotch in one go.

Elliot was more circumspect and took a sip. The warmth was welcome, but he knew he couldn't rush the drink. It would only get an instant refill and it wasn't even eight o'clock yet.

He was looking forward to seeing his old friends again. Six couples under one roof: it was quite a feat Justin had pulled off. But then Elliot had a thought.

'Just?'

'Hmmm?'

'Is Hayley coming?'

'Yeah, although running the latest I think, according to the messages I'm getting. Hope she doesn't get stuck in this weather.'

Danni joined them. 'Has she had to pay the full amount or did you cut her a deal? I bet you've been over-generous again.'

'Didn't have to,' he replied, and went to get himself a top up.

Danni looked to him for an explanation, but Lucy provided it. 'She's bringing someone. A *man*. We're actually going to be all couples for once. No gooseberry lurking around the edges.'

'Lucy…' Justin muttered.

Danni frowned. 'She's with someone? She never said.' She suddenly felt terrible. Danni had been Hayley's best friend in school, perhaps even as adults too, but suddenly Danni realised she hadn't had proper contact with her in, what, a year? No: longer than that. *Christ*. 'Well, good for her.'

Elliot spoke over the rim of his glass. 'I guess we'll soon see, won't we?'

There was silence between them.

It meant they could hear the crunch of tyres outside.

CHAPTER TWO

Justin was the only one to go to the oak front door. He called back through the hallway. 'It's Alicia and Brooke!' The others hung back, propped up against a kitchen island, half-listening to the greetings and pleasantries behind the wall. Then he brought them through and everyone gave a little cheer.

Alicia and Brooke were also blonde and brunette, in that order, but in every other respect they were quite similar-looking. Lucy supposed that was why they were drawn to each other, not really having a clue about how gay attraction might work. It was Alicia who was one of Justin's school friends, Brooke having joined the group about five years ago. It surprised Lucy every time she heard they were still together. Still, there was no sign of wedding bells just yet.

Lucy had had a mind to assign the bedrooms to couples, and as there was one twin room upstairs, she was all for giving it to these two, but Justin had told her that was a silly idea and people would just grab one when they arrived. She had acquiesced, begrudgingly.

She let the rest of them talk and hug. She went to the wine chiller and retrieved a bottle; the boys had started so why shouldn't she?

Justin, grinning, slipped in alongside her. He reached up and retrieved more glasses from the cupboard.

'You're enjoying yourself already,' Lucy remarked.

'Of course. This is brilliant!' he arranged the glasses on the kitchen island. 'Come on, girls: let's get you started!'

Lucy poured herself one and then handed the bottle to her husband. He filled glasses for the others. When Alicia got hers she leaned across to clink it with Lucy's. She obliged. 'This place is amazing,' Alicia said. 'You two have excelled yourself.'

'Oh, it was all Justin. He spends hours researching any trip we have. This one was no different.'

'Yeah, but you let him do it. Thanks for this.' Her face was bright and gleaming, her hair pulled back in a ponytail, clear complexion on show. She looked younger than any of them despite being all the same age. Brooke came over, also sporting a ponytail. Lucy noticed they had matching waterproofs on as well, just of a different colour. Brooke winked at her. 'Luce.'

She smiled back, but groaned inwardly. 'You best go and grab a bedroom before someone comes and takes a good one.'

The couple looked at each other and shared a quick peck. Then they left their wines and went to hunt out their lodgings. Inside a minute Brooke could be heard shouting: 'Four poster, baby!'

The men laughed; Danni too. Lucy topped up her glass.

**

The next car pulled in ten minutes later and filled the fourth and final parking bay; the others would have to block someone in when they arrived. It was Steff and her long-term partner, Nick. This time Danni and Alicia welcomed them in. Justin checked his updates from those yet to arrive and declared with some confidence that it was okay to pre-heat the oven. Dinner would be in an hour.

Steff was slender with short hair, a little shaved at the nape of the neck. Nick was chunky and gruff, sporting tight unruly curls and a substantial moustache. 'Evening, nerds!' It was his pet name for them all; he was the only one in the group that hadn't been to university but had instead worked on building sites since he was seventeen. Elliot sometimes found him a little over-familiar, especially as it was Steff who was the Ashlands connection, but he was in a good mood so he brushed that aside. He offered Nick a hand; he took it and pumped it vigorously. 'Still a librarian, Tilson?'

'I am. Still a bricklayer, Warner?'

'You bet. Although these days they probably call it a *mineral and mortar engineer* to try and attract the snowflakes who want nothing but a fancy title. Some of the wimps coming through... holy fuck!'

'They should stick to the soft, indoor jobs, eh?'

'You know it! Is there beer in the fridge?'

'Go for it.'

Nick left him so Elliot went to hug Steff.

As there were now more of them, Justin suggested they relocate to the sofas. Once they all settled in, talk turned to the people that had yet to arrive. 'I take it Kieran's bringing someone?' Alicia asked.

'He is,' Justin replied. 'A young lady called Rhea.'

Brooke smirked. 'And she will be young, won't she? Has he ever dated anyone over thirty?

Elliot laughed. 'Once, but when we were much younger ourselves. I'd say we were twenty-two and he found himself some forty-year-old cougar!'

'Anne-Marie!' announced Justin and Elliot in unison, and laughed again.

Danni shook her head. 'God, remember when we used to think forty was so old?'

Lucy scoffed. 'Clearly Kieran still does.'

Steff got up and went to the tall window, gazing out at the snow-covered patio. 'It's still coming down heavy. I hope they're alright.'

Justin checked his phone. 'Pings from both cars. Neither of them too far away.' He got up and went to the kitchen. Dinner was straightforward: two large casserole dishes in the oven – one steak, one veggie. He crouched down and took a look.

Nick followed him. 'Fisher, tell me more about that flash car of yours...'

Danni joined Steff at the window and did the general catch-up chit-chat, then they went upstairs to look at bedrooms. The other four stayed on the sofas. Alicia and Brooke muttered quietly to each other. Lucy drank, quicker than Elliot wanted to so he didn't match her. Instead he gazed around, as if taking in their accommodation like a new arrival.

It was nice this, but as always if you came together as a group for the first time in a while, it would take an hour or two for everyone to settle in, especially as they were still waiting for others. Of course, that also meant two new people: Kieran's girlfriend and Hayley's... boyfriend? Elliot assumed as much, but in all the time he'd known her he didn't think she'd ever had a relationship. It was certainly going to be a talking point over the weekend.

That started immediately. Danni and Steff came back down. Steff got Nick's attention. 'One of the remaining bedrooms is a twin. The guys still to come are new couples. Shouldn't they have a double?

Should we take the twin?'

Nick's moustache twitched animatedly as his face screwed up. 'What? There's no way Hayley's boning the guy! We're not giving up a good bed for them!'

Lucy sauntered past. 'I told you we should have assigned bedrooms, Justin. That twin's an issue.'

Steff shook her head. 'We can just push the singles together.'

'We're not having it,' Nick replied. 'I'm putting our case in a double room, right now.' He stomped towards the hall.

'Good thing too,' Elliot said, who'd wandered towards the front of the house and the dining room table. 'Someone else has turned up. Looks like Kieran.'

Nick disappeared upstairs. The rest of them moved towards the window.

Kieran got out of the driver's seat of his Audi, parked in front of Justin's car. He had a beanie on his bald head. His girlfriend got out of the other side. And instinctively covered her jet black hair with a hand. The snow was still coming.

Lucy pushed one of the vertical blinds to the side. 'Oh, she's...'

'Beautiful,' Danni interjected. 'I think that's what you were going to say.'

'Quite.' Lucy walked back to the kitchen.

'Well, let's get them in!' said Justin. He went out into the hallway and threw open the door. 'Kieran!'

The others heard the whoop from the driveway. They were up the steps quickly, Kieran wanting to usher his girlfriend in out of the weather. It meant the three of them bustled through the hallway and into the living area, pitching the newbie into a semi-circle of staring faces. 'Hey everyone!' Kieran gestured with a triumphantly raised fist. He got *heys* back. 'This is Rhea, and before any of you think to ask in some kind of furtive way, she's twenty-eight and nuts about me!'

Rhea rolled her eyes and stepped forward, extending a hand. She had beautifully manicured nails the colour of seashells, in delightful contrast to her warm brown skin. Alicia and Brooke introduced themselves first, and the handshakes became hugs very quickly.

Kieran went the other way around. He kissed Danni on the cheek, but then rubbed Elliot's belly. 'Still cuddly, I see!'

'At least I can get rid of it if I want to. Your hair's not coming back any time soon.'

'Well, if you lose twenty pounds by June I'll wear a mullet wig all summer!'

'I might just take that bet!' They hugged. Elliot could tell under his jacket that Kieran was still a gym bunny. There wasn't an ounce of Christmas excess on him.

When he got round to Steff and Lucy, Rhea was already there, so he pulled them all in for a hug. Lucy squirmed her way out of it, claiming she had dinner to check on.

Nick came back into the room. 'Mooney, you need to go and throw a coat or something on the last remaining double bed. Your options are limited.'

'It's all good. Hey, Nick.' He introduced him to Rhea.

Steff sidled up to Danni and sighed. 'Jesus, that girl is *hot*.'

Danni put an arm around her. 'There's nothing wrong with us, you know. We're just a little more… comfortable.'

'Cosy.'

'Worn,' Lucy said, walking past. She had her own glass in one hand and a bottled beer for Kieran. She handed it over then addressed Rhea. 'I didn't know what you'd want.'

'A beer's fine… thank you.'

'Here: take mine,' said Kieran. 'I want to see what smells good anyway.' He bounced through into the kitchen.

Rhea offered the neck of the bottle to Lucy. It took her a second to work it out. 'Oh.' She clinked her glass against it then they both drank. 'He still has boundless energy, I see.'

'Oh yeah,' Rhea replied. 'He's like the Duracell bunny.'

'I bet he is,' said Nick, walking behind her.

Rhea turned round but he had already moved on. Justin spotted the issue. 'Come on; let's sit back down again.' He put himself in front of Rhea. 'I don't want you to feel overwhelmed. You're so welcome, by the way. I hope you have a great time.'

'I'm sure I will. I mean, what a place.'

Kieran was back. 'Except it was a bitch to get to, and I nearly spun out a couple of times. We all here? Because it's getting quite nasty out there.'

'Just Hayley.'

'Yeah? She's coming? Anyone know what she drives? If it's something like a BMW she's got no chance.'

Nick had found a bag of tortilla chips and was helping himself.

'There's no chance Hayley drives a BMW.' Steff reprimanded him and took away the chips.

They were all hovering again, between the kitchen islands and the sofas. Suddenly no one could settle, conscious that they still weren't complete and the weather was worsening. Alicia chewed her lip and rubbed Brooke's back for comfort. 'Doesn't she have the least distance to travel as well? I thought she lived in Scotland these days.'

Justin confirmed it was Edinburgh. 'But she said she had to work today, so was setting off later than anyone. I'm sure she's fine. I got a message half an hour ago saying she wasn't far away.'

'She's texting and driving?' Kieran asked. 'That sounds reckless for our Hayley.'

'No,' Justin replied, smiling. 'I think her *man* is driving.'

Kieran raised an eyebrow. 'Whooo, what's this now? Hayley Powell finally getting some?'

'We don't know for sure,' Nick replied, 'which is why they're having the single beds.'

Elliot threw a hand up. 'You're all so obsessed about the beds!' Danni knew what he was thinking: he was wishing they hadn't taken the second-best room on offer when they had arrived but the worst one. She went over, stroked his upper arm, and guided him towards the sofas. She suggested everyone else do the same, which they did, slowly, only Justin hanging back in the kitchen.

They got comfy, a little more relaxed, and another bottle of wine was passed around.

Ten minutes later, Justin – still on the periphery of the group with one eye on the dining room window – saw car headlights approaching. 'Looks like they're here! Everyone stay put this time: no need to swarm the guy.'

Because that's it, thought Danni, a little sadly about one of her high school chums. No one was excited to see Hayley; no one ever was particularly. It was all about her companion. What sort of man had she finally connected with, enough so as to bring him into the group for three nights?

She looked around the sofas and just hoped her old friends would be kind.

CHAPTER THREE

Justin opened the door and took a couple of steps down. An old Volvo estate had blocked in Elliot's Dacia and was wheezing in the cold, even though it had come to a stop. At least it was better built to withstand the weather than something more flimsy.

Hayley got out and waved to him. He waved back, genuinely pleased to see her, particularly how she looked. Hayley had always been the one to seem old before they ever got there, and her appearance had matched. She'd been the first to go grey and never did anything about it. She had pear-shaped hips that she'd not shifted, but dressed plain and baggy to try and mask it. Contrary to her figure was a thin and pale face, which meant she had wrinkled early. Now though, in the yellowy cast of the drive lights and the house windows, she looked a picture of health, or at least *better* health. Her hair had been dyed and had volume to it; he could tell from a distance, even through a gauze of snow. Her eyes were brighter, her mouth fuller – probably a trick of the lipstick that he'd never remembered being applied before. She was still thin-faced but had make-up on to give contours and colour. She was *blooming*.

This man was obviously a good influence on her. 'Get up here!' Justin yelled.

She hung back, waiting for her companion.

He got out of the driver's door. Tall, in a mid-length brown overcoat. His hair, a little long and unevenly cut like he'd trimmed it himself, was flat to his skull with a severe centre parting. He wore little round glasses, perched on a strong aquiline nose. He didn't look up to the house but instead went to one of the passenger doors at the back. It looked like it was stuck as he seemed to be wrestling with the handle. Hayley hovered, looking a little uncertain.

Instinctively, Justin took the remaining steps and touched down on the gravel; he didn't know how he might help but he was drawn to do so anyway. He wondered as he got nearer to the car why you wouldn't put luggage in the Volvo estate's huge boot, but then got a peak through the rear window at something bulky underneath the slightly raised parcel shelf. Before Justin could say anything about the situation, Hayley's friend got the door open. Had there been another car parked on that side of him he would have slammed back into it. As it was, he staggered a little but quickly regained his footing.

'Do you need any help?' Justin offered.

'Nope,' Hayley replied. 'Just one bag.' The man held the car door open while Hayley dipped in and fished it out. It was a rucksack and she swung it over her shoulder. She leaned to the side with the addition of weight and Justin wondered why the man hadn't retrieved it himself. *I guess chivalry is dead*, he thought, but then added: *at least he's holding open the door.*

'You made it! Isn't this weather ridiculous?'

'We were very careful,' Hayley said. 'Let me introduce you.' She stood a little taller, as if making a formal announcement. 'Justin Fisher, meet Benjamin Bălan.'

'Hey Ben,' Justin stuck out a hand for a shake.

'It is Benjamin,' he replied, through a thin-lipped smile. 'Pleased to make your acquaintance.' His voice was very low, and almost lost in the wind. He took Justin's hand, long fingers completely encasing it, but the grip was weak. It meant Justin gave it a gentle shake. It was cold too; he was happy to let it go.

'It's now officially freezing out here. Let's get you guys inside.' Justin waved them up the steps towards the light and warmth of the open door and the wood panelling beyond. Hayley bounded after him, as best she could under the rucksack. Benjamin took a little more caution.

Justin turned in the threshold to see him staring up at the house, along the line of the roof and then down the sides. 'Benjamin?'

'You have a beautiful home.'

'What? No, it's rented. Didn't Hayley say? But let me welcome you anyway. Come on in. Come and meet everybody.'

Hayley was by Justin's shoulder. 'Everyone's here?'

'Yes, you're the last,' he replied.

'Very good,' Benjamin said. Justin wasn't sure what about, but the man finally took to the steps and followed them inside.

The others had done as they were told and stayed on the sofas. Danni was first up; she cut across to Hayley, eased the luggage off her back and gave her a hug.

'Everyone,' Justin said, 'this is Benjamin.' There were general greetings, most along the lines of *Hi Ben!* Justin corrected them. 'It's actually *Benjamin.*' He widened his eyes and smirked.

Benjamin watched Justin move towards the kitchen, and then turned to address the group. 'I just believe that once you have been blessed with a name, you should use it in full.'

'That's us in trouble, Danni,' Nick chortled.

Elliot got up, introduced himself, and took Benjamin's coat. Underneath, he wore a grey shirt buttoned up to the neck and an ill-fitting cardigan. 'Take my seat, I'll just put this away for you.' The newcomer followed the instruction but only perched on the sofa; it meant his knees pointed outwards. Brooke offered him a drink but he declined.

Danni still held Hayley. 'He seems nice,' she offered.

'He is. Very.'

'And look at you: hair, make-up.'

Suddenly Hayley looked very serious. 'Is it too much?'

'No, you look lovely. Go and help Benjamin settle in.' She let her go; Hayley scooted off and slipped onto the sofa next to her new friend. *Definitely boyfriend*, Danni thought.

Elliot joined her, having returned from hanging up Benjamin's coat. They checked in on Justin to see if he needed a hand with dinner. He was fine: just boiling a few extra vegetables and warming some crusty bread. Elliot volunteered to put out the cutlery; Danni was going to help but her husband ushered her away. 'Make sure the new boy isn't fed to the lions.' She understood and returned to the sofas.

The question of the moment was about Benjamin's accent. 'Is there some eastern European in there?' Alicia asked.

'You are correct. I am from Sibiu, a town in Romania.'

Alicia nodded slowly. 'Is that where you guys met? Didn't you go travelling there, Hayles?'

'*Hayley,*' she corrected. 'I did, and I did meet Benjamin in Romania, but in Cluj. I was there for some months in 2020.'

Danni knew much of the story: her friend was planning to explore most of Europe – in a journey of self-discovery or some such nonsense – but Covid had limited Hayley's travel opportunities and she got stuck in a couple of places, extending her solo trip by the best part of a year and completely draining her bank account. Danni didn't know about Benjamin though. Hayley had returned to England in the spring of 2021 then secured a position up in Edinburgh. Had she brought him back with her? It was odd to be only hearing about him now.

Really? How often have you enquired about her life in the last eighteen months? Danni felt her cheeks go pink as the guilt seeped in. *Time just goes so fast these days.*

'I work with Hayley at the museum,' Benjamin added.

'You should talk to Elliot,' suggested Nick. 'He's got a boring job too.' Steff delivered a swift elbow to his right pectoral.

Alicia probed a little more. 'And how long have you two been together?'

'Oh,' Hayley replied, sitting a little straighter. 'We're not really *together* together, not yet.' She tried to smile but it wouldn't sit straight on her face.

Alicia held Brooke's knee and put her other hand to her chest. 'Sorry: I didn't mean to pry! I hope you're not embarrassed, Benjamin.'

'You could not possibly embarrass me.' If it was meant to be reassuring in tone, he didn't quite pull it off. It sounded more like a challenge.

It also brought an awkwardness to the square of sofas, only broken by Justin's call to get their backsides to the dining table: dinner was ready.

**

The food was simple enough fare because it needed to be quick and easy to heat up. Still, it was most welcome and a fitting foreground to the backdrop of a snowy winter scene. The layer of white was creeping up the glass bifold doors; it was already two inches deep out there.

There was also wine, water and beer on the table, cloth napkins in decorative rings, small vases of flowers and neat place cards, along with little A5 printed guest lists dotted around the table. As they sat down a few of them picked them up. Nick took umbrage. 'Hey, Fisher? *Alumni and Arseholes?* So just because I didn't go to that nerdy school you all went to, I'm an arsehole?'

'No,' Kieran replied. 'Even if you'd gone to Ashlands with us, you'd still qualify for that category.'

Justin tried to explain. 'I just wanted another word beginning with A, you know, for the alliteration? I was trying to be funny.' His face reddened a little.

Nick frowned. 'Not worked, has it? Now our new boy Ben thinks you don't like him.'

'*Benjamin,*' corrected Hayley's date. He sat tall at the table, hands tucked on his lap.

Brooke clapped her hands. 'Come on – we'll all be arseholes by the end of the night if we do this right.' She picked up a bottle of wine in each hand. 'Let's get this thing going!'

As per Brooke's request, good cheer followed over the next hour. Kieran did the story of how he met Rhea: she was literally working as a waitress in a cocktail bar. Which then led to impromptu karaoke of 80s and 90s hits. Nick ribbed Justin about his excessive display of wealth parked on the drive, which led to Steff apologising for her partner a number of times. Alicia encouraged Danni to share updates on the kids. Inevitably, whatever aspects of achievement she mentioned about her little Tilsons, Lucy would interject with how her Rosalind could match it or do better. Brooke, increasingly aware of this, fired up the singing again with a rendition of the chorus to Carly Simon's theme to *The Spy Who Loved Me*. It wasn't very subtle, but if Lucy noticed, she didn't let on.

Hayley was quiet. Nearly eighteen months backpacking across Europe only to be stranded because of Covid should be fuel for a number of good stories, but nothing was forthcoming. Elliot watched her, waiting to see if she would fill a lull, but she continued with her listening brief, as she always had done since high school. They were nearly forty years old and some things never changed.

Benjamin was quiet too, and Elliot didn't know whether it would be appropriate to ask more of him after the initial grilling on the sofas. This kind of scene wasn't for everyone, and the way he was picking at his food suggested he might be feeling uncomfortable. Still, to not be encouraged to get involved was worse, no?

Elliot took a chance. 'Hey, Benjamin, what kind of music do you like? Nothing near that caterwauling at the other end of the table, I'll bet.'

'I heard that,' Kieran said. 'Nothing wrong with my Britney renditions!'

Benjamin waited to see if Kieran or one of the others might sing again, but when the noise level dropped he gave his answer. 'I am not really an admirer of your modern music: it has no longevity.'

As always when Benjamin spoke there were a couple of titters. Elliot ignored them. 'You play though, right?'

'I do not understand your question.'

Elliot pointed. 'Your left hand. The fingernails are long, whereas on your right hand... for plucking guitar strings, at least that's what I thought.'

'Not for plucking, no.' Now everyone was looking at Benjamin's hand: it still held a fork that seemed to be locked into automatically pushing vegetables around his plate. The nails were yellowy and sharp.

'It's just a thing,' Hayley blurted. 'A European fashion. You wouldn't understand.'

Elliot held up a hand in concession. 'Hey, sure. My passport expired in 2015. I'm no traveller.'

'Yeah,' Nick added. 'We're surprised you even made it up here, Tilson. How was it, Danni? Twenty miles an hour all the way?'

Danni shook her head. 'Nothing wrong with being careful, Nicholas.'

Brooke looked out of the window. 'It does mean we're not driving anywhere tomorrow.' Conversation turned to the weather and the potential for local walks. Elliot however, kept his eye on Benjamin. Behind the round glasses were dark, narrow eyes, like shards of flint. Benjamin brought the fork to his narrow lips in what seemed an automatic gesture. There was actually no food on it. A pink tongue flicked out and licked the prongs, lizard-like. Then he returned to manoeuvring the food before repeating the action.

Elliot couldn't help himself. 'You not hungry, Benjamin?'

The Romanian rested the cutlery on the plate, and tucked his hands under the table. 'I had a substantial lunch.'

Now those stony eyes trained on Elliot, and he didn't much like it. He got Justin's attention instead. 'Is there dessert, Just?'

Kieran took an opportunity. 'You not cuddly enough there, Elly-Belly?'

Whilst Rhea chastised Kieran for being so rude, Justin replied that there was nothing planned but there were plenty of sweet treats in the cupboards. Elliot took the opportunity to leave the table and put some space between him and Benjamin. He picked up his empty plate and put it near the sink built into one of the kitchen islands. He lingered rather than return or hunt out dessert, and this seemed to serve as a cue to others. Chairs scraped back and legs were stretched. Justin set about picking up the other plates, which then prompted others to tidy their own leftovers, not wanting their host to wait on them.

Walking back towards the sofas, Nick tracked behind Alicia and Brooke. 'You know, you two are so similar, it makes me wonder which one is supposed to be the male in this action.' He tugged playfully at Alicia's ponytail.

She spun round and batted his hand away. 'You definitely are an arsehole.'

Brooke interjected. 'Oh, don't mind him, Liss – he just can't understand how two people can actually have a successful relationship without there being a dick involved. And he is *such* a dick.'

'I can show you,' he offered, a hand on his crotch.

'Nick!' Steff yelled from the kitchen.

'I'm just playing! I thought we were supposed to be having a party weekend? Everyone's got so middle-aged in the last couple of years. Jesus!' He turned and walked towards a case of beer on the kitchen worktop. Steff gave him daggers with her eyes all the way.

Lucy watched Benjamin scrape virtually all his dinner into the food waste container. She also clocked Hayley hanging by his shoulder, looking like more of an outsider than *he* did, even though she was supposed to be among friends. Lucy didn't have much time for Hayley – never had. She was so *dull*. In organising this event, Lucy had insisted Justin made it a couples only thing, hoping that this would exclude her. Lucy hadn't – for a *second* – believed Hayley would actually bring someone. Actually *knew* someone to bring.

She resolved to keep away from the pair of them, and got herself another glass of wine.

Kieran managed to access Spotify on the smart speaker, and the requests started to flood in. Justin pushed the leather armchairs to the side and got the fire lit, not without some swearing and a little assistance from Danni. It then meant then that the space between the hearth and the nearest sofa became something of a dance floor. *Beyoncé, Eminem* and *The Black Eyed Peas* got the room moving.

All the women danced except for Lucy and Hayley. Because the latter took up a place on the sofas, the former opted for a high stool by the breakfast bar. Kieran and Nick had discovered the bottle of scotch from earlier and were helping themselves. Justin showed the women his throwback moves.

Elliot, on the periphery, had half an eye on Benjamin. He didn't sit next to Hayley but rather loomed over her, standing behind the sofa, his head hovering above hers, arms locked on the back of the seat either side of her shoulders. They both had eyes on the gyrating group. Benjamin's head would dip to her ear, strands of his lank hair brushing against hers. He would whisper something, and Hayley would nod. Elliot counted this three times; on the fourth the Romanian's eye fell on him, and didn't falter even while he was mouthing something to Hayley. Then he patted her on the shoulder, stood upright and moved away. He said nothing to anyone else, but cut across in front of the kitchen area and disappeared through the door that led to the entrance and the stairs. Toilet break, maybe.

Elliot, curious, weaved between sofas and plopped down next to Hayley. 'How you doing?'

She bristled a little, and shifted away, just enough to notice. 'Fine, Elliot. Just fine.'

'Benjamin enjoying himself?' He didn't look at her but watched the dancers.

'He's had a lovely evening.'

'*Had?* He's gone to bed already?' Elliot checked his watch: it was only just past ten o'clock.

'It has been rather a taxing day.'

'At the museum?'

She paused for thought before replying: 'We've both got a bit of pressure on at the moment.'

'Right. Sucks being a grown-up.'

'Quite possibly. I think I'm going to say goodnight to the girls.' She stood and navigated her way around the coffee table in order to join those dancing in the firelight. He watched her announce her departure; only Danni hugged her and asked how she was. She left them and cut past Lucy. Hayley offered a small wave goodnight; Lucy slipped off her stool and turned away.

Then Nick accosted Elliot with a shoulder pinch and a tumbler of scotch, and his uneasiness around Hayley and Benjamin was forgotten.

They joined the rest of them, and the singing, dancing and drinking continued.

CHAPTER FOUR

Kieran woke up, pretty sure that it was the sound of a door slamming that roused him. He and Rhea hadn't been the last to retire – she wanted him between the sheets before he got too tired or drunk – so perhaps some die-hard was still up. He checked his watch. 4am: it seemed unlikely.

He lay in bed on his back, one hand smoothing the duvet over Rhea's still curves and one ear cocked for more noise.

There it was again. Now awake, he could place it. Metallic, heavy. Clearly outside, and clearly on a car. He got up and crossed, naked, to the window.

Their window overlooked the front of the house, and the parked cars. There were still driveway lights glowing, enough to illuminate Benjamin at the rear of his beat-up Volvo. He was dressed as he was earlier, minus the cardigan and the overcoat. His feet had almost disappeared in the snow and it was still falling, leaving white blossoms on the shoulders of his grey shirt. Kieran was no expert on temperature, but he had a good idea it was probably below freezing. And wasn't Benjamin under the weather? He had been the first to go to bed, and when Rhea had tried to visit the main bathroom to freshen up after their intimate *tête-à-tête*, she heard a man dry-heaving behind the door. Every other couple had their own bathrooms, so by a process of elimination…

Yet here he was, outside in the freezing cold. He was struggling to close the boot. It popped up again, just a couple of inches. He snatched at the lip of it and held it up fully with one hand while he reached in with the other, pushing back what was in there. Kieran couldn't be fully sure but it looked like a large wooden box or crate.

Benjamin shoved it as far back as he could. What looked like dirt was accidentally brushed out over the rear bumper, falling in black clumps against the snow. That was when Kieran noticed that the man's hands were filthy, like he'd been digging up weeds without a trowel.

Benjamin tried the boot again, this time less forcefully but with measured and deliberate pressure. It made much less of a noise, but Kieran could hear it click into place. He took a step back away from the curtain at that point, anticipating a move from Benjamin; he didn't want to be spotted.

Benjamin did turn, but not back towards the house. He walked away from the car in the direction of the main drive. His slow walk turned into a trot and then broke into a fully-fledged sprint away from the building.

'What the fuck?' Kieran thought about waking Rhea, but didn't want to take his eyes off what he was seeing.

Somehow Benjamin wasn't falling in the snow, but finding a grace that seemed impossible. Kieran waited for him to face-plant, especially when he hurdled the low chain that flanked the drive and took to the field. But Benjamin kept on running. He was at the line of trees within what seemed an impossible time and then – without hesitation – he disappeared into the woods.

'Who the hell is this guy?'

He turned back to Rhea and thought again about waking her, but what was there to see? He'd only be able to show her a purposeful-looking trail of footprints. It was a story that could keep until morning.

What about Hayley? He suddenly thought about the crazy yet possible scenario of Bǎlan doing something terrible to his old friend and fleeing the scene. He had to check on her, even if it meant suffering the embarrassment of being caught creeping into her room in the middle of the night. *Only, it won't be embarrassing because I've just seen her boyfriend pull a Forrest Gump, and I need to be sure she's alright.* That sealed it: no question it was the right thing to do. However, he did concede that there was a need for underwear, so he stepped back into his boxer shorts before slipping out into the darkness of the upstairs landing.

Their room was only two doors away, divided by the family bathroom. Kieran put that light on to give him something to work with. He wondered about the benefits of a door knock or a whisper of Hayley's name, but then decided his preference was for discovering whether or not she was alive without the need to wake her.

The door creaked a little as it opened. A vertical rectangle of light was cast over an empty single bed, still perfectly made up. As he pushed further the rectangle became a square and Hayley's bed was illuminated. She was bundled up under the duvet, one foot – still in a sock – sticking out at the bottom, and the top of her head visible on the pillow.

Kieran decided quite quickly that sight alone wasn't enough, so he carefully crept in. He saw Hayley's rucksack on a chair by a dressing table, various items – toiletries and the like – out on the desk top. An open wardrobe door gave him a glimpse of some of her clothes. What about Benjamin? There was no evidence of the man ever having been in the room.

He tiptoed a little nearer, and then, rather than looking, listened more carefully. His body relaxed when he heard a light snoring coming from the Hayley heap.

Stupid imagination. Of course he hasn't killed her and done a runner. He edged his way back across the room, eyes on Hayley so he might explain should she sit up, startled. *But he* has *run off though…* Kieran could only assume it was some unconventional exercise routine. He navigated his way past the chair and the foot of Benjamin's unused bed.

A figure suddenly filled the space at the half open door. Kieran tensed and did his best not to let out a yelp.

He realised almost immediately that it wasn't tall enough to be Benjamin. It was a female frame. 'Hayley?'

'Shhhh.' Hand outstretched and waving, he scurried across to the door. He saw that it was Danni in her winter PJs. He ushered her out, back onto the landing. He slipped through and pulled the door to, somehow without waking Hayley.

'What the hell are you doing, Kieran?' It was an agitated whisper.

'Just checking on Hayley.' He encouraged her to move further away, back towards the other bedrooms. The bathroom light made their shadows dance.

'I heard some banging and then some movement up this end. Why do you need to check on Hayley?'

'Wait: you thought there might be an intruder and you came out here alone?'

She kinked a hip and smirked. 'You've met my husband, right? He's wonderful, but brave he ain't. Now explain.'

He pointed to the stairs. 'Shall we...?'

Danni nodded. 'But put a t-shirt on or something, Kee.' She wiggled a finger at his torso. 'It's quite off-putting.'

**

Five minutes later they were sitting on high stools in the kitchen and warming their hands on mugs of tea. Kieran, now clad in a sweater, had finished explaining what he had seen from his bedroom window.

'That's so weird,' Danni said. She looked to the door to the hallway, half expecting Benjamin to come jogging through.

'He certainly is an oddball. He's not slept in his bed, and I don't think he has any clothes with him.'

'He must have something, perhaps in the bottom of her bag?'

Kieran shrugged and took a sip from his mug. When he set it down he asked: 'What has she told you about him?'

Danni's eyes dropped to her own drink. 'I don't know anything. First I'd heard of him was when Justin told us she was bringing someone. I feel terrible for not asking.'

'You haven't kept in touch?'

'She told me she was back in the UK, I texted back *that's great*, and it was pretty much left like that. Then she let me know about the job at the museum...' she shrugged.

'And you texted *that's great* again... I get it, Danni – we're all moving on. Don't feel bad.'

'Yeah, but she's never really had friends outside of us, at least I don't think so anyway. I just feel shitty for falling out of touch. And maybe if I'd been around for her...'

'...she might not have fallen into the arms of some freaky eastern European? She's a grown-up, Danni. It happens to the best of us.'

Danni managed a smile. 'You trying to tell me you've grown up, Kee? How old is Rhea?'

Kieran laughed. 'Come on. Just because she's young doesn't mean I'm refusing to grow up. I'm just refusing to slow down.'

Danni reached across and patted his hand. 'Well, good for you.

Me though, I need my eight hours these days, especially after what feels like a gallon of wine.' She slipped off the stool. 'You thinking of waiting up for Benjamin?'

'God, no.' He also left his seat. 'I'm hoping to forget this ever happened. Let's just see how he gets on tomorrow.'

They turned off the lights and made their way back upstairs, leaving the tea on the kitchen island. When Kieran got back into bed, Rhea stirred. 'Where you been?'

'Bathroom.'

'Too much beer.' She closed her eyes and snuggled further into her pillow.

'Something like that,' Kieran said, and cuddled up behind her. He'd try to get back to sleep, but he knew one ear would be staying attuned to Benjamin's potential return.

CHAPTER FIVE

The morning was crisp and bright, but not warm enough to put a
dent in the thick layer of snow that surrounded Kilbride House. The
wind had dropped and the air felt cleansing after a night on the drink.
Brooke stood on the back patio and took in deep, healing breaths.
And then she took a few poisonous ones by taking a couple of drags
on the cigarette she'd lit. She didn't consider herself a smoker, but
one or two a day topped up a habit she hadn't fully exploited since
her twenties.

Everything was under snow so the aesthetics of the garden were
not clear. Outdoor ornament and sculpted topiary were rounded off
in curves of white so that the scene seemed constructed out of
marshmallow. A shed that had what looked like cake-icing for a roof,
a foot thick, sagged in the corner. All things considered, it would not
be a space they would utilise. What was of interest though was the tall
gate to the left that led to the second building: a gym and games
room that also promised a hot tub, albeit outside. Still, snow could be
brushed off later, and a dip with a couple of friends and a bottle of
Prosecco sounded appealing. For now though, nicotine and coffee
was the answer. She stubbed out the cigarette in a glass ashtray on the
table and picked up her mug. She felt the steam on her nose as she
took a sip.

The glass door behind her was open just a crack and Alicia's voice
carried through it. Brooke's partner lay on one of the sofas; her face
popped up over the arm rest. 'The consensus is we're going for a
walk in half an hour.'

'No problem,' said Brooke. As far as she could tell, she was the
only one properly dressed and booted anyway. She'd never visited

Scotland before, and was looking forward to getting out and about. She had hoped the weather might have been kinder, allowing them to take a drive at some point. She had imagined her and Alicia discovering artisan shops and cafes, perhaps a drink in front of a log fire in a country pub. What she hadn't reckoned on was essentially being housebound with ten others. As much as she liked Alicia's friends – *her* friends now, she was largely happy to admit – three days holed up in the same place could end up being intense. Yes: a walk – if that was the best she could get – would be good.

She heard the door slide further open behind her; she turned just in time to see Steff step up beside her. She had training shoes on but still wore pyjamas and a dressing gown. 'How you doing, lady?' Brooke asked.

'Good. A little thick-headed but nothing this cold won't blast it away.'

'There's coffee in the pot, or at least there was five minutes ago.' Brooke could see there was now a decent sized group of them gathered in the kitchen.

'Yeah – gonna grab some in a minute. Listen, I just wanted to apologise for last night.'

Brooke turned fully and put a hand on Steff's arm. 'Sweetheart, what for?'

'Nick. He said a few stupid, insensitive things. About you two.'

'That's because he can be stupid and insensitive.'

'I know.'

'But don't you be thinking it's you that needs to apologise. You might be sorry it happened, but it's not something you said so it's not on you.'

'I doubt he'll say anything.'

'Then ultimately, your apology is pointless.' Brooke saw Steff prickle. 'You know what I mean: it's from the wrong person, so…'

'No, I get it. I just didn't want you feeling uncomfortable.'

'Steff, it'll take more than a couple of jibes from Neanderthal Nick to twist my knickers.'

'He's not that bad.'

'I know.' Brooke was conscious that this apology might actually turn into an argument. 'Let's just leave it there and get on with our day. You're underdressed for a trudge in the snow.'

'Yeah, I should go and layer up. We good?'

'Golden.'

This time Steff squeezed Brooke's arm before going back inside. Brooke let her go, just allowing a bit of distance between them, before heading indoors herself. Alicia beckoned her to the sofa so she slipped in next to her.

'Ugh. You're cold.'

'Something to do with it being winter.'

'Well, tune in: I've got a feeling it's about to get a little frosty in the kitchen.'

Brooke looked across. Hovering around one of the islands were Justin, Lucy, Kieran, Nick and Danni. All eyes seemed to be converging on Hayley, sat on a stool.

'I don't know why you're making a thing out of it,' she said. 'He's not coming for a walk with us and that's it. No big deal.'

Justin looked hurt. 'And you're saying it's because of something he ate?'

'He was sick last night and is still under the weather.'

Lucy wrinkled her nose. 'He hardly ate a thing: just pushed his food around. It's nothing to do with our cooking.'

'He ate,' Hayley said.

'Barely, honey,' Danni replied. 'Elliot watched him. At best he licked the utensils.'

'Maybe it was something he licked!' Nick offered, and laughed like he'd told the world's best joke. He walked away, his contribution made.

Kieran leaned in over the worktop. 'This may sound like a strange question, Hayles, but is he actually up there?'

She looked genuinely perturbed. 'What can you possibly mean?'

'Stupid idea, but last night I heard him outside and watched him go... for a run. I didn't hear him come back in. Did he definitely return?'

'What? You think he's run off from me? Left his car and everything, just vanished? And I'm hiding that from you?'

'But it was just-'

Danni interjected. 'Leave it, Kieran.' She turned to Hayley. 'We just want to know he's okay, and that you're okay. We understand if this is a big thing being introduced to such a crowd, for him and for you.'

She narrowed her eyes. 'Because we all haven't seen each other for so long?'

Danni stepped away slightly. 'Yeah, something like that.'

'Look,' Lucy said. 'If the guy doesn't want to be part of what we're doing today, it's no skin off our noses. And if you'd rather stay with him and play nurse maid, Hayley, that's up to you.'

'I never said I wasn't coming along.' This, out of all the comments, seemed to upset her the most. She slipped off the stool in an ungainly fashion and then nudged her way past Justin to set a course for the door.

'Hayley...' Danni implored, but it made no difference: their friend exited the room with a door slam and a stomp on the stairs.

Elliot was putting mugs in the sink. 'You shouldn't interfere; let them do what they want.'

'Yeah?' Kieran offered. 'You didn't see the guy sprint off across the field last night. If he's ill it's because he's got pneumonia.'

'As long as it wasn't the food,' Justin said, and helped Elliot with the post-breakfast tidy up.

Danni knew that Elliot was right; she now wished she hadn't encountered Kieran last night and had all these weird ideas implanted in her brain. She considered going after her, but knew she had no place being in her room with Benjamin in there.

Rhea came in from the hallway, and jerked a thumb over her shoulder. 'She's upset about something.'

'Don't worry, babe.' Kieran beckoned her over. 'You all set for the walk? You look great.'

Lucy walked past Danni and muttered: 'She fucking does as well.' Rhea wore tall brown leather boots with a generous wool trim, thick leggings that still managed to hug her curves, a puffer jacket that pinched in at the waist and accentuated the chest, and immaculate make-up and hair. She looked like a model from a pop star's Christmas video shoot.

'Christ,' Danni mumbled. 'I've got a pair of wellies and one of Elliot's old jumpers.' She turned to the sofas: Alicia and Brooke were smirking at her. 'You two can quit it,' but Danni couldn't help but smile at her and Lucy's reaction. This weekend was supposed to be fun, and that included laughing at yourself. She told herself *no more remarks aimed at Hayley and Benjamin*; it was going to be smiles from hereon in.

**

When Hayley came back downstairs, just at the point of them setting off, she was in brighter spirits and said she was looking forward to spending time with everyone. That didn't enthuse the whole party, but it meant that bar Benjamin they were all together at least, and crunched out into the snow in one buoyant and determined group. Danni linked Hayley's arm and the gesture was welcomed.

Kieran noticed that there was no sign of Benjamin's footprints from the previous night; the snow of the early hours had filled them in. It had also covered the dirt that had fallen from the back of the Volvo. He was tempted to take a look through the rear window at the peculiar cargo, but the company was trudging off down the drive and he didn't want to be cut loose. He looked up at the house, spied his own bedroom window and worked out which one was Hayley's. The curtains were drawn; no sign of Benjamin waving them off. Kieran put it out of his mind and caught up with the others.

It wasn't long before the first snowball was thrown. Once they left the grounds they turned right, obeying Justin's directions. There was the promise of a castle ruin and a village a couple of miles or so away. To say they were following a road was accurate enough, but knowing where the roadside ended and the kerb began was tricky. Instead they just decided to avoid the tracks that had been made through the centre by a farm vehicle and considered the rest of the untouched snow as fair game. So when Nick and Kieran ran across to the other side, snatched up handfuls of snow which they quickly packed into ammunition, and began an assault on the others, a considerable and hysterical skirmish began. Brooke and Alicia deserted and joined the two rebels, and the two sides stumble-ran and pelted each other for the next half mile.

Hayley made as if to join the smaller team in a bid to even up the numbers a little, but in the end she resorted to shuffling along behind and watching. Her oldest friends. With their true loves or new flames. People she loved and people she liked. And just people. She wondered what adjustment to that assessment a day might make.

How differently she viewed them now that she had Benjamin.

Then, before Hayley could think on it some more, Steff made to defect from her side to Nick's, running across Hayley's field of vision. Only, when Steff's boot hit the compacted snow made by the heavy tyre, she slipped. It wasn't serious; she was laughing immediately after she fell, creating a foetal snow angel between the two lines in the road. But it meant the snowball fight stopped, and when Steff held out both hands to Hayley and asked, 'Will you help me up?' Hayley had to oblige. She hoped Nick would come and do it but he was the furthest away. She dug her boots in the snow, grabbed Steff's gloved hands and pulled. A second later they were grabbing onto each other to stay upright. 'Thanks a million, Hayles!'

Hayley, she thought. 'Any time,' she said. Of course, she didn't know if she really meant it. Not anymore.

Because their noise levels had dropped, it meant they could pick up more of the sounds around them. There were voices on the light breeze, coming towards them from over a drystone wall that was six inches taller than it should be due to the mounds of snow. Those on the near side – not in Nick's breakaway group – could see three figures in the field that came sharper into view the further they walked. They were men, dressed in work wear, clearly farmers. They were looking at something on the ground.

Conversation dropped all round as both groups became aware of each other. Elliot and Justin, nearest the wall, took a look at what had the farmers so absorbed.

At first Elliot mistook it for a snow-covered mound that looked like it had been kicked and scuffed, but then he saw it for what it was: a stricken sheep. The markings, reddish-brown, were ragged slashes into the animal's side. There was no movement: the sheep was clearly dead.

'Bugger all fer you to see 'ere,' said a craggy farmer. 'On yer go, lads.'

'Right,' Elliot said and averted his eyes. He turned to Danni and urged her forward.

The dialogue brought the others across. Nick, bolder, walked right up to the wall. 'What have you got there then?'

The youngest of the farmers walked towards them. 'Did yer not hear? Get tae fuck.'

Nick ignored him. 'What's done it, do you think?'

'Away with yer!'

Justin grabbed Nick's elbow. 'Come on, mate. It's not our business. Let them get on.'

Nick conceded, primarily because the weekend was Justin's gig.

NO ONE IS LEAVING

'Arsehole,' he muttered, but moved off in the direction of Justin's small shove.

'Sorry...' Steff said, but then caught herself before she apologised for Nick, despite that being in her mind. Instead she added: '...for your loss.' And felt immediately stupid.

'Losses,' said Kieran, pointing into the field. There were other stricken mounds, other maroon smears.

Now the craggy farmer and his silent companion also walked towards them, so to avoid further conflict the group marched on.

Having crossed from the other side it was now Brooke and Alicia that brought up the rear. They linked arms, for stability as much as it was for affection. Alicia took a couple of glances back into the field they were leaving behind. 'Nasty stuff. Although I thought they might take their sheep in overnight when it's snowing.'

'Round the fire for a game of charades?'

'You know what I mean, cheeky cow.'

Brooke pointed back to the field. 'There's some kind of barn – they might have been in there and maybe something got in? Or maybe they just tough it out in the field.' Brooke was a city girl and didn't really have a clue.

'Are there wolves in Scotland?' Alicia asked.

'Not sure there's wild wolves anywhere in the UK.'

'What do you think's done it then?'

'Dunno. Rabid dog, maybe?'

'And we're out for a long walk, not really knowing where we are or where we're going.'

Brooke pulled her in tighter. 'I've got you.'

They continued to trail the others as they crested a hill and left the killing ground behind them.

CHAPTER SIX

The castle ruin was exactly that, so not much to look at, but as Justin was enthusiastic for it they all gave it some time. When they reached the village, the café was busy and limited for seating so they had to make the tough decision to opt for the Red Lion instead. Three hours soon passed, assisted by a dart board and a pool table. Justin pointed out that they had all these things in the annex building back at the house, but no one was in a rush to launch into the walk again. Of course, the longer they stayed and the more they drank, the harder it would be to slalom their way back to Kilbride House, but what the hell? They ordered some sandwiches and crisps to soak up the alcohol and got on with it. Danni hustled them at pool but Nick was triumphant at the darts.

While Hayley was in the bathroom, Kieran offered what sounded like a random statement. 'Benson and Hedges.'

'Didn't know you smoked,' Danni said, and still glanced around for a cigarette machine. Did pubs still have them? It seemed not.

'I don't mean the ciggy brand,' Kieran replied. 'It's my new code phrase for Benjamin and Hayley. What did you make of all that *one must use one's full name* nonsense?'

No one was really taking him on. 'Nonsense,' Elliot replied. 'A bit like your codes.' He walked past with a pool cue and patted Kieran's bald head.

Nick mused. 'Didn't Noel Gallagher call his cats Benson and Hedges?'

'Not very rock and roll,' Alicia replied, 'being Manchester's equivalent of a cat lady.'

'He's getting old,' Brooke remarked.

'We're all getting old!' Kieran bemoaned in mock anguish.

Rhea had the other pool cue. She leant back against the table. 'I've heard of him. Wasn't he the lead singer of Nirvana?'

'Oh sweet Jesus,' Lucy muttered and rolled her eyes. 'As if.'

'What did I say?'

Justin clarified on his wife's behalf. 'You've just reminded us of how young you are, and of how old we are feeling!'

'Oh okay. For a second there I thought it was *pick on the newbie* hour.' She shot Lucy a look which got returned.

Hayley came back from the bathroom. 'What did I miss?'

'Hedges,' Kieran replied. Nick spluttered into his beer.

'Covered in snow,' Justin added, spying Hayley's confusion and keen to keep the peace. He'd also seen Rhea's look to Lucy. 'We were just talking about the wintry landscapes.' It was weak but all he had. Hayley sat down and sipped her drink. Thankfully, nothing else was said on the subject. Rhea took her shot. Justin noticed Lucy staring at her backside, not in admiration. 'What can I get you, darling?' he asked, to distract and diffuse.

'Liposuction.'

He offered her a kiss instead.

**

The sunlight was beginning to fade when they stepped out into the chilly air. It was 3pm, giving them about an hour of daylight left. Lucy suggested the possibility of a taxi; Justin did his best to let her down gently. They just had to hang on to each other, keep themselves warm, and concentrate on putting one foot in front of the other.

Moaning will get us nowhere, he reminded everyone. Lucy, Nick and Alicia – each at different moments – opted to ignore his statement.

For much of it, Hayley walked alone. Occasionally Danni broke from Elliot and kept her company, but then he'd ask her a question and she'd get drawn back. Hayley didn't mind too much; she just listened to their chatter as they pushed through the still countryside.

It was gone four o'clock when they got back on the drive, and pretty much fully dark. They hadn't seen another property for almost a mile, so the lights from Kilbride House were a welcome sight.

'Girls,' Brooke said. 'First thing I'm doing when we get back is pushing the snow off the top of the hot tub. I say we grab ourselves a bottle and take a dip.'

Nick objected. 'What about us boys?'

Lucy answered. 'You've got dinner to prepare. I'm with you, Brooke, but I'm not sure we'll all fit in.'

Alicia tugged her partner's arm. 'We didn't being swimsuits.'

'No matter. Underwear's good. Wet t-shirt optional. Lucy, we'll fit in if we want it badly enough.'

Hayley spoke quietly. 'I'm fine. I need to check on Benjamin anyway.'

'Oh yeah, him,' Nick muttered. No one had really spoken about him for hours.

As they crunched their way up to the house, the parked cars came into view, Benjamin's battered Volvo the most prominent. Kieran was again reminded of the crate in the back and the dirt on the floor of the boot. 'Justin, I want to ask you something about your car – can we just hang fire?' Rhea gave him a quizzical look. 'I'll be two minutes, babe.'

Justin shrugged. 'Yeah sure. Help yourself to anything, guys – I think you know where everything is now.' The two of them veered off towards the parked vehicles while the others negotiated the icy steps leading up to the door. Having been ditched, Rhea took Hayley's hand and they headed up together.

Justin walked straight to his Bentley, shimmying past Kieran's Audi blocking him in, but his friend hung back. Once he realised he was on his own, Justin turned around. 'What is it?' he asked.

Kieran was standing just outside the group of cars, looking at Benjamin's tired, old estate. 'You said that when Benny boy got their bag out he had to get it from the back seat because the boot was full?'

'Yeah. So?'

'Something like a big box?'

'Yeah.' Justin stepped towards him. 'You can see it lifting the parcel shelf a little. Big deal: he didn't clear the car before coming here. More noteworthy was that he allowed Hayley to lug their shared bag inside.'

'I saw him messing with the box in the middle of the night.' Kieran took a look at the house: everyone was inside. He fished his mobile phone out of his pocket. 'Wrestling with it, almost.'

'I don't think he's the strongest; he could barely get the door open.' Justin was now standing next to Kieran and watched him activate the torch on his phone. 'What are you doing that for?'

'Gonna take a look. The shelf is still up a bit.' He wiped the window with his beanie and shone a light through the glass.

There was the large wooden box, like a storage crate. The lid wasn't fixed properly and offered a small triangle view of the contents, if Kieran could just get the light in the right place. He took a step back. 'Are we parked on a slope here, Just?' He surveyed the ground.

'No. What are you getting at?'

'Well, this: last night he shoved the box as far back as it would go so he could close the boot. Now, it's forward again, right up against the glass.' He went back to shining his torch inside, searching for the best angle.

Justin whipped out his own phone and did the same.

That did it: they got the right combination of cross beam on the dark little triangle between the splintery wood frame.

They both started back at the same time. 'What the fuck is that!?' Kieran exclaimed.

'Shit. It looks like some kind of animal.' They exchanged glances and both went in for another look.

It looked like a patch of hindquarters belonging to some species of mammal. There was a swatch of matted and patchy fur but also skin showing through, all of it looking grey, like it had been rubbed with ash. 'A dog, do you think?' asked Kieran.

Justin wrinkled his nose at it. 'God knows, but whatever it is I reckon it's dead.'

'So here's a question: why's he got a boxed-up dead animal in the back of his car?'

'Museum exhibit.' The two of them spun round at the voice. Benjamin was on the steps, his height accentuated. Hayley loitered behind him, looking nervous.

Justin fumbled with his phone and shoved it in his pocket, torch still on and showing through his jeans.

Kieran was less apologetic. 'Why would you bring an animal carcass on a weekend trip with strangers?'

With the light of the house framing him, Benjamin's face wasn't fully illuminated. His eyes looked black. 'Why would you snoop around the back of a car belonging to someone you do not know?'

There were a couple of seconds in which no-one said anything, just held their positions. But then Benjamin continued. 'I will answer your question first so your minds can be put at ease. It is part of an exhibit that is being relocated from London to Edinburgh. Transport costs as they are and with finances still challenging, the museum staff decided we could facilitate the transfer ourselves. Three other colleagues have similar loads.'

'So why is it still in your car?'

'I only travelled up from London yesterday. Because of this-' he waved his hand at the house '-*engagement*, I did not have time to deliver the crate to work.'

Hayley added: 'He picked me up straight from the long drive, and then we set off for here. Why do you think we were so late?'

'So,' Benjamin said. 'My question to you still stands.'

Kieran was still in defiant mood. 'Because I saw you messing with it in the middle of the night. That's not normal, Benjamin, so of course I'm going to check it out.' He walked away from the car, back towards the house. 'It's just a little weird, that's all.'

When they were on the steps together their heights matched, as did their glares. 'All you had to do was ask me,' Benjamin said.

'How? You've not been seen all day.' He pushed past him into the house.

Justin moved forward. 'Are you feeling better now?'

'Rested.' Benjamin moved the other way, towards his Volvo.

'That's good. Let's have a lovely evening then,' Justin said, more to Hayley than Benjamin. He went inside, keen to check everyone else was okay and to be of use.

He was needed immediately. Lucy was sitting on a sofa, flicking through the manual that came with the property. 'Justin, where's the key for the padlock on the shed? Brooke needs a shovel or spade to clear the hot tub deck.'

'Hook in the utility room. I'm on it.'

Elliot raised a hand to get his attention. 'Erm… Justin?'

'Yes?'

'It appears your right testicle is glowing.'

The group chuckled as he retrieved his phone and switched off the torch. Then he went to get the key Brooke needed, happy to put the spat with Benjamin behind him.

**

Brooke was impressively industrious; it only took her fifteen minutes to clear all the snow from the space around the hot tub. The women negotiated the garden and went through the side exit to the annex. Its entrance was – rather helpfully – directly facing the gate. It was one large, pine-clad box; it looked like a giant sauna. Save for the fact it was freezing. 'You won't notice once you're in the water,' Brooke said, leading the way through the building.

They cut through the main room that housed some gym equipment and weights, a pool table, foosball table and a dart board. Despite the gaming options, the boys were banned until after dinner; for now it was a female haven. Sliding doors at the far end led to the cleared deck and the sunken hot tub. The women had towels draped over their shoulders but were still fully dressed. 'We definitely doing this?' Danni asked, smirking.

Brooke began shedding layers. 'The quicker it's off, the quicker you can get warm again!' She was down to bra and knickers in no time and almost fell in her haste to get into the water. She pressed a button and the bubbles and steam started in earnest. 'It's beautiful! Hurry up!'

The others, laughing, followed suit, except for Hayley who carried the unopened bottle of prosecco; they had decided to forgo glasses and just swig from the neck. Rhea was last in, and had to accept the wolf-whistles from the others for her figure and classy, flimsy underwear. She did her best to hush them as she stepped into the water. Steff smiled. 'If only we could get away with wearing that these days, eh girls?'

Lucy sneered: 'Speak for yourself, Perry.'

'I'm not sure Elliot would notice,' Danni remarked.

'I'd notice,' said Alicia, and she leaned over and gave Brooke a kiss. More wolf-whistles followed.

Danni looked up to Hayley. 'Are you sure you're not coming in, Hayley? We can definitely make room.'

She hugged the bottle against her coat and leaned against the short fence around the decking. 'No, it's not fair on Benjamin.'

Steff made a contribution. 'Nick didn't want me to come in here, but here I am. The boys will look after him, Hayles.'

'I'm fine, really.'

'You do what's right for you,' Lucy said. She reached her arm up. 'Bottle please.' Hayley handed it over and Lucy popped the cork to a round of cheers. Now without a role or a purpose, Hayley slinked off, back through the annex.

'She okay?' Rhea asked.

'She's just Hayley,' Lucy remarked and took the first swig.

**

Back in the house the men had gravitated towards the sofas, with the need to prep dinner a good two hours off. Hayley saw that Benjamin was sitting on a sofa on his own, so went over and joined him. The others greeted her warmly enough but she could tell there was a sense of her invading a male-dominated space. She also felt that whatever had been the conversation was now going to change direction with her arrival. Justin got up, insisting that Hayley have a drink and he be the one to get it her. Perhaps he still felt awkward about the altercation outside.

With that in mind, she looked at Kieran. He was sitting on the sofa to their right, staring across in Nick's direction. She wondered if he'd looked at Benjamin at all since they'd gathered here. She patted Benjamin's knee. 'Are you okay?'

'I am fine. I am getting to know your gentlemen friends better.'

Nick snickered. 'Be careful there, Benny: that can mean something else on these shores!'

'Benjamin,' he reminded them.

'Yeah, *Nicholas*,' Elliot rebuked. Justin gave Hayley a white wine spritzer for which she thanked him. He took up his seat again, next to Elliot, and the group settled into a lull. Justin then asked Kieran a question about work and the conversation inside the square of sofas headed off in a safe direction, Hayley and Benjamin nothing more than observers.

It was in another lull when Nick directed a question to Hayley. 'What's my Steff up to in there?'

Hayley frowned. 'I don't know what you mean.'

'She wasn't going to get into the hot tub so is she just sitting out there, gossiping with them?'

'No. She's... she's in the water with them.'

Nick's brow furrowed. 'In nothing but her underwear?'

'That's… that's how they all are.'

Nick got up, setting his beer bottle on the glass coffee table. 'Back in a minute.'

They watched him slip out through the patio doors and head for the gate. When they saw him slam the latter, Justin, Elliot and Kieran decided to follow.

The women jumped when he bustled through onto the annex veranda; instinctively Danni and Rhea slipped further under the water. Alicia let out an outburst. 'Jesus, Nick!'

Lucy, her back to the door, craned her neck round. 'Girls only! You knew we'd be in our underwear!'

'Like I'm even looking. Steff?' Steff's body was tense and still. Brooke could feel the change in her through the touch they shared upper arm to upper arm. She didn't reply to him so he carried on. 'Steff, I thought you knew how I felt about this?'

She didn't answer, but others asked the question for her. 'What's wrong?' Danni saw the others approaching through the annex.

Nick growled. 'Steff, get out.'

She finally spoke, albeit quite timidly. 'Nick, it's not a problem.'

'It is for me.' He picked up one of the towels draped over the outside seating.

'Being with her friends?' asked Lucy. 'What the hell are we here for?'

'Not that. This.' He waved a hand at the hot tub. 'Being virtually naked next to…'

Brooke worked it out. She stood, spraying water onto Steff and Alicia. 'Wait, you mean us? Because she's in her fucking knickers next to *us*?'

'Well I wouldn't let her sit naked next to these guys.' On cue, Justin and Elliot poked their heads through. Elliot shielded his eyes and turned back.

Brooke still stood, bold and angry. 'Fuck me, you think because she's next to two lesbians she's going to get, what, indoctrinated into some gay cult?'

Rhea muttered: 'This has taken a turn.'

Nick sneered. 'Not a cult, no, but you lot obviously get in people's heads. Why else are there so many coming out of the woodwork?'

'Oh shit,' Justin said. 'Nick, come back to the house.'

'You lot!' Alicia exclaimed and slapped a frustrated hand against the bubbling water.

Brooke snarled. 'You're such – a fucking – dick.'

Nick shrugged. 'And you wish you had one.'

Kieran now emerged next to Justin and the two of them made a grab for Nick. 'Okay, big guy,' Kieran said. 'Too much drink for you: black coffee this way!'

Lucy spat. 'Get him out of here, Justin!'

'On it!' They wrestled Nick into the annex and out of immediate sight. He objected and called out for Steff.

Steff jumped out of the hot tub and grabbed a towel. 'I am so, so sorry!' She disappeared through the sliding doors, using Nick's name like a swear word.

Brooke still stood in warrior pose; Alicia eased her back down. Rhea looked each of the other four in the face before asking: 'Is this what it's always like when you guys get together?'

CHAPTER SEVEN

Dinner was tense. Before everyone sat down Steff pushed Nick into offering an apology, which he did, but with very little sincerity in his tone. As a result, Brooke picked up her utensils and sat on one of the stools in the kitchen. When the steaks came and she didn't rejoin the table, Alicia showed solidarity with her partner and took her plate to the breakfast bar.

'Girls, come on,' Justin pleaded, laying the last dinner down at his place setting.

'Let 'em sulk,' Nick said and got stuck into his meal. The others reprimanded him but his skin remained thick.

After they'd all eaten, (although Benjamin seemed to resort to chopping up food and moving it around rather than trying it) Justin encouraged them not to loiter at the table but spread themselves around, not wanting it to feel like two distinct camps. Some joined the girls in the kitchen area, some went to the sofas. Nick grabbed Elliott and offered him a game of darts. Not wanting to cause further friction, Elliot complied and the pair of them disappeared to the annex.

When Lucy and Justin sat together on one of the sofas, Alicia spied an opportunity and joined them. She crouched down by the arm. Lucy smiled. 'Hey sweetie.'

'Hi guys. Listen, just wanted to let you know, thanks for bringing this all together and everything, but Brooke and I are leaving first thing in the morning.'

Steff overheard from the sofa opposite. 'Oh no – please, Alicia. Not because of us!'

'It's not you at all, Steff; please understand that.'

Justin patted Alicia's hand resting on the sofa. 'How about you sleep on it? It'll all feel different in the morning when we've sobered up.'

'I'm as sober as a judge, Justin. And it's me, by the way, not Brooke. She'd happily stay and take him on. Me, I'm tired of it. We still get it on a daily basis, even in this day and age. We don't need it from friends.'

Steff got up. 'I'll go and tell him what he's done and make him apologise again!'

'It's done, Steff – leave it. We had a great run though. From school to near forty: that's good going. Not many people still know the friends they had as kids. We'll keep in touch, of course.'

The finality of it shook Steff. Her cheeks blushed pink and the tears came. She stormed off in the direction of the patio doors and the annex.

Lucy sneered. 'Even though they've been together, what, nine or ten years, I can't say I've ever warmed to him.' She kept to herself the fact that she'd suggested to Justin that the girls get the single beds. 'Good for you, sticking up for what you believe in.'

'It's not what I *believe* in, Lucy: it's who I am.'

'Yeah, sure. You know what I mean.'

Danni and Brooke walked over from the kitchen, arms round each other, congenial smiles on their faces, but tinged with a look of resignation. 'Let's try to have a lovely last hour or so,' Danni said.

Kieran and Rhea were snug on another sofa. Kieran took umbrage at Danni's timings. 'An hour? It's only just gone nine!'

'Early night for us,' Brooke replied. 'Big drive tomorrow, and probably a load of snow to shift first.'

Hayley and Benjamin had been quiet through all of this, having returned to the same sofa after dinner that they'd been on when Nick first heard about Steff's penchant for a hot tub. Hayley was very anxious about what was happening. She addressed Benjamin quietly. 'What does this mean for us?'

'It means you have to decide quickly,' he replied.

'I can't.' He didn't respond so she stood up and spoke to Alicia instead. 'Please stay until Monday! We've all got so much to catch up on. I haven't told you all about my travels around Europe yet!'

Alicia offered a faint smile. 'That's sweet, Hayles. If you ever want to give me a call to do that, I'll listen, but our minds are made up.'

Then Steff came back in, with Nick on her arm and Elliot bringing up the rear. Nick stood tall and cleared his throat. 'Listen: for what it's worth, I didn't mean to upset anyone.' Steff jiggled his arm; he looked at her and huffed. 'And if it would be better that we left tomorrow instead, then that's what we'll do.'

Alicia shook her head, but she beckoned Steff over and they hugged. When they separated, Alicia was still adamant. 'Let's not discuss it anymore – I don't want to bring everyone's evening down.'

'No one needs to leave,' said Elliot, walking a circuit around the group. Nobody answered him.

Kieran got up, taking Rhea with him. They went to the Bluetooth speaker and Kieran instructed the AI to play the top songs of the 90s. 'Okay, so if this is us for the last time – no, let's say *for a while* – we're not just going to slob about on the sofas, are we?' He instructed the speaker to turn up to full volume. 'Let's finish the night off properly then!' he yelled.

When *Tubthumping* came on and the sofas emptied, Kieran pulled Rhea to one side, despite her taking a step towards the makeshift dancefloor. 'Quick word,' he said.

She stroked his chest. 'Yes, babe?'

'You heard Benson and Hedges there, didn't you? What do you suppose that meant: having to decide quickly?'

'Couldn't say.'

'Odd though, right?'

She furrowed her brow. 'You asking the *cocktail waitress*?'

'I'm asking Rhea Bennett, the-'

She shushed him, and then kissed him. 'Not this weekend. I'm going to dance.' Kieran let her go and followed her for a few seconds with his eyes. She really was something else. But then his gaze fell on Benjamin, loitering behind the sofas, watching the others.

Kieran still didn't trust him.

**

Couples drifted off to bed in dribs and drabs and without much fanfare; the threat of morning departures still meant that overall the evening felt flat. Nick took to drinking scotch in one of the leather armchairs by the fire, which meant that he was fit for nothing but his bed before anyone else. Elliot and Steff took him up; Elliot came

47

back immediately but Steff soon followed him, as she didn't want her night to be done so early, especially as she might be leaving in the morning too. She apologised again to Alicia. It meant that she and Brooke stayed up a little longer.

Justin and Lucy were next. Lucy remarked that hosting had taken it out of her, which raised a smile as everyone knew that she'd done very little compared to Justin. They were wished goodnight by everyone, and Kieran took that as the cue to kill the music.

Danni had expected Hayley and Benjamin to go next, but they stayed on their sofa, chatting quietly to each other or to any of the others that would sit by them. Not many did. Danni tried, but Hayley's conversation seemed a little stilted with Benjamin around, despite her apparent eagerness to discuss her jaunt around the continent. The circumstances of their meeting still remained vague, and Danni soon grew tired of asking questions. She used the excuse of getting a drink but then didn't return to them.

When Elliot sidled over and said he was beat, Danni was happy to call it a night.

Which meant she didn't know what happened next downstairs.

As she and Elliot got undressed either side of the bed, she asked: 'Do you think he's good for Hayley?'

'Who? Benjamin?'

'No, Idris Elba.'

Elliot chuckled. 'I don't know, love. But as far as I know she's never had someone before, so the first one is always going to be a little tricky and awkward.'

She peeled off another garment before stating: 'Wait a sec, I was your first one.'

'I rest my case… and my head.' He slipped in under the duvet. 'What a night. It'll be better in the morning, I'm sure.' He closed his eyes.

'I hope so.' She got in next to him and switched off the lamp.

**

Steff was the last one to go to bed. She sat by the extinguished fire, in the same chair Nick had used, and swirled the last of the wine around the bottom of her glass. She was so frustrated with how the evening had gone, and her partner's role in it.

She was well aware of what she had with Nick; they'd been together long enough to know each other inside and out. He was gruff, rough around the edges, outspoken, and not everyone's friend. In truth, that was something that she loved about him: his certainty about who he was and what he was about. It was the strength she didn't feel she had herself about her own character. She needed Nick to keep her from flaking out and fading away.

But it was – at times – something she hated about him. And today had been one of those times. As she drained her glass she conceded that this would probably be the last opportunity to have a gathering like this, complete with partners. It felt like the end of an era. Turning forty was going to herald a new chapter in their lives. She didn't feel too happy about it.

'Nothing I can do about it here,' she muttered, and decided it was time for bed.

She stumbled a little up the stairs, and felt herself weave slightly as she navigated the landing. She got into their room and closed their door with a heavier thud than she anticipated. She shushed herself and sat on the bed. Nick was fast asleep on his side; his snores sounded like someone rummaging through boxes. He often kept her awake with his night-time snorts and honks, but she thought she'd have no trouble tonight; the alcohol had made sure of that.

Then, in between Nick's saw logs, she heard a new sound. Someone was being sick in the shared bathroom, or at least dry heaving. In her mind she imagined it was Alicia. She pictured herself helping her old friend, which then in turn changed her mind about leaving tomorrow, and then the weekend was saved. The fact the girls had their own bathroom didn't register; in the swirling logic of a drunken haze this felt like a solution to Steff. She got up, intending to lend her support to the stricken.

She wobbled her way down the landing and almost tipped into the closed door of the bathroom. The retching had stopped but there were still the muffled sounds of movement within. She knocked on, and offered in an overloud whisper: 'You okay in there?'

She sensed a hand on the handle so stood back to better greet her friend. Alicia. She would take Brooke too. It didn't matter, as long as she had a last chance to make a good impression.

Steff couldn't hold in the little squeak when she saw who it was. Benjamin, still in his grey shirt and trousers, looking more pale than usual. His hair was slicked back, a sheen of sweat on his brow. Thin, colourless lips and gaunt cheeks. His eyes – missing their spectacles – narrow, like slivers of slate.

'Are you sick?' she asked.

'I'm hungry,' he replied.

CHAPTER EIGHT

Rhea was aware of several things, all at once. One: she was awake but it was still dark. Two: Kieran was not next to her. Three: there was a car horn sounding outside. Mingled in with all of that was the remnant of a dream: Hayley at the foot of her bed, telling her to go back to sleep. Rhea blinked her eyes wide and double-checked the room. There was not much light – just a little coming from under the door – but she was pretty certain Hayley wasn't in here with her.

And Kieran? Her hand instinctively patted across the empty space on the other side of the bed; he definitely wasn't there, but of course she knew that. Her other hand reached for the bedside table. She expected her exploring fingers to light upon her phone, but there was nothing but a glass of water which she nearly sent to the floor. The car horn sounded again.

'Kieran!' she called.

'Out here,' he replied. His voice came from the landing. She swung her legs out and crossed to the door. Once it was open, she shielded her eyes from the overhead light and squinted at Kieran. He was crouched by the bathroom door, in nothing but his shorts, prodding at the carpet with a finger.

'What is it?' she asked.

He rubbed thumb and forefinger together. 'I think it's blood. Perhaps someone had a nose bleed in the night?'

'What time is it? I can't find my phone.'

He glanced at his watch. 'Just gone six.' He cocked an ear at the sound of the horn. 'Is that coming from outside?'

'I think it's a car.' She instantly felt stupid; of course it was. She gave herself a shake. *Come on. Game face.*

Kieran pushed up to his feet, and pointed to the bedroom. Before they got back in, Elliot's tussled head appeared from around a door frame. 'Whatsit? What?' He screwed his face up at the light.

'Don't know, El – just going to check it out.' Back in the room he flicked on the light and he and Rhea walked over to the window.

Outside, there was a light flurry of fresh snow in the air. By the parked cars, stood Benjamin. The boot of his Volvo was gaping open, projecting a weak light into the darkness. The large wooden crate had been dragged clear of it, and was positioned in front of him. The bulb inside the car cast enough of a glow onto the driver's seat. It was Hayley activating the horn.

Benjamin saw them both at the window and waved. There was something on his mouth. He spoke to Hayley and her beeping became more enthusiastic and less intermittent.

Elliot and Danni stepped into their room. 'So what is it?' asked Elliot.

'It's Benjamin. And Hayley. I think they're getting us up like some fucking early morning roll call.' Kieran turned around and ushered them out of the room.

The others were gathering on the landing; Lucy and Justin appeared in single file down the narrow staircase that led to their bedroom on the third level of the house. Kieran described to them all what he'd seen outside.

'Was Steff there?' asked Nick, looking around the group. 'She's up already.'

Kieran shook his head. 'Just them two as far as I could tell.'

'I've got an uber-hangover. I thought that noise was just in my head.'

Justin rubbed life into his face and pointed towards the stairs. 'Shall we go down and see what all the fuss is about then?' He led the way and the others followed – Nick first, calling out Steff's name. When they reached the downstairs hallway, he took the door to the living room still shouting for her; the others – pyjama-clad or in dressing gowns – waited by the front door as Justin tried the handle. It wasn't locked; why would it be with two of them outside in the snow?

They all trundled out onto the steps. 'What's going on?' Justin called.

Benjamin spread his arms wide and grinned. Whatever stained his face was also splattered on his shirt. He looked like he'd been eating chili like a dog. 'Welcome to the message!'

'What the hell does that mean?' Brooke asked. Then she was distracted by Hayley getting out of the car. She moved timidly, sliding along the side of the Volvo. She looked up and offered a simpering smile.

'Hayley!' Danni started to move down the steps towards her.

Benjamin interjected. 'Might I suggest that you stay there until you have heard what I have to say? She does not need your help, at least not the help you are thinking of offering.'

Danni hovered on the last step. Elliot reached out and tugged her back. 'Hayley's fine,' he whispered.

'What is this, *Benson*?' Kieran yelled.

Benjamin chuckled. 'You are all so funny. Really. Hayley has very entertaining friends. This is going to be very difficult for her. I know I could not do the choosing.'

Nick bustled through from the back. 'What the fuck is this? Where's Steff?'

Justin stopped him from getting any further out. 'I think Benjamin's going to tell us about something that's important to him, and then hopefully we'll get on with our morning. Steff'll be around somewhere.' He turned to Benjamin. 'What is it you want to tell us? What's the message?'

He clapped his hands together. 'It has a number of parts. Here is the first: I am not a man in the way you know a man to be.' He paced slowly behind his box, like he was taking a class and it was his lectern. 'What I am is hard to explain exactly, but from the movies and books you have experienced, you might know it best as a vampire.'

'Holy shit,' Nick uttered. 'What a fucking joke this idiot is.' He stepped down once more but this time no one stopped him; instead Justin, Kieran and Elliot went with him. To do what, Justin wasn't sure – possibly get Hayley back inside. They crunched onto the fresh snow that was filling in previous footprints.

Benjamin's hands dropped to the large shipping crate. His fingers lingered for half a second under the lid and then he threw his hands up. The lid flew into the air and flipped over, twice, before slapping into the snow a couple of feet in front of the men. They staggered back, cursing and grabbing each other.

'Here is the second part.' He put his hands back on the open crate, but this time he tipped it forward, spilling out its contents. A torso, limbs, a head. A grey, dead animal rolled into the snow. Lucy screamed; Danni grabbed hold of her.

Seeing it still and in its entirety did not wholly help with its identification. It was much larger than a dog, particularly in the length of its limbs. The hair it had was short and bristly which ruled out any breed of wolf. The feet had recognisable paws but they were longer than the norm, and had larger, knuckled toes with vicious-looking claws. The head had a long muzzle with a menacing jawline crammed with fangs, overlapping the lip in irregular fashion. It was nothing short of a monster.

'It's the thing for your museum,' Kieran stated. 'Why are you showing us this?'

'I am afraid I told you a little lie because of your snooping. This is not for any museum. This is my... how shall I say? *Hell hound!*'

'Yeah? Well, thank fuck it's dead,' Kieran replied.

Elliot stepped across the others, doing his best to exude calm in pinstriped pyjamas. 'Don't you think we've had enough of the theatrics now, Benjamin? It's dark, and it's cold.'

'And time's wasting,' Brooke added. She stroked Alicia's arm. 'Babe, let's go and get packed.'

'I have more to show you!' Benjamin announced. He stuck out his right arm and then tugged at the sleeve with the other. 'Please observe.' He held the skinny forearm over the head of the deceased animal. And then, with a long fingernail from his left hand, he made a two-inch long slit in his wrist.

Lucy flinched. 'Oh, don't do that! Stop him, somebody!'

Fat drops of blood fell down onto the beast's face, splattering its muzzle, jaw, teeth. Benjamin moved his arm to perfect his aim.

Blood, thought Danni, now looking at the stains on the man's shirt and face. *He's already got blood on him.* She also noticed his lips for the first time: they were fuller, swollen almost.

Elliot pleaded with him to stop. Benjamin continued to drip into the mouth of the carcass.

That was when the head of the thing twitched. The muzzle rose from the snow in small jerky movements. Then the jaw opened, exposing a grey tongue like the tail of an eel. More blood spattered on the teeth, the tongue. The throat convulsed and the beast swallowed.

An eyelid flicked open. A black orb rolled. With each new development the group reacted. Shock. Disgust. Fear.

Then it sprang to its feet and they all screamed and yelled, clambering back towards the hallway. It started to prowl in front of its box, head pointing at the steps, jaws snapping at every movement they made.

Benjamin moved the box to one side, like he was housekeeping. He spoke to them as he organised the space in front of the house. 'I did not expect to have to use the hound but some of you were talking about leaving and I cannot allow that just yet. Hayley is not ready with her decision.'

Eyes flicked towards Hayley. She stepped away from the Volvo and moved closer to them, whilst still holding a position behind Benjamin. She clasped her hands together. 'Last night got so tense! It was looking like the weekend was going to be all over by this morning!'

Danni called out. 'What's going on, Hayley?' But then the hell hound zeroed in on her, moved forward and snapped its jaws. Danni fell back onto the threshold.

'Do not worry,' Benjamin said. 'As long as you stay within the confines of the house then the hound will not pursue you.' He smirked. 'I have allowed you the steps so that we might have this audience.'

'No way,' Alicia yelled. 'We're getting out of here!'

Benjamin shook his head. 'I am afraid no one is leaving, until Hayley has decided and we do what needs to be done.'

Kieran pushed forward to the bottom step and roared. 'Then fucking tell us so we can get this over and done with!'

The swell of anger stimulated Nick's emotions. 'What have you done with Steff? Where is she?'

Benjamin lifted his hands to try and appease. 'If you will stop yelling I will explain everything.' Kieran managed his own emotions; Nick needed Elliot's help. Benjamin observed all and waited for the lull. 'Thank you. Now, here is the next part of the message. Much like what you will know from mythology and the movies, I have the capacity to make more of my kind. Hayley will soon join me and we shall live the life of the eternal night together.' Hayley smiled and hugged herself at the mention. Benjamin continued. 'However, it can be a lonely existence, and – unlike myself – she has already lived a large part of her life with good friends. She does not want to give you up-'

'You don't have to!' Danni yelled.

'Quiet!' Benjamin's mouth seemed to extend from his face, and for a split-second he appeared to have more teeth than was possible. Then he regained his composure, and his regular look. 'You have asked me to explain, so please listen. Hayley loves her friends, so I am allowing her to retain some of them, to join us as *Vampyri*. But only four of you: this is why she must choose. For every transference an amount of human blood is needed to nurture the process, much like the suckling of an infant. Four bodies to feed four new vampires, big and strong.'

Now Hayley joined Benjamin's side; He put an arm around her and she leaned into his chest. Standing next to another, it was noticeable that Benjamin looked taller, stronger than before, broader across the shoulders. *He's fed already,* Elliot thought, with considerable alarm.

Justin raised his hand like they were all back at school, top of the class just like 1999 all over again. 'Benjamin, four and four makes eight. There are ten of us here.'

'Nine,' Benjamin corrected.

This got Nick all agitated again and the hound drew closer, snapping at the side of the steps where Nick tussled with Elliot and Kieran. 'Where is she?' Nick's foot brushed the snow and the beast was there; if Kieran hadn't have pulled him back it might have taken it off.

'Correct math, but Hayley also needs a blood supply from one of you, so that is nine. As for your tenth, I also need to keep my strength up for the work ahead. So, to the next part of the message.' He slipped away from Hayley and moved back towards the cars.

Nick was shouting *no*, over and over, in anticipation of what might come. The whole pack of them leaned towards him in support. All save Rhea, so that a small gap formed between her and the others. She too was watching Benjamin's progress back towards the cars, but she had noticed something else.

'The wheels,' she muttered, her voice drawing the hound towards her. 'Look at all the tyres.' Every vehicle except for the Volvo had knife handles sticking out of the walls of the tyres, rendering all of them flat.

The others didn't take much notice: they were too busy watching Benjamin, including Hayley who had turned around. Kieran's Audi was parked behind Justin's Bentley; they were the cars furthest away from the steps. Benjamin bent down behind the side of the Audi then came back up, dragging something.

Snow fell off Steff's body as it was brought into the light of the driveway. There was the same frozen smear of brownish-red along her throat and chest that had been present on the sheep. Her body was rigid. 'I have this one on ice. I will thaw her out when I need more blood.' He picked her up one-handed, fingers locked on the back of the skull, and lifted her up high for all to see.

Nick shrugged Kieran off, and touched down on the driveway. 'You cunt!' he roared and made to sprint towards Benjamin.

The hell hound responded immediately. It twisted its body, changing direction from its position in front of Rhea, then bounded towards Nick.

In his haste to cover the ground, Nick slipped in the fresh snow, crashing down to his knees and elbows. The creature was traversing the conditions with ease and was almost on him.

Hayley jumped forward. 'Careful, Nick!' She skidded over and got a hand on his shoulder.

The hound was mid-leap but it contorted its body, missing Nick and Hayley, instead landing by her feet. Hayley helped Nick up, and with her body between the beast and the man, she was able to push him back towards the steps. Only when contact was broken between them did the hound lunge again, but by then Nick had made the first stone slab.

However, Hayley was still within arm's length of him. He slapped her hard across the face. 'You fucking bitch!'

Benjamin was back over to them with a speed that was barely fathomable. His movement nudged Hayley aside and then he was in Nick's face.

A noise came out of him, something between a hiss and a growl. His jaw opened wide and then seemed to dislocate, the lower half touching his chest. The pink insides of his mouth puffed out, almost filling the cavity, and unfolded a new layer of sharp teeth so that there were two concentric sets. The tongue narrowed as the space became restricted, became longer, and grew sharp exploratory spines that almost touched Nick's face.

Kieran dragged Nick back so hard and fast that his t-shirt ripped.

Hayley's hand reached out and touched Benjamin's arm. He withdrew, and his face collapsed back into a more human expression. 'She is too kind to you. If I had my way, we would feast like gluttons on you all. Instead, I give her this day to choose, to have last hours with each of you. At nightfall she will convey to me her decision. Then we see this through.'

He stepped back. Surprisingly, Hayley didn't go with him but looked up imploringly at her friends. Her left cheek glowed red. 'I'm sorry that it's come to this, but it's what I want. For me, and for some of you.'

'Bitch!' Nick spat, but a little more subdued with Kieran's arms around him.

Benjamin spoke once more. 'This should go without saying but I will say it anyway so we are clear: if any harm comes to Hayley, then I will kill you all in the most painful ways I can conjure.' He indicated the poised creature with his hand. 'The hound will ensure that no one leaves. You cannot make contact with the world.' He then pointed to a tree halfway down the drive. 'Can you see?' There was a plastic bag hanging from a branch, some weight in it pulling it taut and vertical despite the light breeze. 'Your mobile phones are there. And your car keys. Tempting, no? You will not risk it I think.'

Rhea glared at Hayley. It hadn't been a dream after all.

Benjamin pointed into the group. 'Kieran? Brooke? You both have smart watches on. Remove them please and throw them onto the snow.'

The two of them looked at each other from different sides of the group. Brooke called out, her eyes still on Kieran. 'And what if we choose not to?'

Within a heartbeat Benjamin was among them, in the centre of the steps, sending them sprawling. He held Alicia by the throat; she battered against his arm but to no avail, her cheeks a deep pink, her teeth clenched.

Kieran and Brooke tore at their watches and tossed them away. Alicia dropped to her knees, clasping her neck. Brooke was there instantly. Benjamin was somehow back on the drive, picking up the discarded hardware. 'Go inside,' he said. 'There is nothing more to say, until Hayley tells me tonight who is going to join us.'

They didn't quite know what to do, but Justin nodded and made an ushering gesture with his hands. They gathered themselves and pushed through into the living area. Unsurprisingly they moved swiftly to the dining room window so as to have eyes on Benjamin and the infernal hound.

He had returned to where he had dropped Steff's body. This time he didn't hide her on the other side of the Audi but laid her behind it, adjacent to the bumper, in full view. Then he went back to the Volvo. He closed the boot and got in the driver's side. He reversed out, made a clumsy multi-point turn in the space he'd just vacated, being careful not to hit Steff, then headed off down the long driveway. He didn't take the car off the property; instead, just before the exit to the lane, he veered right onto the grass, under the first of the driveway lights: one of a pair of tall ones in the form of lanterns. Then they watched him get out and return to the boot. He popped it open, pushed the parcel shelf back and climbed in. On his knees, he reached up and grabbed the boot lid. As it came down he disappeared inside of it. The parcel shelf popped up a couple of times; when it found its positon, all was still.

The hound crossed in front of the bifold doors, between them and Steff, its black eyes looking in.

'Well, shit,' Kieran murmured.

Bodies slumped as the tension and adrenalin levels shifted. Couples found each other, except Danni and Elliot who rallied round Nick. He was insisting they had to bring Steff inside; they replied that for now at least it was an impossibility. Then they turned their backs on the view and the slowly lightening sky.

Hayley was leaning against one of the kitchen islands. Her shoulders were hunched up and she looked a little sheepish. 'Hi?' she offered.

CHAPTER NINE

A decision was taken: five minutes to get properly dressed and then everyone on the sofas to thrash this thing out.

Nick hadn't moved from the window; he was staring out to where Steff lay, and watching the creature pace around the top of the driveway. Elliot came back with a sweater for him. 'Do you want anything else from your room? I can go up again.' Nick grunted a negative and took the clothing. He didn't put it on though, just kept staring out at the scene of the travesty. Elliot left him alone and went to the sofas.

Hayley wasn't seated yet; she stood behind one of the armchairs near the fire place. The rest were in couples: Brooke and Alicia on the sofa that had its back to Hayley; Justin and Lucy opposite them; Elliot joined Danni to the left of the girls; Kieran and Rhea were to their right. Symmetrical for now, but they had to address the horror of why they were no longer a neat group of half a dozen couples. No one looked relaxed; each pair was close together but sitting forward. Brooke was re-examining Alicia's neck while she was telling her not to fuss. Lucy had had a cry in Justin's arms but she'd just about got through it.

Danni hadn't yet had an emotion reaction to the death of one of her oldest friends. It didn't seem real just now, so in some respects the tears were being held back in reserve until the picture got clearer. To that end, she beckoned Hayley over. 'Come and sit with us. You need to explain exactly what you've got yourself messed up in.'

Elliot, having just sat down, got up and perched on the sofa arm. Hayley sidled into the seated square and flopped down next to Danni. She smiled warmly at the group.

'Hayley, sweetheart,' Brooke said. 'Please take that grin off your face. No one else is fucking smiling.'

Danni raised a hand to calm her, then she turned to Hayley. She cupped one of her hands in both of hers. 'Now, you tell us as best you can, who Benjamin is and why he is doing this to us.'

A look of confusion flitted across her eyes and she looked as if she was going to counter this with a smile but at the last second thought better of it. Instead Hayley made her face as neutral as possible. 'It is exactly as he said. He is a vampire. I am his familiar – his day companion – and have been for over a year. However, this arrangement is not forever; soon he will turn me, grant me enduring life. And he has agreed to turn some of you because he loves me, and I love you. It's actually quite wonderful.'

Kieran rubbed furiously at his bald pate. 'Have you fucking heard yourself, Hayles?' He then punched the arm of the sofa; Rhea soothed him.

Danni continued. 'But none of that is real, is it? There is no such thing as vampires.'

Hayley tilted her head. 'Did you not see everything that happened outside?'

There was a moment's pause for thought: the hell hound revived with blood; the speed with which Benjamin moved; Steff's lifeless body held up with ease. It was a painful silence.

It was Lucy who broke it. 'He's just a madman, a lunatic! Don't they get bouts of enhanced strength or something because they're crazy? Didn't I see that somewhere?'

Justin had his arm around her. 'I think for now we'd be foolish not to believe him – and Hayley – because so far he's done exactly what a vampire would do.'

'What?' Kieran asked. 'You mean going to sleep in the boot of his car because the sun's coming up? Then I say we go on down there and drive a stake through his heart!' He nodded to the stack of wood by the fireplace.

'The monster-thing outside?' Alicia offered. 'We'd have no chance.'

Justin continued. 'Yes, I mean *that*, but also Steff's murder. Her throat was open, Kieran. You said he went out last night, so I think we can include the killing of sheep too, presumably for blood. It doesn't really matter if we think it's true; he certainly does, and he seems willing enough to see it through. So, Hayley, what does that really mean for you?'

All eyes were back on her. 'It means what Benjamin said. Four of you can become virtually immortal with me. I wish it could be everyone, but the… the extra blood is needed for the transference.' She threw up an arm in frustration. 'The process was supposed to be started tonight, while you were all sleeping in your beds, painlessly. But then some of you threatened to leave and I started to panic.' For the first time she looked genuinely upset. 'We decided we would have to tell you to make you stay… unfortunately, Steff caught Benjamin in a moment of weakness.'

'A moment of weakness?' Kieran queried. 'She wasn't a slice of fucking chocolate cake!'

Elliot spoke up, standing from his position on the arm. 'Kee: enough. It doesn't help.'

'That could have been me,' Rhea muttered. 'The night before. I heard him being sick. I waited at the bathroom door, but then moved away so as not to embarrass him. If he'd opened it and seen me…' Kieran hugged her, his energy now diverted away from Hayley.

Elliot carried on. 'So you're serious, Hayley? During the course of today you're going to weigh each of us up and then choose the lucky four to take the trip with you into vampire eternity? Then, when it's dark, Benjamin comes back and makes good on his promise?'

'That's it exactly, Elliot, yes.' She offered him a smile that said *thank you*.

'Jesus Christ.' He dropped back down onto the arm.

Alicia stirred. 'It's dark by four.' She pointed to a clock on the wall. 'We've got less than eight hours.'

Brooke followed. 'Plenty of time to get ourselves out of here.'

Hayley perched. 'Oh, but you can't!'

'Shut up, Hayley. You've said your piece.' Brooke stood. 'Let the grown-ups take it from here.'

Kieran did similar, but encouraged Rhea to stay seated. He called across to the dining area windows. 'Nick? That thing still there, buddy?'

Nick half turned his head, nodded, then returned to his vigil.

It was enough for Kieran. 'Right. So while that thing is out front I'm going to sneak out the back.' He pointed through the patio doors. 'If I go through the side gate there's a gap behind the annex.

Slip through there and I reckon it's a jog across an open field and then I'm at the road. If there are no cars about I'm still going to reach a house inside half an hour if I run.'

Rhea wriggled round on the sofa so she faced the windows. 'Are you sure, babe?' her face took on a stern look. She stood up to be next to him.

'Piece of cake. But would you go and be my eyes at the front? Not sure how responsive Nick's going to be should anything… change.'

'You mean the dog-thing? So just think about this a minute. It sounds dangerous.'

'That's why I need you to spot me. Go on.'

She spoke in a whisper. 'Then perhaps I should do it. I'm probably faster than you.'

He didn't contradict her on that score, but added: 'But they're my friends.'

She weighed it up, throwing their dire situation and Kieran's determined nature into the mix. She then nodded and sprang into action. The others' eyes flitted between the two of them. Kieran did some warm-ups and stretches in his sportswear.

'Could be risky,' Elliot muttered.

'He's got this,' Justin reassured.

Rhea was soon at the front window. She patted Nick's arm and then stepped aside to get a better view of the driveway. 'It's here, prowling!'

Kieran didn't want to think about it anymore; it would only slow things down. He put a hand on the sliding door handle, flicked up the locking mechanism. Because it made a sound it prompted him to look back at Rhea. She didn't react so he assumed all was fine. He did the same when he slid the door open, letting in a cold blast of air. Rhea remained focused on her view.

Kieran eyed the tall gate, the way the latch worked. He visualised his route after that: behind the annex, across a field… 'Okay, wish me luck.'

'Luck,' Lucy replied.

Kieran slipped out onto the patio.

Rhea shouted from the front of the house. 'It's moving!'

Kieran was already crossing the garden so Elliot became a go-between. 'What's happening, Rhea?'

'It's gone! Round the house!' Get him back in!' she screamed.

Brooke and Alicia filled the doorway to the garden. They shouted at Kieran and beckoned him back.

He was at the gate, a hand on the latch. 'It's okay, I can do this!'

Then a thudding crunch slammed into the wood, sending him stumbling back. The beckoning at the door became frantic. Kieran pirouetted to face them but slipped in the snow.

Another thump at the gate, and then an elongated claw scrambled for purchase at the top.

Kieran was back on his feet and scuttling across the snow. It was a large step up to the patio, another potential slipping point.

The thing appeared, hunched and ungainly at the top of the gate, and then it dropped to all fours into the garden.

Kieran negotiated the step, then barrelled forward, clipping the patio furniture, taking the most direct route. There were screams for him and outstretched hands.

The creature crossed the side piece of lawn in a single bound. A small jump up and it was on the patio.

The others backed away as Kieran flew towards them. 'Be ready with the door!' someone shouted. It was Rhea, hurdling a sofa to get there.

The hound was at Kieran's heels. He threw himself into the house. The thing snapped its jaws in a last gasp attempt to get purchase on him. It missed by an inch.

Kieran hit the hardwood floor. Justin was on the door, but wasn't quick enough.

And yet it didn't follow. A steaming snout, slathering jaws and black, soulless eyes came to an abrupt halt at the threshold. Justin slid the door to; the glass fogged up immediately with the creature's breath.

Rhea was dragging Kieran away; he insisted he was alright as others made a fuss of him. Elliot was with Justin at the door, staring down at the hound. It backed off, and started to prowl the patio. 'Just like Benjamin said,' Elliot remarked. 'If we stay in the house it won't follow.'

'Because we haven't invited it in?'

'Something like that I suppose. Unfortunately, we welcomed Benjamin in with open arms.'

They both turned and looked at Hayley, the only one still sat on the sofas. She offered them a reassuring smile. 'If we all just stay inside, and remain calm…'

Brooke's voice, kneeling behind one of the sofas, next to a now seated Kieran. 'Fuck off, Hayley.'

Alicia shushed her, and Elliot thought he knew why. *Don't annoy Hayley. She chooses who makes it out of this.* He looked for Danielle. She was standing in front of the fire, her eyes into the heart of the house. 'Where's Nick?'

Behind Elliot, the hell hound was on the move again.

**

When they got to the front of the house the door was wide open. Nick stood on the steps, looking across at the snow covered body of his partner. The hound was already there, blocking his path, emitting a low growl.

Danni called him in but he reassured her he was alright. 'He thinks he's outsmarted us,' he uttered, monotone, facing away from them. 'Another fancy bastard with his list of qualifications. This thing, fast as fuck, pinning us in, but only dangerous if we leave the property. Steff, left there to taunt me. To try and make me go to her. Same with the phones in the tree. He *wants* us to try it. He wants this thing to eat us, but then it will be our own fault. At least that's what he'll tell Hayley. He wants us dead, but he'd prefer us to bring it on ourselves.'

Said out loud it sounded preposterous but it also had a ring of truth to it. Nick had obviously done some thinking of his own while he had been staring out at Steff. 'He thinks he's smart, but I'm smarter.' He turned around and came back up the steps, then closed the door on the hound. 'But first, some breakfast.' Back in the house proper he crossed to the kitchen and started to root around for food.

The normalcy of his actions took some of the tension out of all of them. Whatever was happening, they should fuel up, hydrate. Carry on. They made towards the islands.

Hayley got up from the sofas to try and join them. 'Not you,' Brooke said. 'Keep your arse there.'

'We'll bring you something,' Alicia added.

Danni stepped forward. 'If Hayley's staying there, then we take shifts to be with her. Then the whole thing is fair.' She didn't fully understand what on earth was going on – none of them did – but she was conscious that some of them were being too quick to burn their bridges with Hayley. In her mind, Danni thought the best thing to do was to kill this situation with kindness. Not give Hayley an easy choice, if she really was going to choose. Everyone should be nice to her, then she might put an end to this whole nightmare. Danni resolved to find a way of outlining the idea with them all, particularly Kieran and Brooke who had shown Hayley the most animosity so far. And Nick, now partner-less and potentially cast adrift.

They had to be as one, and that meant the whole party, including Hayley.

'That sounds like a good idea,' Hayley replied, settling back into the sofa. 'That way I can talk to each of you, to help me decide!'

Danni spotted the worried look between Kieran and Rhea. She stepped across to them, modelled a smile. 'Put on a show,' she whispered.

'What for?' Rhea replied. 'The woman doesn't know me. I'm not part of her plan.'

'Me neither,' Kieran said.

'Just don't make it easy for her,' Danni said through an exaggerated rictus grin.

'You mean like that?' Kieran pointed over her shoulder. Danni turned.

Hayley had company. It was Lucy. She was sitting next to her, holding her hand and leaning close in the manner of a conspiratorial conversation. Danni knew that Lucy had little time for Hayley; she tolerated her because she was an acquaintance of Justin's. Now she was cosying up to her like one of her bosom buddies.

'Yeah,' Danni said. 'Something like that.'

.

CHAPTER TEN

Now the sun was fully up it was a beautiful, bright day: blue skies and the early morning mist burned clear away. The snow sparkled in the light, like it was infused with glitter. It might even melt some, but not quick enough to make any kind of travel easy across what was left of the weekend. There would not be cars on the road unless completely necessary. There was a slim chance some walkers might trudge past the entrance to the drive. But as they were housebound, those open, iron gates might as well be ten miles away.

Nick had pulled up a dining room chair and was staring out at them, more precisely at Benjamin's car parked not too far away from them. He didn't speak to anyone, just gazed out at the wintry scene. The hound walked in front of him, on the other side of the glass.

The others had decided that they should only venture upstairs for the bathroom; apart from that they would all stay in sight of one another.

Justin had had the idea of using the smart TV to make contact with the outside world, but the notion was soon quashed when he realised the router was missing from the sideboard. He tried anyway, in vain. No internet connection. While he was in the vicinity then, he took his turn with Hayley.

Danni passed Elliot a mug of coffee. They leaned against one of the kitchen islands. 'We can't contact the kids.'

'I was thinking that. At what point do you think they'll worry?'

She shook her head. 'I don't think they will. The little ones will trust the adults, so unless they try to get in touch with us...' Harry was seven and Grace was eight; neither of them had phones and so would be relying on their friends' parents to relay any messages from Danni. She imagined those mums would assume her radio silence just meant bad reception or, just as likely, a bad hangover. She guessed they might not worry until the evening, but even then that wouldn't spark any real concern, not until a failed school pick-up on Monday. Danni had left uniforms and satchels – they were all set up for the start of their working week. They were expecting Mummy and Daddy to be at the school gate at three. If they didn't make it, what then?

'What about Oliver?' Elliot asked. He was eleven, and had a phone. He and Elliot had been in contact the day before to discuss Saturday afternoon's football scores. 'He might try to alert someone.'

She shook her head. 'I don't think so. He'll ask Will's mum, she'll check to forecast and see the snow, and tell him it's a signal issue. I'm just glad Lucy banned kids from this thing. Jesus, El – what if we'd brought them with us?'

'Don't think about it. They're safe – that's the main thing.'

'And us?'

He rubbed her hand. 'I'm sure we will be too. Just haven't worked out how yet.'

'I'm not going to beg her, El.'

'And you won't need to. Out of everyone here you've been the better friend to Hayley. You're not in any danger.' Danni noticed Elliot wasn't including himself in the equation.

'I don't fancy being an immortal vampire though.'

'We both know it isn't going to come to that.' He sipped his coffee and stared across at Justin and Hayley. The conversation wasn't as intimate as the previous one Lucy had seemed to be having; Justin looked like he was conducting an interview. Elliot's gaze returned to his wife. 'So what are you going to say to her then, when it's your turn?'

'I don't know,' Danni replied. 'Get her to stop all this, I suppose.'

'Let's hope that does it. With that in mind, I suggest you go next. It's getting a little fraught in here for some of us.' He nodded across to Brooke and Alicia, standing next to the door to the hallway. They were clearly having some kind of muted argument. Alicia was oscillating between being tender with Brooke and showing frustration.

Danni scanned the rest of the downstairs. Nick, by the dining room bifold windows, looking out at Steff. Lucy, in the kitchen behind them, fixing herself something a little stronger than tea. Kieran and Rhea, leaning against the sideboard, taking it all in. They were both dressed like they were about to go out for a run, but after Kieran's brief excursion in the garden that clearly wasn't on the agenda.

Then Brooke was in the middle of the room and calling them all in. 'Right, I've got a plan, people!' Justin left Hayley on the sofa; everyone else gathered around Alicia and Brooke. 'It's simple,' she said. 'Benjamin – and I'm assuming the lovely Hayley down there as well – took our phones and our car keys while we slept. What they didn't count on, was *spares*. They took my keys, but didn't know that Alicia carries a set too.' She fished them from her pocket and jiggled them in the air, making sure Hayley could see. 'I rescued them from her bag when I went upstairs to pee.'

Nick, suddenly animated, roared over at Hayley. 'Not so clever after all!' Hayley jumped a little in her seat and then steadied herself. She craned her neck to listen but didn't get up.

'So,' Brooke said. 'This is it. Someone goes to the patio and lures that fucking thing into the garden. I make a break for the car. I'm not blocked in. Four flat tyres be damned: I'll drive it on the rims.'

Justin waved at her for attention. 'Will you have control? In these conditions you're likely to slide it into a tree or a wall.'

She frowned at his negativity. 'I've got to try it. I can either make a break for it on my own, or drive it up the bank there to the bifolds.' She pointed into the dining area. 'We can pull those back; we know the dog won't come in. Shit, I could even drive the car *into* the house. If you want me to take that option, we can try and get in as many as we can.'

'And then what?' Lucy asked, swirling a gin and tonic around. 'Skid along to the pub from yesterday? Tell them we've got a hell hound and a vampire?'

'I was going to settle for telling them we know who killed the sheep, and suggesting they call the police.'

Discussing it in normal-sounding terms calmed everyone a touch, except for Alicia. 'We've seen how fast that thing moves. What if you don't get into the car in time?'

'It's ten yards versus a fence and the length of the house. I'll make it.' She pulled Alicia in and kissed her cheek. 'Just be sure it goes fully into the garden.'

Kieran stepped forward. 'I'll lure it round.' He looked at Rhea. 'I won't go further than the patio furniture this time.'

'So what do we think?' Brooke asked. 'Am I driving it up to the house so you can get in with me if you want to? I reckon it'll take five more people.' She drove a VW Golf. Not the biggest car in the world.

Justin looked sceptical. 'Just see how it handles first. You're going to have zero grip. It might not make the grass bank.'

'I told you,' Alicia said. 'This is not a good idea.'

'But it's the only idea anyone has come up with, so I'm giving it a go.' She kissed her again; this time Alicia was less receptive. When she slunk away, Brooke shrugged and moved towards the front of the house. 'I'm going to open the door first, so I've got a clean run at it.'

Justin and Elliot followed her into the hall. When she opened the front door the hound moved away from the bifolds and prowled at the foot of the steps. It made no attempt to mount them. It was a straight line to her car. 'Should be easy,' she said.

Elliot spoke. 'Alicia doesn't want you to do it.'

'But no one else objected, apart from you, Justin. And it wasn't really an objection, just advice really.'

'It won't be easy, Brooke,' he confirmed.

'And yet, everyone but Alicia wants me to try, yes?'

Her question wasn't answered, so she took that as an affirmative. 'I'll stay here. Tell Kieran to do his thing.'

Justin slipped back inside; he was replaced by Alicia. Elliot stepped back so she could get to Brooke. They hugged and kissed again. 'You be careful,' Alicia said. 'I'm going to watch from here. Nick is ready with the dining room doors. If you can get it up the slope, me and him are going to come with you.'

'Love you, babe.'

'You better.'

In front of them, the hell hound cocked its head. It looked up, then took a couple of steps to their right, towards the annex. Elliot popped his head back into the house. The patio doors had been slid open at the rear. Kieran shouted across: 'Ready!'

Elliot assessed the situation and then called back: 'Okay! Go!'

Kieran stepped out onto the patio; he grabbed the edge of the table and dragged it across, making a thudding, rumbling noise, but also forming a barrier between the gate and the glass doors. Even if it bought him half a second it was worth it. He got behind it.

At the front of the house, the creature considered the three stood in the hallway one last time, and then tore off around the side of the house. 'It's coming!' Elliot yelled.

Kieran braced himself. Rhea was behind him, on the threshold. The others hovered in a rough chain between the front and back of the house. Hayley stayed on her sofa.

There was a slam against the gate, and then the claws splintering the top. 'It's here!' he yelled. It heaved over, slathering. It landed once more in a poised crouch.

'Kieran!' Rhea yelled.

Kieran pushed away from the table and flung himself back into the house. The hound sprang forward and landed on the table, glowering down at him. Hot slobber fell onto the snow. But he was over the threshold, and safe.

Danni saw it all from the kitchen. 'Now, Brooke! Now!'

Brooke took the steps one at a time, quickly but carefully. She crunched down on the gravel, planting both feet firm, wanting to be sure of her grip.

'Run!' yelled Alicia.

In the garden, the creature contorted its body – almost performing a back flip – and then lunged towards the gate. It got purchase just in front of it and leapt up. It hit the top of it in a single bound, smashing the edges, weakened by the repeated battering.

Rhea yelled back through the house. 'It's coming!'

Brooke was running to the car, not quite at full speed, careful not to tip her weight too far forward or unbalance herself in any way. Half way there she held out her hand and pressed the key fob; the side lights on the VW winked at her.

She was almost within reach of the handle when she heard a quick, ferocious rustle from the foliage at the side of the house. She didn't turn around. She continued moving, almost sliding into the car. She grabbed the handle and squeezed it in.

For a split second she wondered if she'd accidently pressed *lock* rather than *unlock*, but then the door gave in her grasp and popped open. She flung it wide, hearing snow being crunched behind her. She threw herself in sideways, cracking the top of her head on the door frame. She ignored it, made sure she was all in then reached for the internal door handle.

That allowed her a sideways glance at what was coming.

It was already airborne.

It meant she hardly needed to grab the handle herself; the creature thudded into the door, ramming it into her hand and bending a finger back. She yelped at the same time as it clunked into place. The muzzle of the beast pushed up against the window, exposing sharp yellow teeth and smearing the glass with a gloopy froth.

But it was outside, and she was in.

Her finger throbbed; she ignored it. Instead she guided the key towards the lock, using habit and memory rather than sight.

Something was wrong: there was not the satisfying union of two engineering feats custom made for each other. Instead the key seemed to be rattling inside a space.

The hound flung itself at the window again, wobbling it in its fixture. A sudden thought occurred: *this is not the same as being in the house.* The creature wasn't backing away.

Brooke dipped her head and looked at where she'd shoved the key. The ignition cylinder was missing, leaving a hole and a couple of exposed wires.

'Fuck!'

The hound crunched against the door again. One corner of the plastic inlay popped its seam as the metal behind it dented.

Inside the house, everyone was either at the door or at the bifolds. Nick was there, ready to push them back once the car was on the slope. Only, the engine had yet to fire, and the hound kept throwing itself against the driver's door.

'Can it smash the glass?' Alicia wailed.

'Why's she not driving it?' Lucy asked.

Nobody knew, at least until Hayley slid past the kitchen and lingered behind them. She cleared her throat and tried to get their attention. 'I know. I know.'

Danni and Justin heard her; the latter shushed those nearest although Alicia could not be quieted. She was still screaming at Brooke to start the car.

Hayley, standing quite formally, hands folded in front of her tummy, addressed them. 'Benjamin knew about the spare key. It was easy enough to locate most – phones and keys, I mean – but when we couldn't, he *tuned in* to your sleeping minds and asked you.'

Justin was incredulous. 'He did what now?'

'You were one, Justin!' she replied, almost laughing. 'We found your regular phone easy enough but I suggested to Benjamin that you might have a separate work phone with you.'

He frowned. 'I left it at home. Lucy insisted.'

'I know! You told Benjamin as much in your dream. It's in the top drawer in your study.'

He turned to Danni. 'It is. That's... that's where I left it.'

Nick shouted out. 'Come on, Brooke!'

The creature continued to throw itself at the car door; Alicia shrieked with every impact.

Inside, Brooke was flinching, but trying to remain calm. She'd shuffled over the gear stick into the other seat. Her thinking was that if it did smash through the glass there would be a few seconds when it might be stuck in the window frame. If that happened she would be out through the passenger door and tearing off towards the house. But while it was still very much outside the car, there was nothing else she could do, other than react to any development.

In the house, Hayley continued her explanation. 'I knew that Brooke and Alicia shared their car, unlike most of you who have a car each. That made me think there was a chance two keys were being carried. One set was on the dressing table. Benjamin tuned into their minds to see if there was another. Alicia told him there were keys in her bag.'

'Alright,' Danni said. 'So what's happening in the car? Why doesn't the key work?'

'Because there's no ignition,' she replied, pointing to the tree outside. 'The cylinder is in the bag with the keys and phones.'

'You fucking bitch,' Nick said, knocking a dining chair over. 'You left the keys in Alicia's bag so one of them would try this! You set them up! You want us to die!'

She addressed him like she was appeasing a stroppy toddler. 'Nicholas, I have a difficult choice to make this evening. If the field shortens somewhat it'll make things easier. At least that's what Benjamin suggested.'

'The fucking *field*? You make it sound like a job interview.'

Hayley's brow furrowed. 'It is, sort of.'

Danni remembered the manner in which Justin was speaking to Hayley earlier. Had he been making a pitch?

'Just so you know,' Nick replied. 'I'm not fucking applying. He killed Steff. I'm going to kill *him*.' He went back to the bifolding doors and slid them open. 'Brooke!' he roared.

The hound turned to regard him. It padded away from the car, just for a moment. It meant they could see the dents battered into the door and a spider web crack in the glass. Brooke was inside, but pushed against the passenger door. Alicia called out to her; Elliot grabbed her arm just to make sure she didn't do anything foolish.

Nick strode out onto the snow-covered grass bank. He planted firm steps, knowing that a slip could mean a slide right down to the drive and then a mad scramble to recover.

The hound paid him more attention, dropping into a half crouch and stalking towards him, without fully leaving the vicinity of the car.

Elliot spotted it: the creature repositioning based on Nick's actions. He shouted into the house: 'Someone go to the back door and see if it can be lured away again!'

Kieran ran through the house, back to what was quickly becoming his personal domain. He slid the door open and ran onto the patio. 'Tell me what it's doing!'

The hound pointed its head in one direction and then the other, sensing all the movement around it. It didn't commit to one course of action though, not like before. Instead it kept within striking range of the car, as if it knew Brooke was the most vulnerable. *Which she is*, thought Elliot, taking it all in. He called through the house. 'Kieran! Try the gate!'

'What? You sure?'

Rhea came across to the entrance hallway. 'What are you playing at? You've seen how quickly it moves.'

'Trust me,' he said to her, then shouted the same words to Kieran.

'Okay!' Kieran crossed to the back garden gate and flipped the latch. That notion he'd had earlier of making a run for it came back.

The hound took three bounding steps across the drive, away from Nick and towards the straight run that would lead to Kieran. At what point would *he* become the most vulnerable? Elliot didn't want to find out. 'Back up, Kieran! Back to the door!' Rhea ran to the sofas to make sure he complied.

Elliot's conclusion: this was a supernaturally smart animal. And it knew the odds. It also meant he didn't know how to get Brooke out of the car without potentially sacrificing someone else. But if they let it keep battering itself against the VW, it would eventually force a way in and Brooke was done. He did his best to soothe Alicia who was still screaming Brooke's name at the car.

Nothing else could be done.

Nick had other ideas. He marched back into the house, straight up to Hayley. Before she could say anything he grabbed her tightly by the arm and started to drag her away towards the large glass doors. She protested, and Lucy asked what he was doing, but Nick ignored them.

When he was within the reach of the chilly air he pulled her around so that she was in front of him, but not face to face: he could not see her wide, frightened eyes, just her straight, lank hair. She bucked against him, kicking backwards and trying to free her arms to launch fists. 'Let go of me! Let go of me this instant!'

'Okay,' he replied, and pushed her through the opening and down the snowy slope.

CHAPTER ELEVEN

Hayley lost her footing instantly and fell on her hip. She slid, rolled, then landed onto the snow-packed gravel with a grunt.

The hell hound made straight for her.

Only, it didn't attack, just sniffed around her, and then nudged her with its snout as if encouraging her to stand. She got onto her knees and regarded it nervously, but once she remembered it posed no threat to her, she brushed snow from her arms and chest and got her breath back.

Alicia called to Hayley from the front door, allowing herself a second's worth of focus away from Brooke. But then her eyes were back on her stricken partner. Could she leave the car while the dog was preoccupied with her friend? No, not far enough away. Brooke knew it too; there was no sudden or decisive movement from inside the VW, although she did relocate to the back seats.

Danni barged Nick at the bifolding door. 'What have you done?'

'She's fine. Look – the thing fucking loves her. It's just like earlier: it knows who she is and that she's not to be touched.'

'So if you knew that already why did you shove her outside?' She pushed him away from the opening and beckoned Hayley back up the slope.

Hayley shielded her eyes against the sun and looked up, no doubt searching Nick out. She got to her feet but then hesitated. Danni noticed this and turned back to Nick. 'Will you clear off! She's coming back up.'

'Sure, why not?' He walked away towards the kitchen. 'Just make sure you don't invite her fucking pet in too.'

As Hayley started to scrabble up the slope towards her, the word *pet* got Danni thinking. She held out her hands, ready to pull Hayley in. But when her friend took them – her fingers cold and damp – Danni held still, like they were preparing to dance and just waiting for the music. 'Hayley, can you call that thing off?'

'I have no control over it.'

'But it came to you.'

'Because it thought I might be under threat.' Danni glanced down. The creature hadn't followed Hayley up, but was instead stalking off in the direction of the cars, getting ready to plough another violent and chaotic furrow through the snow towards Brooke.

Danni jumped when it crashed into the driver's door once more. She didn't think the glass would hold for much longer. 'Well, couldn't you just lead it for a walk around the house, or something? We need to get Brooke out!'

Hayley gave her head a small, impatient shake. 'It won't follow me if I'm not in danger. And Brooke made her choice. I can't help her.'

Danni felt like pushing Hayley back down the bank herself. Instead, she let go of her hands and stepped aside. Hayley came back in.

Kieran and Rhea, making their way back to the front of the house having closed off the patio, saw Nick by the cold fireplace. 'What's been going on up there, buddy? What we doing about Brooke?' Kieran looked up and saw Hayley leaning against the bifolds, rubbing her arms. 'Is Hayley okay?'

Nick grumbled. 'She's far from fucking okay.'

They left him there and re-joined the others. Lucy first, at the breakfast bar, staying out of the way and nursing what looked like a gin; Danni staring out through the folding doors, Hayley now walking away from her; Justin, Elliot and Alicia at the house entrance and steps, calling out to Brooke but ultimately helpless.

'What a mess,' Rhea muttered. 'We need to formulate a plan. How are we getting out of here?'

'I don't know. Maybe we take our chances with Benson later, rather than his dog.'

'He's a murderer. He killed your friend.'

'I know that, babe! Sorry...' He considered Hayley, who had now sat down on one of the elegant dining chairs. *A murderer's accomplice.* She had to be the key, somehow. First of all though, they had to get Brooke out. 'What's that thing doing?' he asked.

'Still pounding on the car!' Justin called. He was half in and half out of the hallway.

'You any more of those steaks left, Just?'

'We had them all last night. I don't think we can tempt it with diced chicken breast.'

'Maybe we can throw something at it?'

'What, another snowball fight? There's nothing, Kee. All the knives are in the tyres.'

Kieran hated being without an option. He rubbed his head furiously. 'Fuck!'

Then Nick strode past him, purposeful. There was something in his hand, a flash of black. He marched through the kitchen area, straight up to Hayley, grabbed her by the hair and dragged her off the chair. Kieran spied what Nick held: it was a poker from the set on the hearth.

He yanked her hard and she yelped. In that split second he changed his hold on her and wrapped his arm around her neck, her chin on his elbow.

Danni cried out. 'Shit! This again, Nick?!'

He held up the poker. 'If anyone tries to stop me I'll skewer her with this.' He leant in to Hayley's ear. 'You see this, bitch? Stop fucking wriggling or you're a kebab.' He hauled her towards the front door.

He told the others to back up, which they did, despite the chorus of protest. He pulled Hayley onto the steps. The hound was there in an instant, padding around the bottom stone slab and snapping its jaws.

Elliot was wide-eyed. 'Jesus Christ, Nick – what are you doing?'

'Testing this thing out.' He stepped down onto the snow and gravel.

It made to bite him but he pulled Hayley around just in time and it veered away. When it looked at him again, ready to spring, he dug the point of the poker into Hayley's side. When she yelped the creature dropped low, almost to its belly. It had been silent in its systematic and relentless attempts to reach Brooke, but now it growled, as if annoyed. When he drew the poker away, it stood taller and refocused. 'Clever monster.' He walked backwards away from the house, eyes firmly on the hound. It followed, but kept a distance so that it could properly observe him, black eyes like polished jet.

Hayley squirmed so he jabbed her again with the poker. 'Keep that up and I'll ram this in your thigh.'

'What is this achieving?' she squeaked.

'First of all, I'm gonna see if we can lure that thing away from Brooke. Which is why you're coming with me.' He continued to walk backwards, slowly, firmly planting his feet, conscious of the possibility of icy patches. A fall now, even just ten yards from the house, could be fatal.

He stopped, to look at Steff's snow covered body behind Kieran's Audi. Thankfully her neck was hidden so he couldn't make out the wound. What he could see of her flesh – a cheekbone, a hand – was bone white. Her hair was frozen rigid, spiky, like it was in shock. *Second of all...* he thought to himself.

He continued, and the hound followed.

Alicia was on the steps, getting excited. 'It's working! It's going to move far enough away.'

Elliot suggested caution. 'Not if you slip off the step. Touch the ground and it might be right back over. Be patient.'

'Easy for you to say! It's not Danni in there, is it?' She looked at the Volkswagen. Brooke was leaning over the back seat, her head in the boot of the hatchback, watching Nick intently.

'Alright, but let's be careful.' He too watched Nick, shuffling backwards, alternating between beating the poker against Hayley's thigh and waving it at the hound. The creature stalked him; it shimmied to the left and right occasionally, looking for a weak spot.

Nick got to the point where the drive turned a corner, heralding the long stretch that led to the entrance of the property. In the other direction was the side of the house. They all watched, wondering which way he would go. Even Lucy joined Danni at the bifolding doors. 'He's going to fuck this up, isn't he?'

'God, I hope not,' Danni muttered.

In the car, Brooke realised she would soon have a decision to make. How far was far enough away? Opening the door would no doubt alert it. Would it head back – at speed – as soon as it heard the clunk? She had to assume so. Her short sprint versus... how long? Fifty yards? That was roughly the same as metres, wasn't it? Usain Bolt could cover that in five seconds. She couldn't trust herself to get out of the car and onto the steps in five seconds. It needed to be longer. Nick needed to keep going. She muttered to herself: 'Go on, you homophobic Neanderthal: draw that thing away from here.'

Out in the open, Nick turned slightly so that he was heading up the drive. The hound, sensing this change, ran around him, causing him to pirouette with Hayley. It did it a few times, making the others fearful that Nick was going to get dizzy or lose his footing.

He smashed Hayley in the knee with the poker. She screamed. The hound went to its belly and behaved.

Nick continued to shuffle backwards, towards the edge of the property.

Alicia believed it to be far enough away. She stood on the bottom step and shouted across to Brooke. She was already repositioning herself inside the car so that she was looking directly at Alicia through the rear passenger window. They fluctuated between looking at each other and at Nick's progress. He'd turned a corner, putting a couple of trees in the way of the most direct path.

It seemed more than enough now. When Alicia looked at Brooke, she was nodding. Alicia did the same, like they were getting in synch with each other.

Brooke pushed the door open. The release of the catch made a noise that alerted the hound. It flipped round like it was looking to bite its own ragged tail.

There was no going back now. She pushed herself out, planted a foot and launched herself forward.

Alicia screamed: 'Run!'

That meant the hound was coming.

Brooke didn't waste time checking but ran, fast and steady. A couple of times her boot slipped but she was able to right herself and keep her momentum going. Alicia changed her position from reaching her arms out to backing up and giving Brooke space; the last thing they needed was a clumsy collision. Out of the corner of Alicia's eye, a grey streak was approaching at speed. Other voices roared Brooke on.

Her boot hit the second step, overstretching. The different material and height underfoot affected her balance and it skidded away from her. She knew she wasn't going to be running any further; it was all about how successfully she fell. She pitched herself forward and flung her body onto the steps.

Two firm ridges dug into her middle. She got an arm out to stop her chin slamming into stone. In propelling herself, the foot that had touched down first had now been cast behind her along with the trailing leg. The toe of a boot still dragged in the gravel.

She thrust her feet into the air and arched her back, so that she ended up in the bow pose from her yoga class. She reached back and grabbed her ankles, pulling them in as tightly as possible. But now she had no purchase at all on the slippery, icy steps.

She didn't look but heard the arrival of the hound. It skidded in behind her and made a gnashing sound with its fearsome jaws.

Her body slipped down half a step. She had no idea how close she was to be outside of the protection of the house, but it snarled more audibly behind her, as if in anticipation.

Then there were hands: Alicia, Elliot and Justin, all reaching for her, grabbing a shoulder, an arm, a foot, and then hauling her up the steps in an ungainly but effective manner. Once clear she unfurled herself like a flipped bug trying to get right. She looked back towards the car. The creature was there, teeth jittering and nostrils twitching. Great globs of saliva fell onto the snow, a centimetre from the bottom step. It regarded her briefly with its ebony eyes then sprang sideways, bounding towards Nick and Hayley.

Alicia was in her ear. 'That was too close, oh god that was too close!' Brooke shot her arms out and wrapped her up in an embrace.

All eyes now fell on Nick and how he would navigate his and Hayley's way back to the house. The hound took to circling them again, which meant they were rotating once more, Nick making sure that Hayley remained an effective human shield. To stop the creature he had to do what he'd done previously: he thwacked Hayley hard with the poker. At her cry, it dropped to its belly, and Nick was able to plot his course again.

Only, it wasn't back to the house. He was carrying on along the drive, towards the entrance.

Now they all moved to the dining area, pushed the bifolds fully back, and stood in a line watching him. Kieran called out: 'Where you going, buddy?'

'To see a man about a dog!' He laughed at his joke, but kept his eyes firmly on the hound. Hayley wriggled a little so he squeezed a little tighter so she got the message.

It took a while but once they veered from gravel to grass, it was obvious to everyone that Nick was bound for Benjamin's Volvo.

Hayley got her breath back and aimed a comment over her

shoulder. 'And what do you think you'll do when we get there?'

'You'll have to wait and see, won't you?' The truth of it was he wasn't a hundred percent sure himself. In his head he was popping the boot open and pulling out the parcel shelf. He didn't really believe the sunlight would burn Benjamin to a crisp, but he supposed he could entertain the possibility for a second or so. The actual plan was to beat him to death with the poker. Unfortunately, Nick had the issue of what he would do about the dog as well; it might tear him up before he got one good swing in.

He then had another idea: get into the rear passenger side of the car and rip through the back seat to reach Benjamin. It would be an awkward fight but he could claw the fucker's eyes out.

That might do it. Not long to go now.

As they got close to the car, Hayley became more jittery under his arm, and the hound more animated. It continued to pace left to right, looking for an in, but did so quicker than previously, meaning Nick had to sharpen his focus even more.

Hayley had both hands on his forearm around her neck, fingers pushing his muscle just enough to give her throat licence. 'You can't get out of this, Nick. Take us back while you can.'

'What would be the point? You're not choosing me to survive your ip-dip-dog-shit murder game later, so we'll do things on my terms. For Steff. For your friend.' Again, he flung them both around to stop a potential lunge from the hound.

Hayley wheezed under his hold. 'I'm sorry about that, Nick. It was an accident. If it's any consolation, I think I would have chosen Steff.'

'Nope, that's no fucking consolation.'

His calf muscle pushed against the rear bumper of the Volvo. The creature growled more audibly than before. *Here we go,* Nick thought.

He sidled around the car, Hayley in front of him, the hound grizzling and shifting from side to side. His right arm was around her neck so – after passing the poker to his other hand – he felt behind him with his left, searching for the door handle. His fingers found it. There was an indentation to slip his hand in, then he gripped the handle and squeezed.

Nothing happened. It didn't give. He tried again, more forcefully. The door didn't move.

Hayley snickered. 'Benjamin will have locked it with the fob key once he was inside. How stupid do you think he is?'

Nick, suddenly very hot, thought back to when Benjamin had climbed in earlier on. 'There were no blinking lights to suggest...'

'That function has stopped working. The car still locks though.'

It was at that moment the creature spied his weakness: the poker was effectively disabled in the hand that secured Hayley. It made a dive for the passenger door, and Nick's exposed left.

Fangs tore down his hand and ripped deep into the flesh of his thumb. Nick swore and let go of Hayley so he could wield the poker. Released, she dropped to her knees and scrambled away.

The poker came down on the head of the hound, but it was undeterred. It launched itself at Nick's exposed middle and sunk its teeth into his gut.

At the house, cries, shrieks and gasps. Kieran and Justin left the dining area and slid down the bank, but their instinct to help took them no further than the first few yards of driveway. What could they do? Even if they ran over they'd have nothing to fend it off with, and it would probably be too late. They could do nothing but watch the hound tear a hole through the middle of their friend.

Hayley, clear of the fight, got to her feet and turned. The beast worked with ferocious speed, snarling and snapping in a blur. Snatches of material from Nick's sweater blew out like confetti, followed by blood splatter. Nick swung the poker at its grey flank and pawed at the creature's face with his left hand, but in the blink of an eye lost two fingers. The pain sent a bolt of lightning through his body, and – in solidarity with their fallen brothers – the fingers of his right hand straightened and relinquished the poker. All he could think to do was aim his remaining fingers at the hound's eyes. But the head was whirring too quickly, and his vision becoming too blurry, for him to act with any decisiveness. And the pain. Oh, the pain.

It continued to chew through his guts.

Nick's legs buckled and he slid to the ground.

That's when it tore off his face.

CHAPTER TWELVE

There was no way Nick could have survived such a vicious attack. They screamed for him, but ultimately they were helpless. When the hound left his prostrate and bloodied body and started to run towards them, they all stepped back inside and pulled the folding doors shut. It got back to the front of the house in no time, now smeared scarlet and dripping blood onto the snow.

Hayley was not as fast. She limped back, slow but dogged. She stumbled her way along the front of the house, conscious of their eyes on her. She mounted the steps and pushed in through the front door.

When she stepped through into the main room she said: 'That wasn't my fault.'

Brooke snorted. 'It's *all* your fault. Go sit on your fucking sofa.'

She walked through in silence. Again, they tracked her; it felt like no one dare move until she sat down in the living space dip and was partially out of sight. Then they let out a collective breath around the dining table. Some sat, others leaned. All felt beaten.

There followed some more tears and confusion; frustrated cries and largely futile attempts at soothing. Faces against the window to check that it was definitely real and not some prank. Glasses of water offered as the potential remedy to everything. Guidance given on regulated breathing. The group moved sporadically around the table, swapping partners at random as different bouts of anguish were consoled by different counsellors; they each took their turn as parent and child, as the stoic and the stressed.

Then, when they were too tired, they sat quietly for a time, each playing their own perspective of events through their minds. Danni found herself shaking her head each time she got to the point where she realised Steff and Nick were lost to them forever.

Alicia eventually broke the silence: she clutched Brooke's hand and offered the obvious question. 'What do we do now?'

Justin looked not at his friend but at his wife, sipping at a fresh gin and tonic. 'I say we all need to hydrate properly, perhaps eat something. We don't want to run on empty. We've a challenging day ahead.'

Rhea massaged her brow. 'Jesus. Understatement much?'

Kieran agreed with Justin. 'No, it's a good plan. Help us reset. Just, how about me and you rustle something up? Sit down, everyone: we'll get things going.'

It was agreed, either through consent or apathy. They sat at the table like...

The last supper, thought Brooke. She had gone to a Catholic school, unlike Alicia and the others. Of course, she'd long abandoned its teachings – the nuns weren't a fan of her kissing another girl behind the science block, aged fifteen – but the religious imagery remained with her. The only difference was, their Judas currently sat in another part of the house. Was that the right thing? She'd banished Hayley there but now she'd calmed down a little she wasn't so sure. 'Should we get her back up here?'

'Not yet,' Elliot replied. 'At least I don't think so. What about anyone else? I just think we have to work out what happens next, and it might be we don't want Hayley in earshot of whatever we have to say.'

'Good point,' Lucy said. She got up with her drink and walked across the open plan. She tipped her glass to the boys in the kitchen and then took the step down into the sofa pit. Danni stood up to watch her. Lucy grabbed the remote from the coffee table and turned on the TV. She knocked the volume up a couple of notches; the dialogue suggested it was one of those Sunday morning current affairs shows. Danni then expected her to come back, having encased Hayley in a wall of sound. Instead Lucy sat next to her on the sofa, and started to chat.

Danni raised an eyebrow. 'It looks like Lucy has a plan of her own.'

Alicia bared her teeth. 'Trying to force her and Justin into Hayley's top four.'

Rhea looked at the others at the table: four of them. What was Hayley's real intention for the four that were left at the end of all his, assuming Benjamin was going to make good on ensuring the other six died? *He's got off to a good start, girl: two dead outside already.* She thought she didn't believe in vampires, but after what she'd seen so far... 'You guys know this is real now, right? When he climbs out of that car at around four, five o'clock, he is going to try and kill four more of us. Look at this table. Just imagine the other four dead. We need to work something out before it gets dark.'

'I don't know,' Elliot replied. 'Nick tried that, and look where it got him? We can't escape that thing out there. Negotiating with Benjamin and Hayley later might be our only option.'

Alicia was still bubbling. 'You mean negotiating like Lucy's doing? Selling each other out so we're chosen?'

'No, I mean convincing them both that no one else has to die.'

Danni reached over and rubbed her husband's shoulder. 'I know you see the best in people, and think that everything can be talked out, but I don't think that's going to work here. Benjamin is a maniac. And Hayley is under his spell. If she's been with him for a couple of years, I'm not sure an afternoon with us is going to shift what he's made her believe.'

Elliot sighed. 'So you think we're beaten?'

'No, I just think you're not going to be able to smooth this one out.' He was the calm parent, the one that got in the middle of the disputes between the children and ironed out the creases. Danni tended to ride on the wave of hysteria with the kids and work on the principle that if she shouted loudest she should win the argument. It worked some of the time, but Elliot had a higher success rate. Although his calm was a good asset now, she wasn't convinced it was going to be the quality needed once night fell. 'I don't think we can break Hayley from this, and I'm not for trying to ingratiate myself with her at the expense of others, but I do think we need to talk to her. If we show an interest in Benjamin, learn more about him from her, we might get some kind of clue about how we tackle this situation later.'

This brought positive noises from the table. For the want of a better plan, this one had legs and was worth pursuing. Rather than wait for their food, they joined Justin and Kieran in the kitchen.

**

Lucy looked genuinely disappointed when the rest of them came down to the sofas with plates loaded with toast, bacon and eggs, and bowls of fruit and yoghurt. 'The TV's not *that* good,' she murmured.

'You looked like you were getting on so well,' Alicia said, 'that we thought we'd come down and see what was causing you to be so cheerful!' The smile she gave Lucy was a not very well disguised attack. Lucy sneered at her and finished her gin.

'Tuck in,' Justin said. But most of the dishes were placed on the coffee table. They mainly had eyes for Hayley, not breakfast.

'Hayley,' Danni began. 'We've been so dismissive of your time in Europe and your relationship with Benjamin. But we're here now. He is obviously very important to you, so we'd like to hear all about him.'

Hayley smirked. 'Keep your friends close but your enemies closer. Is that it?'

'You can think what you want. But if you're happy to talk, we're here. If not, there's bacon.'

Hayley relaxed a little, and leaned back into the sofa in the same way as Lucy next to her. 'We met in Cluj. I'd been making slow progress through Europe on my journey of self-discovery. Previously I'd been stuck longer than I wanted to in a number of cities because of Covid: Paris, Milan, Vienna, Budapest, but I finally made it to Romania. That was October time, 2020. I only intended to stay in Cluj a week, particularly as I was behind schedule. I did some of the touristy spots. Visited a nightclub or two – never my thing and still not now. More interesting were some of the events that the university was holding, and that's where I met Benjamin, at a poetry recital evening.

'He wasn't with anyone, and neither was I, so we got talking at the break. We seemed to hit it off straight away. He listened intently to my interest in 16th century pottery. I'd seen some wonderful pieces in Milan and told him all about them. He shared his love of ancient weaponry. I almost didn't want the second half of the readings to begin!'

Danni watched her friend's face light up. In any other situation she'd be delighted for Hayley, to have finally found someone who seemed perfect for her. But they were in the middle of a horror, and she couldn't bring herself to smile. 'Go on then. How did you come to be a thing?'

'He took me for coffee. He had nothing but water, and even that seemed to disagree with him. I asked him if he was okay, and he said yes, but he had a particular condition that made the consumption of certain foodstuffs challenging. He said if I'd meet him again the following night he'd tell me more about it. So I did.

'It was on the fourth night that he told me he was a vampire. We'd been watching some terrible undergraduate slapstick, and he just told me, once I promised him that – just like the comedy – I wouldn't laugh at it.'

Kieran frowned. 'And you believed him, just like that? So I could tell you I'm a werewolf and you'd say *yeah, okay*?'

'No, of course not. But I was convinced *he* believed it. And was living his life in accordance to certain rules from vampire lore. I wanted to know why someone so nice would do that, so I wasn't put off but kept seeing him. I extended my hostel stay for another week.

'By the time that ran out, I'd seen him kill and feed, and I was committed to him forever.'

'Whoa,' Brooke said. 'That's quite a leap.'

Hayley's smile spread wide across her face. 'He's quite a man.'

Elliot had a finger on his chin and looked like he was approaching this as a seminar. 'Is he a man though, if he really is a vampire? Doesn't that make him a monster? Surely you two can't be together?' He went a little pink in the cheeks for the next bit. 'You haven't... done it?'

'No, Elliot, we haven't. But once he has made me like him, then we can.'

'Let's rewind,' Brooke said, 'back to you first seeing him kill. How did *that* happen?'

'He walked me through a park in the middle of the night, where he knew some homeless people slept. We found an old man, isolated from the rest, and Benjamin opened up his face to feed. Like some snakes do. It's called cranial kinesis.'

'Right,' Rhea said. 'Sounds like you watched this like some kind of nature show. What's the TV guy called, babe?'

'Attenborough,' Kieran said.

'Yeah, him. You studied this man like he was something at this museum you work at? You're talking about him killing a guy.'

'*Feeding.* He can't consume regular food the way we do. He needs the flesh and blood of humans, to keep him *super*human. Without it, he'll die.'

Danni picked at something. 'Isn't he dead already? Isn't that what vampires are: the undead?'

Hayley shook her head. 'Part of the old myths and fictional lore. He's alive, just like us. But a different species.'

Justin looked to the patio doors. 'Like his pet dog out there.' The hell hound had relocated to the garden and prowled across the stone flags, keeping its watchful eye on them.

Danni's thoughts whirred. This was helpful. *If he is alive he can die.* 'Aren't vampires supposedly immortal? I think earlier you said *virtually* immortal. Yet if he's a living thing…'

Hayley nodded enthusiastically, enjoying the discussion. 'He's not immortal, but his kind live a long, long time. He's aging, but very slowly. He's over a hundred years old, but looks – what? – in his thirties? He could live for a thousand years…'

Kieran thought about this morning. 'But if Nick had opened Benson's car up earlier and ripped out the parcel shelf, he would have been killed by the sunlight?'

'He's called *Benjamin.* And yes, the sunlight would – possibly in the space of a minute – age him back to his actual year. If Nick had done that, Benjamin would have become over a hundred years old and his organs would have probably failed him. I'm sorry about what happened to Nick, but I'm glad he didn't succeed in disturbing Benjamin.'

This brought a ripple of discontent, and Danni didn't want to lose the narrative Hayley was giving them. She orchestrated the group with a couple of hand gestures, and then asked: 'Go on then, Hayley: what else have the movies got wrong? I bet Justin's brought some garlic with him.' She tried out a laugh. 'What would happen if we rub ourselves with it?'

'You'll smell bad. That's a nonsense, as is the idea of no reflection in mirrors.'

'A stake through the heart?' Rhea asked.

Hayley narrowed her eyes at her. 'Would kill him. As would damage to the brain. Because he is a precious, living thing! The wood thing is just for the movies; a mortal blow is a mortal blow.'

'So if we stabbed him in other places too, we could kill him?'

'Rhea,' Danni chided. She didn't want them to look so obvious with their questions. Rhea raised a hand in a half-hearted apology and leaned into Kieran.

Hayley continued. 'He heals faster than us, moves faster than us, is stronger than us, so if you're thinking about landing some kind of deadly injury on him you're going to find it very difficult. I know what this is. You aren't really interested in Benjamin and me, you're just fishing for clues. I don't mind, because I'm happy to talk about him, because I know you can't stop what's going to happen. I just wish you would *embrace* it a little more, like Lucy and Justin have.'

Danni started. 'What's this?'

It was something of a showstopper. Everyone sat up a little taller, not least Justin and Lucy. Then Lucy shrugged and said: 'Listen, hardly aging and living to a thousand sounds good to me. I've had a proper chat with Hayles and said I'm down for it. All of it.'

Elliot looked at his oldest friend. 'Justin?'

He held up palms in defence. 'We said we would all take our turn to talk to Hayley individually. Catch up on things. Make sure she had time to reconnect with everybody. That's all I did.'

'Look at you all,' Hayley sneered. 'Cross with them both because they were nice to me.'

Danni sighed. 'Hayley, we are all trying to be *nice* to you, but it is very difficult when your plus one for the weekend kills two of the group and threatens to kill four more. We're just trying to understand your situation, and *our* situation, because this is somewhere we've never been before.'

'But it is where *I* want to be. I'm so happy to see you all, and although I can only bring four with me, I can't wait for us to go on that journey together. You'll love Benjamin once you get to know him, just like I do. I've told him so much about you all, he's going to love you too.'

'Just not all of us,' Kieran remarked.

'That is regretful, but it's a blessing that I can even take four of you with me. It's an opportunity not given lightly. I've been Benjamin's day familiar for over two years now, maintaining his affairs during the day and spending time with him at night. Our love is so strong that he is willing to do this for me. Normally a day companion will fulfil the role for decades and either die in post or be fed upon themselves once they can no longer function at their job.

But that's not Benjamin and me.'

She considered each of them, lingering on her oldest friends the longest. 'I was never anything special, I know that. But I am when I'm with him. And this time tomorrow I'll be in an incubation stage, transitioning into the most amazing phase of my life, like going from a fat, frumpy caterpillar to a beautiful butterfly.' She looked up to the light fitting, as if she was actually watching a butterfly in flight, bashing against the bulb.

Kieran dropped his head nearer to his knees and rubbed hard at his face. 'Jesus, this is nuts.'

An idea occurred to Justin. 'When you arrived yesterday and I greeted you on the steps, Benjamin was hesitant about coming in, until I welcomed him. So is that a thing? It's in the movies, but it's real?'

Hayley shrugged. 'Hard to say. It's more historical I think, from when people used to try to ward off evil by blessing their house. Benjamin said that it's caused him quite a lot of discomfort at times, depending on the home and the people in it, so it's always easier when he's given permission to enter.'

Brooke jumped on this. 'So by extension, you're admitting there that Benjamin is evil.'

Hayley smiled. 'I'm telling you that some people hide behind their faith when they're confronted with a difference they don't understand. I seem to remember you sharing with us something similar from your teen years, Brooke? Not that you're evil, just gay.'

'No need to spell it out, Hayley – I'm sure everyone got it.' This had been the situation: her parents were devout Catholics and had invited the priest to their home to more or less *exorcise* her of homosexuality. Needless to say she didn't live there much longer, so in a sense it worked: it left the house in one way or another. Brooke addressed Rhea's puzzled face. 'A creep in a dog collar blessed the house and drove the demon lesbian away.'

Rhea smirked. 'Gotcha.'

Elliot had another thought on the topic. 'I think the idea to take from it, if it's worked on him in the past, is that there must be a god after all?' In certain parts of the room this brought more scepticism than the notion of a vampire lying in the boot of a Volvo.

'I can't answer that,' Hayley replied, 'but if there was a god who vehemently opposed Benjamin's species, it would do more than just make them queasy if they walked into a house of faith, don't you think?'

Kieran sneered. 'So because God isn't punishing him, it must be okay?'

'*Porphyria's Lover*,' Elliot said, but no-one understood the reference.

'Maybe that's it then,' Rhea said. 'Just faith. We have to believe we can beat this fucker.'

'Rhea!' Danni blurted. Again, the girl was too vocal about their future intentions.

'It's fine, Danni,' replied Hayley. 'At least she's being honest.' Then she gave her a look that lingered too long, and Danni – usually strong – had to look away. Hayley continued. 'Benjamin is not evil. What I am proposing is not evil. It is just... an evolution.'

Kieran sat back up from his hunched position. 'Well, I for one am delighted you see it that way. It must make it so much easier to deal with two dead friends out there in the snow. For us it's a fucking tragedy, but for you, well, it's *progress*. Good for you, Hayley. Good for-fucking-you.' Kieran shot up, making them all jump a little. Then he strode through the gap between two sofas, stepped up a level and crossed the house.

Rhea followed him, and it was taken as a signal that the group discussion was now over.

Elliot took Danni's hand and led her to the patio doors and the prowling hellhound. 'We need to find a way out of this,' he whispered. 'For the kids. We have to make it home.'

His grip on her hand tightened. She leaned into his shoulder, both of them still looking outside. 'I know, love. I know.'

On the sofas, Hayley tucked into the eggs and toast.

CHAPTER THIRTEEN

They allowed Hayley to go upstairs, chaperoned by Justin, to fetch her knitting. She went back to the sofa and set about click-clacking the needles as a means of passing the afternoon.

Rhea looked at her, bewildered. Did forty-year-olds knit? Sure, Kieran was nearly twelve years older than her but she didn't think of him as middle-aged. There was something absurd about this woman – having been party to the deaths of two people and effectively holding them hostage – now setting about creating a scarf.

She hadn't sat down with her yet, for *a get to know you* session, and she didn't intend to. As an outsider looking in, she had her ideas about who was getting chosen to be in the fantastic four, and there was no way she was making the cut. Danni and Elliot were a given; as far as Rhea could tell, Danni was the only one who was genuinely nice to Hayley before any of this happened. And probably Justin, their generous host, who with his greying temples put the capital F in Fantastic, if you liked your comic book movies. Would Lucy then tag along? Maybe, after all her ass-kissing, but ultimately she was a bitch, and possibly an alcoholic, so there were things to contend with there. One, could Hayley see through the act? And two, could Lucy live for a thousand years without gin and wine?

Rhea gave a dry chuckle and passed on Hayley, walking by the sofas and on to the kitchen. Lucy was pouring herself another one while Justin whispered to her about whether or not that was a good idea. Rhea kept going until she got to the dining area. Kieran was sitting at the table unboxing some playing cards but she kept going until she stood next to Elliot, looking down the slope. The hound was down there, probably because someone was standing by a window. So too was Steff's body. There was a new flurry of snow and she was being covered once more, having thawed a little in the morning sun. 'We had maths together at school,' Elliot said. 'Steff and me. I used to sit behind her, and ask her for all the answers. She'd slip me bits of paper or turn round and whisper. It got to the point that whenever we had something complex to do she'd spit numbers out to me before I even asked. She once got a detention in a test for shouting out "For God's sake, El, the answer's sixteen!" I'd been nudging her with my pencil. I hardly remember anything from actual lessons in school, but I remember that.'

'She seemed like a very nice person.'

'She was. She just wanted everyone to get along, for everyone to have whatever they needed, even if it was answers to tough maths questions.'

Rhea looked out towards the entrance to the property. Snow was beginning to cover up the scene there, but there was still evidence of blood – quite a lot of it – showing through the white bumps and humps of Nick's remains. 'Nick was a little rough and ready,' she said. 'They seemed an odd fit.'

'Nah. He was crude at times, and insensitive; blunt. But he'd do anything for you. They shared that trait, and it was probably what brought them together, and the glue that made them stick. They enjoyed making each other happy.' He turned to Rhea and smiled. 'How about you and Kieran? You a good fit?'

'Like I'm gonna say here and now with him in earshot?' They both looked back at the dining table. He was dealing cards to himself, setting out a game of *solitaire*, but he was smiling and nodding. He had an ear on them. Rhea smirked. 'I just wish he had hair. No fun running your fingers over a bowling ball.'

Kieran put a hand to his heart. 'That hurts,' he said to the cards.

Rhea turned back to Elliot. 'Kee told me that you and Danni have been a couple for ever.'

'I'm sure she'll tell you it feels like that at times.'

'And what about it actually being *forever*? You know Hayley's gonna choose you two, right?'

Elliot met her eye, now looking grimly determined. 'Absolutely not. We've got a family to get home to. We are not about to embark on a night-time vampire adventure with Hayley, as much as we love her.'

'You still love her?'

He stared outside again, at his dead friend. 'Ask me when this is over.'

'Let's hope I can.' She patted his arm and turned towards Kieran. She playfully knocked one of his columns of cards off the table and announced she was going to the bathroom. Kieran swore under his breath and set about tidying up her mess.

She and Brooke crossed in the doorway. The latter came back into the house proper with her hands full. 'They love their golf in Scotland,' she announced to the room. She had a club in each hand, old-fashioned looking, a driver and a putter. 'They were mounted on our bedroom wall. I didn't take the time to read the plaque. I thought we should gather some weapons. We've got less than three hours.' She let them clatter on the table, disturbing Kieran's game before he got it re-started. He abandoned it and got up.

'There's the rest of the poker set on the hearth,' he suggested. He felt a twist in his heart when he thought about where the missing iron was.

Lucy chirped up from the kitchen-island-cum-gin-bar. 'We could just bash him with the rolling pin!' She laughed and set about slamming the kitchen drawers. Justin followed her and got her to stop.

Alicia went to fetch the fire tools from behind the sofas. She brought back a couple of stokers. 'I thought the little shovel one was probably no use.' It was a pretty pathetic haul when they looked at it.

'Is this our plan?' Danni asked. 'Are we going to try and fight him when he comes back to the house?'

Brooke shrugged. 'You heard Hayley. He's tough, but not invincible. He's a living thing so he can be hurt. And killed.'

Kieran stuck a hand out. 'Just so we're clear though, like, on the same page. We are all now having it, that he is some kind of vampire, a supernatural being?'

Danni ran a hand along the shaft of a golf club. 'Kee, that hasn't really been in doubt since the moment he nearly took Nick's face off on the steps. We've just spent the morning trying to find ways not to believe.' She picked up the club, felt its weight, perhaps not substantial enough. 'Do we risk trying to get the knives out of the tyres?'

Alicia shook her head. 'That thing moves too fast. Even if we lured it into the garden, as soon as the front door opened it would be away.' She put an arm around Brooke as a way of saying *thank God you're here* and *you're not trying anything else stupid.*

Kieran stared at the bifolding doors. They were double-glazed, reinforced against harsh winters. 'If he's extra-strong, but not – I dunno – all-*powerful*, perhaps if we lock up tight he might not even be able to get back in. Or in trying to he might make himself vulnerable.'

There was agreement. That had to be something. Barricade where they could and if it took him some time to break through then they might be able to land blows on him while he was in the act. Elliot nodded. 'We've nothing else to do.'

**

The plan was shared with Justin and Lucy. Lucy decided she would sit this one out and join Hayley on the sofa; Justin joined the others. First of all, the dining table was pushed up against the glass doors, almost an exact fit. They picked up the hefty chairs and laid them on top, overlapping their backs, and pushed them against the glass too. It wasn't by any means impenetrable, but if he got through the two panes, the furniture would slow him down a little.

They did similar for the patio doors at the back of the house, using the sideboard and two of the sofas. There were narrow windows in the kitchen; they were able to wedge stools between sill and ceiling. 'We're gonna end up with nothing to sit on!' Alicia quipped.

Upstairs – once they'd decided that Benjamin could probably climb – they turned beds onto their ends and pushed them against windows, wedged in place by whatever moved: wardrobes, dressing tables, chests of drawers. They wedged a bookcase in the family bathroom window. Some of the ensuites also had windows; the best they could do there was to close the doors and barricade them.

Gradually, the upstairs darkened as the natural light was shut off. Outside it was getting duller by the minute. After two hours of humping furniture, they gathered around the kitchen islands for water. Justin doled out the glasses. As the day was fading, Elliot decided to take his over to the dining room barricade, to look out through the chair legs. Danni, Brooke and Alicia clinked glasses, tired but feeling like they'd achieved something.

On the remaining sofas, Hayley had made good progress on her scarf. Lucy was asleep.

Kieran nudged Justin. 'What are you going to do about her?'

'To be honest, it's better that she's snoozing. She needs to sleep off the afternoon tipple.'

'And the morning one. You could have just stopped her, you know.'

He shook his head, grinning. 'It's Lucy, it's how she copes.'

'Nah, it's you. Not wanting to create a fuss, a scene. If ever there was a time when it was okay to have an argument with your wife about her drinking, in front of all your friends, today was the day when it was more than acceptable.'

Justin stood taller, his face suddenly stern. 'Thank you for the marriage guidance. Come back to me when you've had a relationship last longer than six months.' He walked away, and didn't turn when Kieran called after him.

Hayley got up and walked over to the main group. She hadn't reacted to any of their work, not even when they'd shifted two of the sofas right next to her. But now she had a view. 'You've all been very busy.'

'Well,' Brooke said, 'when there's a guest you wish you hadn't invited to the party...'

'Whatever you're thinking, it won't work. When Benjamin wants to come in, he'll come in.'

'Because *I* invited him in,' Justin muttered bitterly. He went to the sink and ran himself another glass of water.

'No. Because I'll let him in.'

'We won't let you,' Kieran replied.

'How will you do that? To stop me you'll have to hurt me, and if Benjamin sees that you've hurt me, I won't be able to prevent him doing terrible things to you, even if you're one of the four I've chosen.'

Kieran frowned. 'So you think we're just going to allow you to open the front door to him?'

'I'm sorry, but it really is inevitable.'

Alicia pushed to the front of the group. 'What the fuck has happened to you, Hayley? What's made you like this? We're your *friends*, and you're wishing half of us dead!'

'And half of you will get the greatest reward. I'm giving you something no one else can. I'm being as much of a friend as I can possibly be.' She scanned the group for Danni. 'You'll come with me, Danni, won't you?'

Rhea reacted. 'Here we go. Seat one on the plane.'

Danni screwed up her face. 'None of us are going to do this with you, Hayley. *None of us.* It's insane. So when Benjamin does come to door, you need to call this off, because you're not getting out of it what you want.'

Hayley held out a hand. 'Don't be like that: you're my best friend.'

Alicia batted it away before Danni could choose whether or not to take it. 'She *was* your best friend. Perhaps you're only true friend, if we're all being honest with ourselves. But not anymore; you can forget about it from here on in. None of us are your friend, and that includes Danni!'

Danni didn't contradict Alicia; instead, tears welled in her lower eyelids.

Hayley looked at her hand like it burned. 'You're right. Friends would talk to each other every week, check up on how they're doing. Not go months, *years*, without any proper contact.' She took in the rest of the party. 'I know none of you really like me; you've put up with me as part of the group ever since we were kids. At best we're acquaintances. But mark my words, before the night is over, you're going to be begging me to be your buddy, and you'll be praying that you're chosen.'

'Dream on!' Alicia spat. Brooke pulled her back and gently shushed her. Danni wiped her eyes but said nothing.

The silence was broken by Elliot, yelling out from the front windows. 'Guys! Something's happening!'

Danni glanced up at the kitchen clock. It was almost 4.30pm. 'What is it?' she called, a tell-tale squeak in her voice, the residue of the ache she felt at the altercation with Hayley.

'The boot of the Volvo: it's just popped up!'

'It's nearly time,' Hayley said, and returned to her sofa. 'I need to make my final choices.'

CHAPTER FOURTEEN

There was no immediate movement from the car. Outside it was twilight; there was still an orange tinge to the edge of the sky. The solar-powered bulbs along the driveway were beginning to come on, but there was enough natural light to make out the Volvo for themselves, at least for now. The large boot lid was all the way open, and as a result the parcel shelf raised, but nothing else was happening.

Their weapons were in hand. Kieran and Brooke had the golf clubs, Alicia and Justin had a fire iron each.

Elliot maintained his place as chief lookout. 'I can't see any other movement. Just that it's getting darker with every passing minute.'

'He must be waiting for it to be safe,' Danni said, arm linked with his.

'I know how that feels.' He pulled her towards him.

More minutes passed. They each held their positions, eyes either on the Volvo, the hell hound or Hayley.

And then, making them all start, the creature prowling outside began to howl. It arched its back, raised its front legs and puffed out its chest. It then let out a piercing cry which seemed to almost deflate it. Its limbs trembled at the effort. Kieran was watching it the most closely. 'That thing is truly ugly.'

At the Volvo, movement. A leg extended outwards and sought purchase in the snow. Once it was steady, a hand appeared on the lip of the boot, and then the rest of Benjamin followed. He stood slowly, uncreasing and uncrumpling himself, as if a puppeteer was tugging at each of his strings in turn so as to right him. Once he was fully upright he straightened up his glasses, rolled his head around and thrust his shoulders back and forwards. Then he shook himself out and began to walk.

He stopped almost immediately at the sight of Nick's ravaged body iced with snow. He bent over, reached out for purchase on Nick's clothing, somewhere around the collar, and started to drag him along, snow falling off him as he moved. 'He's coming,' Elliot said. There were gasps from the others when they saw what he was bringing with him.

Hayley started clapping and got to her feet. Brooke saw her move out of the corner of her eye. 'Hayles, we are not letting him in, so you can sit back down.'

'He's as much as a guest here as you are. I'm opening the door.' She walked through the house. Behind her, Lucy finally stirred on her sofa. She asked what was going on but didn't get an answer.

Brooke was still brandishing the club and didn't want to relinquish it. 'Danni, Elliot: you might want to stop Hayley.'

They left their post at the window and cut across to her, Danni grabbing her arm just before she moved into the hallway. 'No, honey – let's see what happens first.'

'Get off me!'

'Come on,' Elliot said, taking the other arm. 'You're not letting him in.'

'You can't stop this!' She pulled and wriggled. Her friends gripped tighter and with both hands. Hayley thrashed and shouted, and the two of them had to heave her away. They were never getting her back to the sofa so they settled for against a wall. They instructed and soothed in equal measure; Hayley complained and swore.

Lucy stumbled through, still waking up. 'What's happening?'

Three of them answered simultaneously: *Benjamin's coming.*

He was making steady progress along the drive, more upright now as his limbs stretched out, Nick's body two-thirds off the ground, the heels leaving tracks alongside Benjamin's footprints. He'd covered about half the distance.

'What are we doing when he gets here?' asked Justin. He beckoned his wife to him; she looked puzzled at the poker in his hand.

Kieran shimmied across the room, towards the hallway and the front door. 'Let's just see what happens when he tries to get in.'

They had lights on, so when Benjamin looked up at the full length window he could see exactly what they'd done with the dining furniture. He chuckled, deposited Nick's body next to Steff's, and walked towards the steps. The hell hound approached him; he held out a hand and it licked it. 'You have made quite a mess of him, have you not? Yes, you have. Yes, you have! Good boy.' He patted it on the head and then pushed its snout away when it got to enthusiastic. His hand came away tacky. He licked his fingers and then wiped them on his grey shirt. The hound hung behind him.

Benjamin called out. 'I can see you have had a busy day! Shall I waste my time and try the door?' He kept walking; when he reached the first step he carried on but the creature stopped dutifully. When he got to the top he tried the handle; it wiggled a little but wouldn't move fully. 'It looks like you have locked me out.'

He dropped to his knees and flipped up the letterbox. His dark, bespectacled eyes appeared in the rectangular slot. Only Kieran saw them, half in and half out of the hallway. He instinctively pointed the putter in their direction. Benjamin continued. 'Open the door, Kieran, and let me talk to Hayley.'

She yelled from the other room: 'I'm in here! They've got me against the wall!'

Benjamin's eyes narrowed and focused on Kieran. 'I hope you remember me saying that she is not to be harmed.'

'She's fine, but you won't be if you come in here! Get in your car and just drive away!'

'You know that is not going to happen.' He stood up; Kieran jumped as the letterbox clattered.

Brooke called from the other room; she was on the table, her face pressed against the bifolding doors. 'He's heading this way!' She backed up, and replaced the chair she'd moved. They all took a step away and waited to see him through the legs and slats of the furniture. Elliot and Danni moved Hayley across to them, still squirming in their grip.

Benjamin walked along the top of the slope, in front of the doors. He knocked on the glass. 'You need to let her go. Now.'

Danni and Elliot looked at each other, nodded and relinquished their hold. Hayley shook herself out of their hands and moved closer to the table. She hollered at the doors. 'They don't want it, Benjamin!'

He spoke low, but his voice travelled through to them behind the glass. 'You cannot be surprised. But that is not important. What is important is what *you* want. Tell me. Have you decided?'

'Mostly,' she replied. 'I would like-'

Danni interjected. 'Say no more, Hayley! We've got to work this thing out!'

'There is no *we* in this,' Benjamin said. 'You do not have a say. Four of you will transition and four of you will feed the process. This is how it is going to be.'

Brooke sneered. 'You've got to get in here first.'

He smiled. It did not improve his looks but gave his face the impression that someone had just stuck a needle in him. 'When I want to come in I will come in. Once I know who I am coming in for. Hayley?'

'I've not got four. Not yet.' She glanced between them all, like she was doing a choosing rhyme in her head.

'He's bluffing,' said Kieran. 'He's quicker and stronger than us, but not enough to break in.' He looked at Benjamin, expecting a reaction, and then at the others, searching for agreement. Brooke and Alicia seemed on board; Justin and Elliot presented more nervously.

He glanced back at Benjamin. The outsider gave him another smile. 'Let us see, shall we?' He backed away from the glass and headed down the slope. When his feet touched the gravel he kept on going.

'Brace yourselves,' Justin said. 'I think he's going to charge the glass.' He put Lucy behind him and held out his poker.

Benjamin kept going, back to the parked cars and the two bodies. He crouched by the nearest: Nick's. He placed one hand on what remained of the chest, and locked the fingers of the other in Nick's curls.

Then he pulled in one, swift motion. The head tore clean off, sending fresh globs of blood onto the snow, the arm of his shirt and the knees of his trousers.

Lucy shrieked.

Then Benjamin stood, wound his arm back, and launched the head.

It thudded into the glass with such velocity and power that the whole set of doors shivered in their frames and the boom reverberated around them. A large spider-web crack appeared in the outer pane. The pulpy mess of what remained of Nick's skull rolled unevenly back down the slope, leaving a streak of red. When it reached the gravel, the hell hound picked it up in its teeth and took it back to the body.

'Holy fuck,' Rhea muttered. 'So this shit just got real.'

Justin nodded. 'I think we've been in that postcode for quite some time.'

Then Benjamin did charge, this time towards the steps. Kieran and Elliot made a move towards the front door but then instinctively shrank back when Benjamin collided with it, the oak bowing in the middle. There was a pause of a few seconds and then another crunch; this time the door rattled in the frame and a crack appeared from the middle running all the way to the bottom, along the grain. 'I think he's strong enough, Kee!' Elliot said, his voice higher than he expected it.

Benjamin gave it a third assault, and one of the hinges popped. It wouldn't hold him for long. Alicia called from the other room. 'Have we got anything left to barricade it with?' The general consensus was no.

But then there were no more charges, and a moment later, Benjamin reappeared in front of the bifolds. 'Just like I told you, when I want to come in I will come in. Ten minutes, Hayley, and then I will ask you to give me the names.

'Then we will begin.'

**

They moved away from the barricade, apart from Elliot who volunteered to keep watch on Benjamin. The latter was just standing still at the top of the slope, peering in through the furniture. The rest of them moved deeper into the house, some on the remaining sofas, others around the breakfast bar.

Ten minutes.

Time for another drink.

Lucy couldn't really process everything that was happening, but then she wasn't sure any of them were, not properly. She watched them jostle for position: Kieran tried to take charge, then Danni, then Brooke. Even Justin: this whole thing had been his idea after all and she could tell he felt responsible. He went round all of them, checking they were okay, or as okay as they could be, all things considered.

Even Hayley. Lucy had told him that he shouldn't have invited her; she'd never brought anything of worth to any gathering Lucy could remember. But he had been soft, and called her anyway. Now look what she'd brought: death, on all their heads.

Unless they were one of the four chosen. Then they would live, but a completely different life than the one they currently had. But a life nonetheless.

She could drink to that. She poured a couple of fingers of gin. Didn't bother hunting down a new bottle of tonic water.

Of course, there would be the issue of their daughter, Rosalind. Lucy supposed that they could collect her at a later date, and once they knew how to perform the *transference* themselves, they could make her just like them.

They just had to make sure they were chosen by Hayley. She'd laid some good groundwork earlier, presenting her and Justin as a couple, knowing that he was a bigger draw than she; all that school history they shared seemed to go a long way with Hayley. Lucy had to assume then that she wouldn't want to split up couples. She saw it as being her and Justin, and Danni and Elliot.

She sought out Kieran and Alicia, the other two to have known Hayley since short trousers and snotty noses. They'd both been quite confrontational, and if she got a chance in the next few minutes she would remind Hayley of that. Currently Alicia was grilling Hayley about something and throwing rhetorical questions at her; Lucy didn't think she would interrupt yet as there was a chance Alicia might do enough damage herself. Brooke was leering over her like her frigging shadow, as always. Hayley was shrinking into what was becoming her sofa. *She'll make her own butt crease in that thing before we go home.* And she had knitting with her. Jesus wept!

Kieran was pacing behind one of the sofas in an intermittent dialogue with that young, tight body he brought as his plus one. Surely a place wouldn't find its way there?

But then, Lucy didn't know who had tried to worm their way into Hayley's affections while she'd been snoozing on the sofa. She didn't feel better for it at all; she wished she'd just powered through the day.

Still a chance to make up for lost time, she thought, and down the gin. Then she slipped off the stool and sashayed over to Hayley as confidently as she could.

She addressed Alicia first. 'Maybe you should back off and give the girl a break? No one's thought about how Hayley must feel in all this.'

Alicia straightened up, and looked Lucy up and down. 'And suddenly you're all about other people's feelings? That's rich.'

'Hayley's my friend.'

'At least for the next six minutes? It's okay, you're welcome to her.'

Hayley spoke up from the sofa. 'Don't be like that, Liss! I still don't know – not for certain.'

Alicia screwed up her face. 'I'm sick of whatever game you're playing. Just spit out the four names so the rest of us can get on with it.' She moved off, taking Brooke with her.

Lucy stepped into the vacated space and then flopped down onto the sofa next to Hayley. 'Don't you worry about them: me and Justin have got your back.'

'Thank you,' she muttered, then dropped her face into her hands.

It went against her instinct, but Lucy put an arm around her shoulders.

Kieran, now in the kitchen, called some of them over: Brooke, Alicia, Danni and Justin. He would have pulled Elliot in too, but he was content enough in his post, keeping an eye on Benjamin. Rhea was next to Kieran as he gestured for the others to line the other side of the island. 'What have you got?' Brooke asked.

'Not much. We've seen how strong he is, but surely smashing through that door is going to take something out of him. That's when we've got to do it: we beat the shit out of him the minute he's inside.' He held up the putter; Brooke matched him with the wooden-headed driver. Alicia followed suit: she still held a poker.

Justin looked about. 'I don't know where I put mine.' Then Lucy called for him from the sofa, *wailed* for him. 'Listen, I just don't know. I mean beating a guy unconscious…'

'I say we go further than that,' Brooke said, and slapped the head of the club into her palm.

'Nick and Steff are dead,' Kieran reminded him. 'And he doesn't intend to stop there. We don't have a choice. Find your fucking weapon.'

Lucy continued to whine at him.

'There needs to be another solution,' Justin said. 'I'm going to see my wife.' He spied the poker on top of the sofa back. 'If any of you want it, there it is.'

Danni followed him, but when she got to the sofa she reached for the fire iron and turned back.

Rhea was scrabbling around in the kitchen drawers. All the dangerous looking knives had been taken, but she came out with an old-style vegetable peeler and a small pair of scissors. When they looked at her she shrugged. 'Just in case I can get up close.'

Kieran looked at the kitchen clock. 'We've only got a couple of minutes. Should we go and wait by the door?'

They all looked in that direction, towards the hallway, and then at Elliot by the barricade. Benjamin was on the other side of the glass, looking in. Brooke huffed. 'It's hardly going to be a surprise attack, is it? He can see what we're doing.'

'Then we play to his ego,' Kieran replied. 'He thinks we can't touch him, so we throw down the gauntlet.' He held up his club, strode forward and shouted at the face behind the spider-web crack. 'We'll be waiting to welcome you in! See you in the hallway! Two minutes!'

On the slope, Benjamin applauded as the rest of them joined Kieran, makeshift weapons aloft.

Elliot pushed right up against the table, as close to the glass as he could get; he made sure Benjamin could see his face. 'You're a monster. Not because you've killed people and want to kill more, but because you're enjoying this.'

'It is because you are all so very amusing. See how they perform for me?' They watched the others file into the hallway.

Elliot turned back to him. 'If this whole thing was just a necessity for your survival and the creation of new... *vampires* – or whatever you are – you'd take the theatre out of it. You and Hayley would have decided earlier and done this quickly, last night, while we were sleeping.'

Benjamin's eyes narrowed. 'Hayley was rushed because others threatened to leave. She wanted this final gathering to help her make a decision. You know this.'

'Bullshit on that too. She knows exactly how these things go. Who's going to talk to her and who isn't. I think this is all about you, about the *sport* of it.'

Benjamin raised his hands as if to say *you got me*. 'What can I do? I have never been able to go to the match on a Saturday afternoon, as you good time boys do.'

'I hate violence,' Elliot muttered, 'but I hope we kill you.'

He grinned. 'So let us play the game.' He punched the circular crack hard, sending Elliot stumbling backwards, onto his backside. Shards of glass fell out of the centre, and the rest of the pane got swallowed up in a wave of fissures, so that the whole thing looked constructed out of puzzle pieces. Benjamin brushed at it with his hand and it all fell apart, meaning there was only one sheet of glass between him and Elliot.

Those in the hallway came back into the house; those by the sofas rushed towards the barricade. Elliot scrambled to his feet, but was still the closest to Benjamin.

Benjamin had his palms flat against the glass, as if he was just going to push it in like a revolving door.

Then Hayley was next to Elliot. 'No, not him! I mean don't kill him!'

Benjamin relaxed. Elliot turned to Hayley. She was smiling. 'I choose you. I choose you and Danni.' She looked back at Benjamin. 'Those are the first two names!'

'Okay,' Benjamin replied. 'Then I will come in to help you with the next two names.' He walked back down the slope in the direction of the steps.

Elliot didn't know if Hayley was expecting some kind of thanks, but he ignored her and looked at Danni, wielding a poker. Her nose was wrinkled – he recognised her angry face. 'That changes nothing,' she said.

'I know.' Then he did turn to the woman next to him. 'Sorry, Hayley.' He hefted up a dining chair, held it like a lion-tamer, and joined the others as they went back to their positions by the front door.

There was a tentative rap of the iron knocker. 'May I come in now?' Benjamin asked.

CHAPTER FIFTEEN

They didn't respond to him but just waited, tensed. Kieran thought it would only take one more charge: the crack in the middle was substantial, and with one hinge gone the other two could easily follow. 'Brace yourselves,' he whispered.

But nothing happened.

When nothing continued to happen, Kieran called back into the house. 'Justin?'

'Yeah?'

'Can you see where he is?'

'You want me to go right up to the glass?'

Elliot put down the chair, using it as a means of wedging open the door to the house proper. 'I'll go and check.'

They remained poised while they awaited an update. Brooke practised a swing; Rhea tested the point of the vegetable peeler with a finger.

'I can't see him,' Elliot said. 'I think he's gone. Round the back, maybe?'

That got others moving. Justin, Lucy and Hayley headed towards the sofas.

Alicia lowered the poker. 'Should we... stand down?'

Kieran shook his head. 'Let's just wait until we've got eyes on him.' He glanced across to Elliot in the other room. 'Buddy? Anything?'

'Wait a second... is that?' He leaned right in to the glass. 'Oh shit.'

'What? What is it?'

'He's in his car. And coming this way.' Elliot backed up, then turned and ran to the rear of the house.

They heard the engine, and the crunch of packed snow and gravel under tyres. Getting louder and clearer. Danni made to run to Elliot, but Kieran caught her arm. 'No time. What if he drives it up the slope?'

Rhea then grabbed *his* arm. 'What if he drives it up the *steps?*'

They looked to the distorted oak door, the redundant hinge. They heard the engine getting noisier, nearer.

'Up the stairs!' Brooke yelled. She grabbed Alicia and set off. The rest scrabbled after them.

The crash was immense. The loudest thing Danni had ever heard; it shook the whole house. She lost her footing on the stairs and slipped, bumping down a couple of risers. She had been the last one to follow Brooke and so had the clearest view behind them: Benjamin had not driven the car into the front door.

When the house stopped creaking and the noise was reduced to tinkling glass and small pieces of falling debris, she scurried the rest of the way down the stairs. She had to know that Elliot was okay.

The chair he had brought still held the door open.

Inside the house, Benjamin's Volvo was three quarters of the way into the dining area. The bifolding doors were no more, just a mess of mangled frames either side of the vehicle, the last pieces of glass hanging on in vain. The barricade of table and chairs had been reduced to firewood strewn across the polished floor, some of it reaching as far as the kitchen islands.

Danni looked beyond them: there was Elliot, in the living room dip, crouching behind a sofa with Hayley, Justin and Lucy. Her heart was still hammering, but not as much.

Benjamin was still behind the wheel. He looked back over his shoulder and reversed out and back down the slope.

Danni walked into the room, glass crunching under her shoes. Elliot came out from the living room and beckoned her to him. They met by the kitchen and hugged, then checked each other over for injuries. Both okay.

The rest of the weaponised group trooped in, taking in the devastation. The car gone, a stiff icy breeze blew in through the gaping whole. They moved quickly off the floor that bore debris, like it could still hurt them, and congregated in the kitchen.

'Somebody must have heard that.' Alicia muttered.

'Who?' Justin asked, having led the others to the group. 'There's no other property for at least a mile.'

'Passers-by?'

'At this time on a Sunday evening?'

Then they saw Benjamin walking back up the slope. He crunched into the house and stood in the middle of the devastation. 'I told you I would come in whenever I wanted.' He held out a hand. 'Come to me, Hayley.'

She started to move, and the others reacted, unsure whether or not to grab her. There were comments of concession from Danni, Kieran and Justin, and Hayley was allowed to pass through.

When she reached Benjamin he took her chin between thumb and finger and lifted her face to his. 'Are you okay? Have they harmed you in any way?'

'I'm fine. They just don't understand. They're scared.'

'Of course. Then we must make this as easy as we can for them. The other two names.'

Hayley's shoulders sagged. 'I'm still not sure...'

Brooke nudged Kieran. She whispered: 'As soon as he has four names the rest of us are dead. But before then-'

'-he can't kill us, just in case. We should-'

'-yeah.' Brooke ran forward, swinging the driver up behind her shoulder. Kieran followed, but the others hadn't tuned in to the plan.

Hayley flinched and fell in behind Benjamin.

The head of Brooke's club zipped through the air, aimed directly for Benjamin's face.

His hand shot up and grabbed the shaft, stopping it dead, sending a judder into Brooke's wrists. Then he wrenched it from her grasp and tossed it away. Her arms were still extended, pulled forward by the effort to keep a hold of her weapon. Swiftly, Benjamin grabbed her left forearm.

Then Kieran was swinging his club. It smashed into Benjamin's shoulder, but it just bounced off, unfazing him. With his spare hand now a fist, Benjamin lunged forward and punched Kieran in the face, shattering his nose. He stumbled away, lost his footing and his club, and tipped backwards into some broken glass.

Benjamin then returned to Brooke's arm. His other hand joined in, gripping it like a trapeze swing. Then he snapped it in half.

Brooke howled and slumped. Benjamin let go to allow her to fall to the floor. Her arm was almost at a right angle at the impossible

110

new joint, and bone poked out through the skin. She tried to hold it with her other hand but that just brought more exquisite pain.

Then Alicia and Rhea were at her shoulders, dragging her away.

The whole episode – starting from when Brooke first took off optimistically with her golf club – took nine seconds.

'I know what you are thinking,' Benjamin said. 'Until the moment I have all four names, you believe that I cannot kill you, *must not* kill you. This is so. But I can *hurt* you. If you are chosen for the transference, you will heal anyway. So, if anyone else wants to try something stupid against either Hayley or myself, I will break both your arms and legs. Brooke, you got off lightly.'

'Fuck you!' she spat from her heap on the floor.

Hayley came back out from behind Benjamin and took a step towards them all. 'Please don't try anything; I don't want you to get hurt.'

Kieran got up, collecting blood in his palms from his gushing nose. 'Bit late for that, Hayles.' Rhea led him across to the sink.

In all this, Danni had moved away from Elliot and was walking around the edge of the room, keeping a good-sized distance between her and Benjamin, making the circumference of her invisible circle as even as she could. She'd got close to the hole in the wall before anyone questioned her. It was a combination of Elliot and Hayley, although she had to assume Benjamin had noticed too. She stopped and turned towards him. 'You heard that Hayley has chosen me, right? To be one of you?'

'I did. You must not let it concern you.'

'I'm not concerned. No, I'm glad to be chosen. You can't kill me now though, not if you're honouring Hayley's wishes.'

'This is also correct. But I will-'

'-break my arms and legs, yeah, I heard that bit. Hayley?' Her friend started a little. 'Would you allow him to do that to me? Would you still love this man if he caused me that much pain?'

Hayley grabbed Benjamin's arm. 'You mustn't do that to Danni, you mustn't. She's not attacking you, she's not attacking me.'

Benjamin smiled at Hayley and stroked her arm. 'I will only do what is necessary to make tonight a success for both of us.'

'Don't hurt them.'

'I will try not to.'

Alicia, kneeling on the floor next to Brooke, called out. 'He's going to kill half of us, Hayley! Don't forget that!'

Hayley shook her head, as if she could displace that notion from her brain with a physical action.

Benjamin's attention was back on Danni. 'So what is it you are doing, Danielle?'

She stood on what had been the threshold between the outdoors and in, now just a heap of rubble in an icy vortex. She folded her arms against the wind, the poker still in her grasp. 'I'm going to go outside.' She stepped onto the slope.

Hayley panicked. 'Benjamin! The hound!'

He closed his eyes for a couple of seconds while Danni eased herself slowly down the bank. Others called to her, including Elliot. When she reached the flat she looked up and saw him at the top of the slope. 'Danni! What are you doing?'

The hell hound had been standing guard at the bodies of Nick and Steff. It now tore across the drive towards Danni.

She didn't have time to react; she only managed to get her poker hand up in front of her face.

The creature ran past her and bounded up the slope. Elliot stepped back across the threshold just in time. Its jaws snapped and drooled on the other side of a metaphysical barrier. Elliot dropped his hands to his knees and almost threw up.

'Benjamin!' Hayley cried. 'I've chosen Elliot as well!'

'Of course.' He closed his eyes again, communicating with the hound.

Kieran and Rhea went to Elliot, giving Benjamin and Hayley a wide berth on the other side of the destroyed wall. Kieran had tissue shoved up both nostrils and a bib of blood. Rhea look at the state of the two men and decided it was up to her to ask the questions. 'What's your thinking, Danni?' she called.

She had eyes on the top of the slope: on her friends, on Benjamin, on the hound. They were all waiting to see what she would do. She walked away from them, along the drive. 'I'm thinking that I'm gonna get that bag down from the tree, retrieve my phone and call my kids.' She turned towards it. The branch was high but the bottom of the plastic bag would be within her reach with the help of the fire iron. If she couldn't get it down she could just poke a hole in the bottom.

She'd taken a total of five steps before Benjamin was standing in front of her. She hadn't for a second believed he'd let her get there.

'Go back to the house, Danielle.'

She was gambling, she hoped not quite with her life, but certainly with her safety. Whatever had happened to Steff, it had been in the dead of night and just between her and Benjamin. Nick had been savaged by the dog-thing. She had to believe that if she was Hayley's first choice, her best friend, the most important person in her life besides Benjamin, then she wouldn't let this man harm her in front of her very eyes. And if he did, she could hopefully use it against him and make Hayley see sense. 'Get out of my way, Benjamin.'

He didn't move. 'You must know that I am not going to let you place a telephone call?'

'Perhaps not. But what are you going to do about it if I try? How upset is Hayley going to get?' She sidestepped to get round him; he matched her movement. She went the other way and he did the same. He hadn't touched her though; not yet.

She looked back at the house. 'Hayley: if me and Elliot are going to be part of this thing with you, I need to speak to my children one last time. You know I need to do that, right?'

There was shuffling atop the slope, and Hayley was ushered to the front. Danni could see that pressure was being applied by the others. Hayley hushed them before answering. 'I... I know that, Danni... but maybe just not right now?'

She scowled up at her. 'Hayley, you chose me because you love me, so I hope that means you support me. And I want to talk to my kids. Right now.'

She turned back to Benjamin and made a dart past him, giving him a choice to make. She wasn't surprised when he grabbed her; it was the ease with which he lifted her off the ground that took her breath away and made her drop the poker. He had locked fingers around the top of her arm initially but then another hand was at her hip and up she went. Not high, but enough so that no amount of leg-kicking could get her feet on the floor. She shouted at him to let go, and shouted to Hayley to make this stop. It didn't change anything. The more she struggled the tighter his grip became.

Logic suggested that he couldn't possibly hold her in this position for long, that the lopsided nature of her body weight would draw her towards the ground. But there they were: Danni wriggling to be free, Benjamin locked in position like a statue, holding her out in front of him almost horizontally.

'There is no getting out of this, Danielle. You must see this by now.'

She couldn't get her feet to the ground, but what else could they do? She swung her right leg as hard as she could, and planted a kick to Benjamin's side. He flinched slightly, but it didn't seem to cause him any pain. He grinned at her efforts. And dug his fingers in deeper.

The pain was like electrodes pushed into her body. In a couple of places she thought she felt the skin break. She screamed for him to stop, and somehow managed to also spit out Elliot and Hayley's names in one long stream of verbalised agony.

Benjamin relented and the pain lessened. He looked back towards the slope. 'Get back to the house, Elliot, or I will squeeze tight again.'

She heard her husband's voice but couldn't see him from the angle she was in. 'Put her down, you bastard!'

'To the house, Elliot. Do not be the cause of unnecessary pain.' Benjamin dug a solitary finger in and Danni yelped. It must have had the desired effect, as no further instructions were aimed Elliot's way.

Then Benjamin looked at her, and spoke softly. 'You think you know me, and can control this situation? The arrogance of you people. What if my real intention is to kill you all, including Hayley? This little rebellion of yours has done nothing but leave you completely vulnerable.'

Danni's eyes widen. Oh God, was that it? They were just an all-you-can-eat buffet to him? Had she just taken a stroll to certain death? How could she have been so stupid? 'Hayley… Hayley loves you.'

'Yes. Yes, she does. So because of that I will not – even though I could – snap you in half like a twig. Instead…'

He let go. It was unexpected and she couldn't right herself before hitting the frozen ground. The wind was knocked out of her and bolts of fresh pain shot through her body at the points where his finger holds met the floor.

As he had done before, he extended one of the long fingernails on his left hand. This time, he placed an incision across his right palm. Rivulets of blood ran down across his pale skin.

Danni scrambled to her feet but didn't get far. He grabbed her hair with his left and hoisted her towards him.

Then he clamped his bloody right palm across her mouth.

NO ONE IS LEAVING

CHAPTER SIXTEEN

Elliot had made it back up to the house, but seeing Benjamin wrap his bleeding hand around Danni's face got him running down the snowy bank again. He fell at the bottom, face-planting in the gravel, but corrected himself as quickly as he could. The others shouted his name. The hell hound watched on, disinterested.

As he covered the flat ground towards them, Benjamin tracked him. He held Danni to one side. Her hands had been grabbing at his but now they hung limp, which terrified Elliot. He screamed as he approached. 'Let her go!'

Just before Elliot reached them, Benjamin removed his hands and took a step back. Danni dropped to her knees and then keeled over. Elliot slid in and lifted her head. Her eyes were closed and there was blood smeared all over her mouth. 'Danni! Danni!' He parted her lips and put his ear to them: she was breathing.

'She will sleep for a short while,' Benjamin said, 'but then she will be back with you. Do you want me to help you carry her to the house?'

'Don't you fucking touch her!' He got one arm under her back and the other behind her thighs and lifted. For a second he thought he wouldn't make it, that his legs would fail him and they'd topple over, but with gritted teeth he managed to get upright. He turned and took small and steady steps back towards the slope.

It was Justin who suggested the steps; Elliot shifted his course slightly. When they opened the door it collapsed in on itself, rendered useless. However, it did mean they could come down the steps and help him. The dog-thing followed him, and was reinvigorated when the others came out into the chill air, but it didn't touch the stone, and as soon as Elliot shuffled up onto the first step, they were able to help. Justin and Kieran got Danni from him and took her into the house. Rhea helped Elliot the rest of the way.

They laid her on a sofa and Elliot knelt, trying to wake her, but to no avail. Hayley was hovering. 'She'll wake when she's ready.'

'Go away, Hayley.' He licked the edge of his sleeve and dabbed at Danni's mouth, desperate to remove Benjamin's vile blood from her beautiful face. He sobbed a little at the struggle, then Rhea was there with a damper cloth which worked better.

There was moaning from the kitchen. It was Brooke. They'd done what they could to reset her arm and Alicia was now bandaging her up with virtually everything they could find in the house's emergency first aid kit. They'd stemmed the bleeding but not the pain. Justin ran upstairs and came back with a box of paracetamol. Brooke took four without a drink, just swallowed them dry.

Lucy approached. 'Might I have a couple of those? I'm getting a little-' Alicia snatched up the box and told Lucy to back off.

Then Hayley was on the move. She made her way to the front of the house. Benjamin was waiting, standing in the rubble once more. They hugged and then separated. 'I need the other two names, Hayley.'

Everyone else stopped what they were doing in anticipation of what Hayley might say. 'I need... I need a little more time.'

He nodded. 'Seeing as we have already made a start, I will allow you thirty more minutes. If you cannot choose then I will have to choose for you. We cannot allow this-' he wafted a hand into the house; Kieran and Rhea were the closest, poised with pokers. '-to go on for much longer.'

Kieran yelled, passionately but powerlessly. 'Stay back!' Then his face crinkled in pain; the outburst hurt his swollen nose.

Benjamin laughed. 'I understand. I have not managed to break into the inner circle of friends. I do not have such rich shared history. My presence here is a little awkward!' He looked around, spotted the chair that had been holding open the door, checked that it was still functional, and sat on it, blocking the doorway and the access to upstairs. 'I will wait here. For thirty minutes.' Hayley seemed in limbo, caught between both camps. Benjamin addressed it. 'Go and be with your friends. It will help you decide.'

She nodded and walked back into the kitchen area. She faltered when she got near Kieran and Rhea. 'It's alright,' Kieran muttered, and pokers were lowered.

Benjamin, whistling, checked the time on his watch. It was 5.40pm.

**

Danni had one sofa, Brooke the other. It seemed redundant having a barricade at the patio doors, so the rest of them rescued the other two sofas and put them back in place. It was almost like trying to put together the scene from when they first arrived, filling up the seats as friends showed up. So much had happened since then. So much had changed. In less than forty-eight hours.

Danni was still unconscious. 'What's wrong with her?' Elliot asked, to anyone who might have an answer.

Hayley offered one from the fringes of the group. 'She's in transference. She took in some of Benjamin's blood. The process has started.'

'What?' Elliot dabbed Danni's face again with the cloth, at blood that was no longer there. 'She's... clean.'

Justin chaperoned Hayley inside the newly assembled square of sofas and encouraged her to sit. 'Do your best to explain it, Hayley.'

'There isn't much to say. I don't know the science behind it; just what Benjamin has told me would happen. The chosen ones take in some of his blood, the effect of which puts them to sleep for a short time...'

'How long is a short time?' Kieran asked, tissue still wadded on his face. They had just over twenty minutes before Benjamin wanted to proceed.

'Undetermined. Could be as little as ten minutes, could be a couple of hours.'

Elliot was fraught at the idea of Danni being out for that long. 'Is there no way we can wake her?'

'Not until her body is ready for the next stage, or the next stage is brought directly to her.'

'And what's the next stage?'

Hayley sat a little straighter; pulled her knees tight together and place her hands on them. She was bracing herself for a backlash. 'Human blood.'

There was very little reaction. There was processing, but perhaps also an acceptance. Hayley thought that maybe they were finally beginning to understand. 'Elliot, we could see Benjamin and start your transference now if you like.'

'No thank you,' he uttered, without the politeness in tone the words suggested. 'She drinks human blood – what then?'

'She takes a little more of Benjamin's... then more human blood... and then the process repeats until she's ready. Until she's changed.' Hayley knew that was the simple version: there were physical changes, particularly to the mouth, jaw and tongue so that she could feed at a swifter rate, but she didn't think that was worth getting into just yet, seeing as it seemed to be going quite well for a change.

It meant she wasn't quite ready for Elliot's next question, even though – when she thought about it – it was probably the logical one to ask. 'What happens if she doesn't take in any human blood?'

'Oh, right. Well, if she doesn't feed within the first couple of hours, she'll... well, she'll start to die.'

They could hear Benjamin laughing from the other side of the house.

Elliot prickled at the sound. 'Can he hear us? Is he listening to everything we say?'

Rhea was the only person currently standing. She looked in Benjamin's direction. 'Er, no: I don't think so. He's talking to Lucy.'

Justin stood. 'What?' He'd been lost in his own thoughts, mainly about how this perfect weekend he'd planned had gone spectacularly wrong. He'd not had eyes on Lucy for about a minute. 'What's she doing?' He excused himself and left the group.

They watched him go. It was a long, straight diagonal line across to the other side of the house. Benjamin was still on the chair by the door to the hallway, and Lucy was standing in front of him, hands on hips and swaying slightly. Benjamin laughed again.

'Didn't think she was one for jokes,' Rhea remarked, and sat down next to Kieran. 'How's that nose?'

**

When Justin got to Lucy he could tell that she was not only drunk but in one of her furies: her teeth were bared and her eyes were wide.

She was enraged and indignant about something. 'What is it?' he asked, putting a hand on her shoulder, to steady her as much as anything.

She shrugged him off. 'This *tool* won't let me go to the bathroom!' She leant towards Benjamin and said the next words loudly and slowly like he was just learning the language. 'I need a *piss*!'

Benjamin remained seated. He directed his response to Justin. 'I have told her. She is not allowed upstairs. You are not to leave the vicinity. Who knows, she might have a wooden stake hidden under the bed, no?' He laughed again.

Justin held Lucy back but couldn't prevent her swearing. Once she'd finished he tried to readdress the situation. 'Come on, mate – what's she supposed to do? She needs to go.'

Benjamin pointed to the kitchen. 'There is a sink-' Lucy made a noise of disgust '-or there is outside.' He cocked a thumb behind him.

'But your hound...'

'Remember, you have the steps. You are her husband: I will let you assist seeing as she is inebriated.'

Lucy wrinkled her lip. 'Peeing outside? Fuck that.'

'Half of the door still hangs. You will be afforded a little privacy. That is my best offer. I will be right here, with this door open. If you try to run upstairs, I will be there to break your ankle so you cannot run anymore. Do you understand this, Justin?'

'Yeah, I got it. Luce, come on: it's the best you're going to get.'

Lucy muttered a stream of disbelief mixed with expletives as Justin led her to the first door. Benjamin stood and held it open for them. The front door was like one half of a saloon entrance. Justin guided her through into the night air. They went down a couple of steps then stopped. She looked less angry now, just frustrated. 'This is ludicrous.'

'Yeah, you haven't quite got that right. Look, I guess you squat over the side of the steps and I hold you? Does that work?'

'I'm actually doing this?'

'If you need to go...'

'Fine!' She popped the button of her jeans and started to shuffle them down. The next bit was supposed to be a whisper, but came out too loud, making Justin flinch. 'That dowdy bitch better choose us two next!'

'Let's just get this over with.' He took both of her hands and she stuck her behind out over the side edge of the steps, bending her knees a little. 'For God's sake, don't slip, Luce.'

He heard the pee. She'd taken in too much fluid for it to smell strong.

There was a shape in the darkness. Approaching. Fast.

Justin yanked her forward so that she peed into the crotch of her jeans. 'Bastard!' she yelled.

The hell hound snapped its jaws right where her backside had been. Then it dipped its head and licked at the puddles of urine.

Justin pulled Lucy into an awkward hug. 'Holy shit, that was close!' The creature had been in the garden since they took down the barricade by the patio doors; it must have run round as soon as they came out.

'I should have reminded you,' Benjamin said from the other doorway. 'Anything beyond the boundary of the steps is his. Better to pee *on* the stone rather than off it!' He laughed again.

Justin righted Lucy, then – keeping one hand on her shoulder for balance – looked away as she clumsily got herself dressed again, cursing the wetness in the clothes. This whole episode had got Justin thinking, and not about how difficult it was going to be to plan one's toilet from hereon in. He stared at the hound, prowling the around the steps but not touching them. He remembered something he and Elliot had discussed when Kieran had had a close encounter with the thing in the back garden.

If we stay in the house it won't follow.

Because we haven't invited it in?

Something like that I suppose.

Exactly that, thought Justin. At that point the two of them had lamented welcoming Benjamin in. But now Justin thought that didn't have to be the problem it currently was.

'Inside now, please,' Benjamin instructed. Justin led Lucy back in; they didn't converse with Benjamin other than for a few more slurred expletives hurled his way. Justin was keen to get back to the others to disclose what he'd been thinking.

**

Back at the sofas, Lucy flopped down and shared the disgraceful way in which she'd been treated. They listened, for the practical information rather than the outrage. Justin was quiet, and seemed to be more drawn to Hayley than his wife. Rhea didn't blame him: Lucy Fisher was an arsehole.

Rhea surveyed the group. Danni was still *sleeping*, as Elliot like to call it. He was kneeling by her head, waiting for her to rouse. Brooke was heavily strapped up, her broken arm secured as well as possible. She had dewdrops of sweat on her face and occasionally blew out her breaths; she was clearly still in a lot of pain despite popping paracetamol like Tic Tacs. Alicia sat by her. Kieran paced as he was wont to do, bloody tissue still hanging out of his nose. She'd leave him to it for now; she knew better than to follow him around like a lap dog. Hayley sat, prim and proper and getting on with her knitting, in contrast to Lucy, sprawled and picking at her sticky jeans.

Considering they were facing potential death in the next quarter of an hour or so, it was remarkably sedate. But then what could they do? Try to fight him again? That hadn't gone well the first time. Run? Dash out the back and the hound would be on them. Benjamin held the front. Some of them would get further, sure, but between the vampire and his monster, she was certain they'd be all picked off before they made the road. No wonder the feeling was to just sit and wait for the next part, and perhaps hope you react well when it happens.

Rhea looked back at Justin. Here was something different. Yes: eyes on Hayley, but then eyes in Kieran. And repeat. Rhea thought she understood, could read the need in his expression. Justin wanted to speak to Kieran – and others maybe – but not have Hayley listening in.

'Yo, Hayles.' Rhea said. 'You give me a hand with something in the kitchen?'

'Of course, what is it?'

'We've not eaten in a while. I don't know what's coming next but I've got a feeling dinner isn't on the cards. I just think a bit of quick and easy food might do us good. Even if we have only got...' she checked the clock. 'Under fifteen minutes.'

'I'll help.'

'That's my girl: come on.'

Elliot lifted his head to object. 'I really don't think it matters if we have a *Last Supper*, Rhea – there are more important things going on!'

'No,' Justin said, standing up. 'I think it's a good idea. Who knows what we'll need energy for.'

Kieran waved at the glass coffee table. 'That didn't work out for us last time, Just. There's still stuff out from breakfast. We didn't bother then; I can't see us bothering now.'

Justin leaned over and picked up the dirty crockery. 'Then it's just something to keep us occupied.' He directed Hayley through with a nod of his head.

Rhea waited as Justin overtook them with the used plates and platters. He dropped them on one of the islands and hurried back, giving Rhea an acknowledging look. Rhea then walked with Hayley into the kitchen. 'I'm actually pathetic at this stuff: I asked you because I thought you might have a better idea?'

'That was nice of you,' Hayley replied, smiling. 'I'll root around in the fridge; you take a look in that cupboard: I think that's where the boys have been hiding the snacks!'

They got to work in their given stations. Rhea was just going through the motions, hoping this was giving Justin time for whatever he wanted to do. Between crouching down and loading the worktop with chocolate bars, tortilla chips and Mr Kipling's cake boxes, she caught glances of him talking to Kieran and Elliot.

Hayley brought out cold meats, a large pork pie and a lettuce. *A fucking lettuce,* thought Rhea. *What did she think this was?*

Rhea asked her. Hayley came back with spring onions and cherry tomatoes before replying. 'For the side garnish. My grandmother always said there was nothing wrong with making your food look pretty.'

Rhea looked at the crap she'd pulled out of the cupboards and pushed it to the side. 'Looks like you've got this then, girl. You have a talent for entertaining.'

'Thank you! But I've nothing sharp to get through the lettuce. I guess I'll have to tear.'

Rhea rooted around in her pockets. In one was the vegetable peeler. In the other, the small scissors. She offered the latter to Hayley. 'Not ideal, but good for the spring onion at least.' Hayley was again vociferous in her thanks; she seemed excited about this joint venture and fully engrossed in it. She sought out serving bowls and plates while Rhea kept an eye on the others. Now Brooke was being included in the conversation, and Elliot.

'How about dips?' Hayley asked.

'Yeah, go for it.'

Hayley went back to the fridge. Back at the worktop, she peeled off the lids and arranged the pots on a plate. She chatted as she worked. 'You and Kieran seem to get on really well!'

Rhea couldn't help but smile at the normalcy of the conversation and the genuine interest in her tone. 'Yeah, I like him: he's a great guy.'

Hayley set about the side salad. She looked at the ingredients she was snipping as she spoke. 'I'm very torn about you being here, Rhea.'

'Oh yeah? How do you mean?' Rhea glanced up at Benjamin sitting on his chair next to the devastated dining area and thought she knew exactly how she meant.

Hayley looked at the food as she spoke. 'On the one hand it isn't fair on you because I haven't had the opportunity to get to know you. On the other hand, I'm glad I've met you and had the chance to see you and Kieran interact so well together.'

Rhea thought about this for a second. 'If it isn't fair, you could always let me and Kieran get away?'

Hayley looked up, and for once her face reflected the gravity of the situation. 'It's not going to work out like that, is it?'

'I guess not.'

'Sorry.' She arranged the cold meats on a platter.

'Think about it though, Hayley. It's not me you have to apologise to the most. What about the old friends you're not taking with you? Some of them are going to die for your happiness. Have you thought about how messed up that sounds? How selfish? How did you let it get to this point, girl?'

Hayley continued to arrange the food, slowly. 'When you've been unhappy for thirty-seven years, the chance to change that forever means everything.'

Rhea leaned closer. 'Unhappy all that time?'

'I have no siblings. My parents died in a train derailment when I was seven-'

'-oh Hayley, I'm so sorry-'

'-it's okay.' She continued to stare at the platter. 'My grandmother raised me, but died when I was nineteen. I have been alone for a long time.'

'What about the group? Your friends?'

At this point she looked up again. 'Let's be honest, Rhea. I have been a better friend to them than they have been to me. Even as a newcomer I'm assuming you can see that.'

Rhea's smile was a knowing one. 'I guess I can. But no relationship's fifty-fifty. We take what we can get, right? We don't need to seek out... extreme solutions.' Again she glanced in a particular direction.

'I didn't seek Benjamin out. But I am happy he found me. And that's what matters most.' She lifted up the platter. 'I'm ready!' Cheer spread across her face, like the last conversation had never happened. With her spare hand she scooped up the dips.

Rhea lifted up what she had: a serving bowl inelegantly crammed with samples from the unhealthy bounty she'd retrieved from the cupboard. She stared past Hayley's shoulder. It looked like whatever conversations needed to happen were done. 'Okay. Let's set these on the coffee table. If people want something they can help themselves. Yours looks more appetising than mine.'

'I was happy to help.'

'I can see that about you, Hayley. Come on, let's go back.'

They caught the last lines of a conversation when they returned to the sofas. Brooke saying: '...pretty sure I left it open.'

'And the other thing?' Kieran said hastily, an eye on the two carrying dishes.

'I think I got it,' she said, giving him a serious stare. 'It'll take some remembering, but yeah.'

Hayley looked like she was about to ask, but Rhea nodded to the wares in her hands. 'Put yours down first, girl.'

No one showed any immediate interest in what they set down on the table, instead the group watched where the two of them went next. Hayley returned to her knitting, smiling, asking them to *tuck in*; Rhea, still standing, sidled over to Kieran.

He put his mouth to her ear, just a little wary of the tissue still in his nose. 'When things start moving, just follow my lead.'

'Gotcha,' she replied. She stepped forward and grabbed a few chips; she thought someone had to engage with the food. Alicia seemed to understand. She reached out, grabbed a bread stick and dipped it in the hummus Hayley had brought over. When Alicia crunched it, Hayley looked pleased.

Kieran looked at the clock and then over at Benjamin, still sat in his chair at the other end of the house, watching them. There were five minutes left before he would push Hayley for the other names.

'Okay,' said Kieran, walking behind the back of Danni's sofa. He got the attention of those that had been colluding. 'We ready?'

There were furtive nods, to avoid alerting Hayley.

'Right,' he replied. 'Let's see if we can speed this along.'

He pulled out the blood-sodden rags of tissue from his swollen nose and dropped them onto Danni's face.

Elliot was too shocked to protest.

Danni's eyes flickered open.

CHAPTER SEVENTEEN

Elliot batted the tissue away almost instantly but did not see where it fell; he was drawn to his wife's eyes, open, blinking and gazing up at the room above her. 'Take it easy, Danni: you're okay, I'm here!'

She ran her tongue around her mouth and lips. 'Dry,' she muttered.

He helped her sit up. 'We'll get you a drink in a minute.' He spoke quieter but with an insistent tone. 'But first we're going to move. Quickly. You'll need to keep up.' She looked confused. 'Say nothing,' he said. 'But get up and stretch your legs; walk around the sofas.' He stood and took her with him. They passed Kieran; Elliot shot him a look. He shrugged as if to say *I thought it was worth a try.*

Hayley's knitting needles stopped clacking. 'You okay, Danni?'

'I think so.' Fists clenched, limbs stiff, she walked a circuit around the seating. Elliot encouraged her all the way. When they got back to their starting point, he said: 'Alicia is going to guide you when we move.'

'What?' she croaked. Her throat was really dry.

'Just go with it.'

Alicia and Brooke stood, the latter very carefully.

Hayley nudged Lucy. 'Have I missed something? Is something happening?'

Lucy gave a slow, lazy wink. 'You just stick with me, Hayley Wayley!'

Then Justin got up and announced he needed to take a pee. He made his way through the kitchen area and towards the front of the house.

Alicia turned to the fireplace and picked up a stack of the split logs. 'Danni, you okay to grab a couple of these?'

She went over, still a little stiff. 'Sure?'

She pushed out her forearms and Alicia placed some wood on them. 'Stick with me.' Danni nodded. Alicia then turned to Brooke. 'You gonna be okay?'

Brooke cradled her strapped up arm with her good one. 'Don't worry about me.'

Now Hayley stood. 'I'm really not following.'

Kieran and Elliot walked over to the patio door, but then they waited, listening for Justin.

**

Benjamin, still in the chair, saw Justin approach. His eye flickered between the movement at the back of the house and the man heading towards him. 'Are they getting ready to welcome me back?' he asked.

Justin was uncharacteristically stern. 'And we did welcome you, didn't we? Extended the hand of friendship. And this is where we are.' He gestured towards the gaping hole in the dining area. Snow had started to build up inside the house.

Benjamin raised an eyebrow. 'It is not how we planned it, but it is the situation we have got. Regardless, the end result will be the same. But what is this? I assume you did not come to chat?'

'No. Solo visit this time to the new bathroom. I came to pee.'

Benjamin stood, moved behind his chair and opened the middle door with an outstretched arm. 'You remember how this works?'

'Point and shoot.'

'You know what I mean.'

'Keep everything on the steps: got it.'

He walked through, then stopped at the battered front entrance to look back. Benjamin was in the same position, watching him closely. When he looked forward he stared through the half hanging door and waited.

And then it was there, having run back round from its patrol at the back of the house: Benjamin's dog-thing, taking up position at the foot of the steps.

Justin gave a big sigh. 'Not sure anything's going to happen now. It's freezing!'

The last two words felt loud coming out of his mouth, as was the intention. Too loud? Was Benjamin suspicious? Justin turned, feeling nervous, awkward – he just hoped Benjamin read that as being in keeping with the potentially embarrassing situation of having to find one's penis in the cold.

Benjamin continued to stare at him, dispassionately. Justin took to the steps.

**

Back at the patio doors, those in the know acknowledged with nods that the trigger word had been heard: *freezing*.

Kieran undid the locking mechanism on the patio door and slid it open. Elliot darted out into the darkness. Brooke shushed Hayley's outburst of surprise.

Elliot unfastened the garden gate and slipped through onto the path that ran along the side of the house. He looked down it: no hell hound bounding towards him. He'd been chosen by Hayley, and he still had protection because of it. That had been their first risk in this half-baked plan, but it worked. He made the couple of steps to the annex, fished the key out of his pocket and unlocked the glass double-doors. He didn't go in but pushed them open as wide as they would go.

He went back through the gate and part way up the patio towards the light inside the house's sliding doors. Kieran was there on the other side of the glass; Elliot offered him a thumbs up.

Kieran looked down the length of the house and then returned the gesture.

Elliot then plotted a straight line direct to the shed. Brooke had been in there for a shovel and had said she'd left it open. She wasn't wrong: the door squeaked open with little resistance. Inside though, it was pitch black. Brooke had had the luxury of the torch on her phone. However, while she'd been in there she'd seen what Elliot was after; she'd described its placement to him. He was going in blind but not clueless.

**

Back in the house, Benjamin moved away from the adjoining

door, letting it swing closed on Justin, and walked across the rubble to be in a more central position. He saw them standing up, moving, looking into the garden. 'Hayley! I think it is time to give me two more names!' Instead of walking towards them though he walked backwards, through the destroyed house front and onto the slope. He looked to his left: Justin wasn't peeing, but merely standing there, looking down at the hound. 'What is it you are doing, Justin?'

His mouth was moving. He was counting. When he stopped, he turned to look at Benjamin. He looked afraid, but also determined. He called out, in the direction of the house: 'Back off, *Fido!*'

Benjamin observed. He wasn't directing it at the hound prowling in front of him. It wasn't a reaction. It was… a signal.

He looked back into the house.

They were all rushing into the garden.

'Hayley!' he called, in the manner of one embroiled in a game of hide and seek. He walked forward, unconcerned but a little bemused.

**

They ran – as best they could across the slippery ground – in single file into the annex. Or at least that was the intention. Kieran and Elliot formed a gully on the path for them to pass through. Brooke went first, sturdy and firm in her footing. Lucy next, urged on by Rhea, but then she looked over Elliot's shoulder down the path and saw movement. Frightened, she pirouetted and slipped.

At the same time, Justin, still on the steps and having seen the hound twist and scurry for the side of the house, stepped off stone and onto gravel. It was like the creature was on a leash that suddenly ran out of length. It flipped mid-air and came back for him. It was a simple equation: he was closer than them, therefore it had a higher chance of shredding someone with its fangs right here.

And it nearly did. As he returned to the bottom step it flashed past his waist, spittle from its jaws speckling his shirt. He felt the draft it made, and either that or barefaced fear rocked him. Literally. To avoid falling back and risking a foot slipping off the step, he overcompensated and nearly took a nosedive onto the gravel. He juddered in his stance and swore loudly, ordering himself to stand fucking still.

The hound assessed him, then instinct took it back to the path.

Fresh meat was exposing itself behind the building.

Justin hoped he had bought them a little time. He didn't think he could step off again.

Kieran hoisted Lucy up and more or less threw her into the annex. 'Come on, come on!' Danni next, a little stiff still, with Alicia behind her, encouraging, both still holding logs.

One more remained, between the posts of the open garden gate. 'Hayley?' Elliot asked. 'You coming?'

'No time!' yelled Kieran. He pointed over Elliot's shoulder. The dog-thing was hurtling towards them. 'Give it to me!'

The *it* in question was what Elliot had retrieved from the shed: the axe for splitting logs. The plan had been for Elliot to hold the thing off with his newfound immunity, but in truth he was more than happy to surrender the weapon. He tossed it across to Kieran who caught it one-handed.

Elliot felt the air change at his back and neck, and a fleeting shadow passed over his head, blocking out the stars. Just having the hound close to him for a split-second made his skin crawl. But by the time he ducked it had already leapt over him.

Kieran swung the axe with all he had.

**

Justin walked back into the house. This was the bit of their hastily constructed plan that had the most variables. If they all got into the annex then most of it was done, but it did leave him alone in the house with Benjamin. If in fact he was still in there.

He crossed the destroyed dining space, then moved into the kitchen zone. That's when he spied Benjamin, crouching down by the cold fireplace in the living area. He stood, holding a split log in each hand. 'They have taken some of the wood. Why do you think they have done that? Are they perhaps hoping to give me splinters?'

Justin treaded carefully, both physically and with his thoughts. He approached the sideboard, on the opposite wall to where Benjamin was. 'It's human nature to try and protect one's self; to survive. You surely can't blame us for that.'

'Like the tiny spider that scurries away when you put obstacles in its path.'

Justin forced a smile. 'That's it. But you can capture that spider at any moment, kill it even. Still, you see where it goes for a short time. Play with it. At least that's what I did as a kid. Were you a kid, Benjamin, in the same way we all were?'

He stepped away from the fireplace, still holding a log in each hand. 'I was. I was born just like you, to a very simple Romanian family, in 1888. I played with insects in this way. So you are saying that all of you are like the insects?'

'That's right. And for now you're humouring us, playing with us. I get it, you can take us at any time, but there's some sport in seeing what we will do. This is just a game. And you have all night to end it.' He edged over towards the patio doors; they were still open. 'You can let it run a little longer. Let *us* run a little longer. So I'm just going to join the others, and then you can be amused by our foolishness all over again.'

Benjamin smiled. 'That is quite clever, to try and get me to think that way.'

'It's true though, isn't it? Can I go?'

He shrugged. 'How are you going to get past my hell hound? You now have no one at the front of the house to distract it.'

Justin put one foot out into the cold, and glanced around warily. 'If they all got into the annex, I'm guessing they immobilised the dog.'

The smile fell from Benjamin's face. 'You better hope that is not true.' He closed his eyes for a couple of seconds, and then – looking alarmed – strode over to the door. It prompted Justin to step out fully and move along the patio towards the gate.

It was open, and so too was the annex, directly opposite. The whole group of them were gathered there, framed by the doorway. Except for Hayley; she stood in the spot in between, approximately where Elliot and Kieran had formed their gully. She was looking down at her feet. The crunched snow was darker where they'd beaten a path.

No, it was more than that: there was blood. Hayley seemed immobilised by having stood in it. It also trailed into the annex, under the feet of Elliot and Brooke who were the nearest. Elliot was beckoning Hayley inside. When they saw Justin approach they called for him also.

Before Justin could make another move, Benjamin was standing beside him. 'Hayley, come to me and give me the two names. This has gone on long enough.' He was ramrod straight, with no humour in his face. 'Tell me now, or I will hurt Justin.'

Justin flinched, and did so again when Benjamin's arm shot out – still holding a split log – blocking his path.

At that point Brooke raised her good arm, and started to recite something, chant-like. 'Heavenly father, almighty God, bless and sanctify this house and all who dwell in it. Grant this home the grace of your presence.' She closed her eyes, straining to remember some of the words used against her by her parents' priest as a teen. She knew they were in there somewhere; they'd visited her enough in nightmares well into her twenties. 'Banish from it, all that is... unclean, making it a secure place for those who dwell within. Through Christ our Lord. Today and always...' She shrugged. 'Amen.'

Elliot nodded: 'That's good.' She stepped back, allowing Kieran to come forward. He had something in his hand that she shrank away from.

Justin tried to step around Benjamin's arm but he wasn't allowing it. Behind the glasses his eyes were black and shining. 'I have not finished with you yet.'

Elliot called out. 'Come on, Justin! Hayley!'

Hayley was still frozen. It felt critical somehow: a choice between Benjamin or her friends. She couldn't get her head around the last couple of minutes, but she had the dreadful feeling everything had changed.

Then Kieran stepped forward, out of the annex. In his hand he had the severed head of the hell hound. He launched it at Benjamin, narrowly missing Hayley. It struck Benjamin on the chest and landed at his feet: a dead, dried-up husk, like mummified remains.

'Fuck you, Benson!' roared Kieran. 'That's for Nick and Steff!'

Justin realised he had to run. He got around Benjamin's arm and made for the gate. But then there was a thump against the back of his head and a white hot shooting pain from his skull to his groin. He put a hand to his hair and it came back bloody.

Then there was a second jolt of pain as another log smashed him by the ear. The pain of that one seemed to jangle every tooth in his head. He suddenly felt very woozy and dropped to his knees. He could make out Hayley in front of him, looking distressed. Noise came from the annex but for some reason he couldn't see that far;

not clearly. Just shapes and colours, animated, but so, so far away.

Kieran moved further out of the doorway, Elliot close behind him; both within touching distance of Hayley. However, Justin was out of reach. Benjamin stood behind him. He put a hand under his chin, pressing the back of his head against his middle, unbalancing him slightly. Justin's eyes looked unfocused and when he lifted a hand to try and remove Benjamin's he missed, pawing at his own neck.

Benjamin snarled. 'No more games!' The last word was distorted slightly as his jaw dislocated and the inside of his mouth unfolded to reveal that second row of menacing teeth. His tongue twirled and thinned, and vicious-looking, needle-like spines appeared. He wrenched Justin's head into an almost impossible position, exposing more neck than seemed natural. Then he lifted him up so that his twisted flesh met Benjamin's dismantled and horrifying face. The tongue latched on like a fishing hook, then the rest of his elongated mouth fastened itself around Justin's neck.

Immediately, blood began to pour down Justin's shirt front.

There were shouts and screams, hands grabbing, feet slipping, a mass of scrambling limbs in the entrance to the annex. Those whose instincts were to try and save Justin, and those that knew he was lost and saving themselves was key. As a result, they more or less stayed on the threshold, writhing and raging in response to Benjamin's actions.

Hayley, still in the no-man's-land between the building and the garden, was aghast at what was occurring. 'I… I was going to…'

The sentence didn't need finishing for everyone to understand. *I was going to choose him.*

Benjamin let go of Justin. He fell to the floor, his neck torn out, a streak of red coating everything up to Benjamin's face. 'Choose someone else,' he spat. 'This one is meat.'

Lucy was screaming in the doorway, an unintelligible, guttural sound. Elliot got both hands around her middle and dragged her away, almost falling on top her once they were inside.

Benjamin moved towards them. Instinct pushed Hayley away from him; she darted towards the annex. Kieran grabbed her and pulled her in.

They didn't have time to close the door before Benjamin was there, blood-stained mouth agape and that impossible, vicious tongue flicking. They stumbled back, almost as one.

But Benjamin stopped dead at the threshold, emitting a low hiss of frustration.

'It worked,' muttered Brooke. She had feared her own lack of belief would be to the detriment of what they were planning. 'Holy shitballs.'

Kieran leaned forward and hastily pushed both glass doors to. They came together with an airtight click, just in front of Benjamin. Kieran still expected him to push them back; they had hoped that Brooke's *Bless This House* routine might slow him down, weaken him maybe, but they still expected him to try and follow them in. However, it looked like Benjamin could go no further. He didn't touch the doors or even acknowledge them, just continued to stare at the group beyond. The bottom half of his face pulsed, fluctuating between its two forms. The top half of his face became fixed, as his eyes fell on Hayley, and stayed there. 'Invite me in, Hayley, so we can finish what we have started.'

She started crying and moved deeper into the wide room. They'd only got as far as turning on the entrance light so she disappeared into the shadows behind the pool table.

Benjamin observed this coldly, then stepped away from the door and disappeared from view, down the path. There was a collective exhale from the group, and bodies lost some of their tension.

Lucy was still wailing; Elliot sat with her on the floor.

But then he was wrenched away by Alicia's words.

'Oh shit, Danni – don't do that!'

CHAPTER EIGHTEEN

When Alicia had first got Danni through the double doors to the annex, they kept going to the wall on the far side. Past Brooke and Rhea, past Lucy stumbling around and swearing. Alicia dropped her logs on the floor; Danni just lowered her arms and let them fall. In the gloom Alicia could make out the foosball table to the right. Around it, lining the wall was some padded bench seating, forming an L shape. Alicia took Danni and sat her down in the nearest spot, bolt upright. 'Wait one second.'

She dashed over to the others nearer the door, only to be flung back by Kieran's hasty retreat. He held the axe out in front of him, and on the business end of it, the blade embedded into its neck, was the hell hound, writhing and kicking. Alicia didn't know what made him bring it inside; perhaps not wanting to be *outside* with it when Benjamin approached. It didn't matter: what mattered was whether or not he could make it dead.

They cleared a large space for him; he swung the axe towards the floor and the creature slid off the weapon and onto the boards. Before it could right itself, Kieran swung hard again and again at the neck. It wasn't just blood that flew but a coarse dust and flakes of skin like shredded papyrus. When the blade jammed into the wood, having gone fully through the dog-thing, he declared it over. 'Get everyone in! Where's Justin?'

That was when attention focused on the door. Just before, Brooke shot a glance back at her. She looked anxious about what was coming. 'Good luck!' Alicia said, and nodded enthusiastically.

'They're coming!' said Elliot at the door. Brooke joined him.

Elliot started calling for Hayley, but Alicia was distracted by someone saying her name. It was Danni, still on the bench behind her, propped against the wall. Alicia wondered about finding the main light switch: there was some of the evening glow and the property's security lighting coming in from the side door, and the sliding exit leading to the hot tub, but it wasn't enough to fully make Danni out.

'I'm so thirsty,' she said, in an unusually cold, dispassionate voice.

Alicia went back to her, reassured her outline that it would all be okay. Behind her, Alicia heard Brooke saying the parts of prayer she remembered.

Then everything happened so fast.

Danni started to moan at her, a low, consistent rumble.

Kieran charged forward and swore, did something with the dog, possibly?

Danni's body, still stiff and upright, began to shake.

Alicia tried to soothe her, but she was chilly to touch, making Alicia pull her hand away.

They were screaming at the door: something about Justin.

'I don't know why – I just need it,' Danni explained, in an abrupt, business-like tone.

Elliot fell in with Lucy, almost landing in the creature carcass still on the floor, the axe still prominent like a grave marker.

Danni, her fist still clenched, moved from her sides and up to her chin, like a boxer getting ready for a bout.

Hayley came stumbling through, then did a U-turn and went back to the door.

Danni. Something was terribly wrong with Danni.

The door clicked shut.

Danni.

There was more chaos at the entrance.

Her hands.

Hayley came back, crying this time, and shot off down the side of the pool table.

Danni opened her fists, displaying her palms. She had been holding something in her hands all this time. She put it to her mouth and started licking.

'Oh shit, Danni – don't do that!'

Someone turned on the main light. Alicia closed her eyes and then blinked at the bright assault. Once adjusted, she looked back at

Danni.

She held the blood-soaked tissues from Kieran's nose, her hands and fingers stained by them. She lapped at the soft paper like a dog.

Alicia reached across to try and pull Danni's hands away. She reacted by shoving her palm into her lips. She took the whole tissue in one mouthful. 'Danni, no!'

Elliot left Lucy and scrambled across. 'What is it?'

Alicia gawped at Danni's masticating before saying: 'She's eating the bloody tissue.'

Elliot didn't comprehend; he just knelt by Danni and held her hands, then wondered why they had the remnants of blood smears on them. 'Are you hurt?'

At the same time Lucy made a dive for the doors, screaming her husband's name. His body could still be seen, just in the garden beyond the gate, collapsed on itself like he'd been deflated. Before Lucy could reach for one of the handles, Kieran grabbed her and dragged her away. 'He's gone! There's nothing you can do!'

'I need Justin!'

'It's dangerous out there; we can't let you go!' There was a two-seater settee beyond the pool table, near the exercise gear: he wrestled Lucy in that direction. 'Rhea – help me out here!' Together they pinned Lucy to the cushions and let her scream.

Alicia and Brooke found each other in the middle of the room. Behind them, the foosball table and dart board, adjacent to the L-shaped benched seating where Elliot knelt in front of Danni. Next to them, an axe in the floorboards and the grey corpse of an abnormally long-limbed dog. In front of them, the pool table then the small settee not built to accommodate three. Across from that the exercise bike and the rowing machine set out in front of another set of patio doors that led to the hot tub deck. Was it only yesterday that Brooke shovelled snow off that thing and they all took a steamy dip? Now she had a broken arm, and Steff, Nick and Justin were dead…

Alicia didn't even realise she was crying until Brooke told her everything would be okay.

'How can you know?'

She pointed to the glass double doors. 'Because that shit actually worked. But instead of praying the gay away, we banished a fucking vampire. Now we just sit tight until morning.'

Alicia looked at her, and then at her arm in the rudimentary sling.

'And we get you to a hospital straight away.' It was beginning to spot with blood.

'Damn, that means I've got to trust your driving.' She smirked, and then they rested their heads against each other's, closing their eyes.

Now that Danni's jaw had stopped moving, Elliot asked her a question. 'So what did you just swallow, honey?'

She looked at him like she'd just been caught taking something illicit. 'I needed it, okay.'

Hayley spoke up from behind Elliot. 'It was Kieran's tissue. That he bled on. She did need it. It's part of the transference.'

Elliot's eyes flitted between the two women. 'What? What are you talking about, Hayley?'

This time she looked genuinely apologetic rather than annoyingly hopeful. 'You saw her take in some of Benjamin's blood after I chose her. She's starting to change. She needs to alternate between some of his blood and then the blood of regular people as her body starts to adapt. After several rounds of this, she becomes like him. *Vampyri*.'

Alicia and Brooke drifted over. 'How many rounds is several?' Brooke asked.

'Hard to know. Benjamin said it is different for everyone. It can take hours.' She looked at the door. 'That's why he's now in a hurry to get things started.'

Elliot, looked up, incredulous. 'What? Danni's not becoming a vampire! She's just sick because of what he made her ingest.' He looked back at her. 'We'll just keep an eye on you, keep you hydrated: you'll be fine.'

'I don't feel fine,' she muttered. She was ghostly pale and had beads of sweat on her brow. They held hands.

Lucy was approaching, flanked by Kieran and Rhea, poised in case she decided to make another rush towards Justin's body. She headed in Hayley's direction, standing nearest the dead, headless creature and the axe in the floor.

Her cheeks were streaked with grey lines; tears had found the remnants of mascara and left faint trails across her skin. Her eyes were bloodshot, her lids heavy. She spoke carefully and deliberately. 'If time is of the essence, Hayley, then you need to make your choices now so we can get this over with.'

'She's not choosing anyone,' Kieran said softly. 'We're safe now.

It'll all be over in the morning.'

'But she still wants to be with Benjamin, don't you, Hayley?' Lucy extended a hand and gently stroked Hayley's arm.

Hayley looked around the group, unsure. 'I'm… just a little upset right now-'

'-*you're* upset?' Lucy interjected, her tone changing.

'-and I ran in here because I was frightened. For a second. Things just went crazy. Poor Justin.'

'Poor Justin?' Lucy's breathing was becoming ragged. Kieran took another step and had an arm ready to wrap around her if necessary. He didn't think it would be consolatory, but a potential restraint.

'Wait,' Alicia said, addressing Hayley. 'You're still thinking of going through with this? Danni just ate a blood-soaked tissue!'

Realisation dawned on Elliot. 'When you said a bloody tissue I thought you were just…' He looked at Danni with new eyes.

Hayley continued to explain. 'This whole thing is just terrible, but to live this life with Benjamin, and with four of you… that's still what I want.'

Lucy was right up in Hayley's face, so much so that she had to take a step back and almost slipped on the dusty, sticky carcass. Kieran was primed.

But he wasn't expected what came next.

'Choose me,' Lucy whispered. 'You've chosen Danni and Elliot. You were going to choose Justin, so I must be next. Choose me.'

'Lucy?' Kieran's hand lingered.

'Choose me and we can go out there together and start this thing properly.'

Hayley remained quiet but Alicia interjected. 'Lucy, you can't be serious? Justin just got killed in this thing. *By* that thing.'

Lucy flipped. 'I fucking know! We are losing this fucking thing and if you think your bitch's stupid fucking prayers are going to prevent anything you must be fucking insane!'

'Fuck you!' spat Brooke.

'So Hayley is going to say my name, and one other if she likes – I don't care – and then the chosen ones are going outside to get this show moving. Then, when it's all done, a few nights from now, I am going to pull my little girl from her bed, and she is going to be made one too. And then we live together, untouchable, for a thousand years.'

Hayley had a hand to her mouth. She spoke through her fingers. 'Lucy, I don't think we're going to be able to do that.'

'Shut the fuck up, Hayley. Apart from choosing me next; that you can do. Let's hear it.'

'No, not like this.'

'Fucking say it!' At that point Lucy grabbed Hayley and gave her a shake. Kieran swooped in and pulled them apart.

'Come on!' he yelled. 'This shit is supercharged, so we all need to calm down!' He backed away with Lucy wrapped in an arm.

'Get the fuck off me, Kieran! It was your fucking antics with the dog that got Justin killed!'

Kieran's face twitched but he pushed on. 'No, Luce. On the settee. Now.' He flipped around and pushed her in that direction. Rhea took over and guided her away. It seemed to work. As the physical gap between Hayley and Lucy grew, she became more in control of herself.

Kieran addressed the whole group. 'Can we not all just take... a fucking... minute! We don't have to rush anything. But we do need to get off the ceiling. At the moment there is nothing that needs dealing with, so just... chill.'

Elliot spoke up. 'Danni's not great, Kee. She needs a drink maybe.'

Kieran pointed to the corner. 'There's a mini-fridge by the rowing machine. There might be something in there.'

'On it,' Alicia said and moved towards it. Brooke headed over to the bench seating and sat near Danni. She encouraged Elliot to get off his knees and do the same. He sat next to his wife, still holding her hand. The three of them in a line looked like they were waiting for appointments in a doctor's surgery.

Alicia came back with a bottle of water. 'There's also energy drinks and full fat Coke. We're good for the night.'

'Alright,' said Kieran. 'So here's the plan. First of all, we have fifteen minutes where nothing happens. And that's it. That's the plan, for now. Give ourselves a little room to breathe, and think.'

Think about whether or not it was you who got Justin killed. His chest hurt at the thought.

The room, without having to necessarily say anything, concurred with him. 'Alright,' he continued. 'That's better. I might even sit down myself. First of all though, I'm going to throw out this flaky, gloopy dead shit so we don't trip on the fucker.' He pulled the axe out of the floor and laid it down. Then he walked to the doors: his intention was to pull them both open and then push the headless body out onto the path with the head of the axe, being careful not to cross the threshold himself. Was Benjamin still lurking somewhere? He had to assume so.

This was confirmed when he looked out into the night. Lights from the living room cast their glow across the garden.

Justin's body had gone. The hurt, and the doubt, hit him again. *I angered Benson so he killed him.*

Whether that was right or not, he knew he couldn't let it get to him; he had to keep going. Slowly, watchfully, Kieran dragged the hound's carcass across the floor and then eased it over the threshold of the annex, keeping his distance by the length of an axe handle. Outside, the wind offered a low moan, but there was no other noise or sign of disturbance.

Still, Kieran was relieved to be able to close the doors again.

CHAPTER NINETEEN

There was a welcome lull, a passage of time without the need for frenzy or chaos. Elliot took Danni into the corner where the bench seating made its L shape, out of the direct line of sight of the door. Alicia and Brooke sat on the same furniture, at the furthest part away from them, on the other side of the foosball table. Rhea had taken Lucy back to the settee beyond the pool table. Hayley floated around; currently she was by the patio doors, staring out at the deck and the hot tub, perhaps waiting for Benjamin to appear on the other side of the glass. Kieran had half an eye on her. He was sitting on a chair by the rowing machine – plastic like one of those you had at school. There to catch your breath on, but completely resistant to a river of exercise sweat. He had his knees apart and between them were the logs they'd brought in. He was shaping them into points with the axe. *Stakes through the heart*, thought Elliot, *to kill a vampire.*

He looked at Danni. She was in something of a daze: fluctuating between being responsive and affectionate, tactile and warm, and then falling into a trance or state of stupefaction, barely responsive to his words or touch. When she was lucid it was like she'd just woken from a sitting snooze. She'd stroke his arm or his face and ask if he was okay, and once he reassured her he was she'd ask after everyone else, including Benjamin. She was very curious about where Benjamin was.

'He's outside somewhere, honey. We're trying not to worry too much about him. We're worried about *you*.'

'I'm fine. But I'll be better when I see Benjamin.'

'Not happening,' he replied, patting her hands on her lap.

She looked at him a little confused, and then smiled, relaxed, and closed her eyes. 'Maybe in a minute then.' She was gone again, head tilting to one side, chin pointing at her collar bone.

It'll wear off, he told himself. He had to believe it. He looked at a wall-mounted analogue clock on the wall: it was past 7 o'clock. He couldn't remember the last time they'd contacted the kids, or the adults they were staying with. Had Danielle given them the address for this place? He had no idea. And anyway, what were the chances that anyone would send a search party to Scotland just because there hadn't been contact for twenty-four hours? A few days, maybe, but less than that...

All being well, they were out of here in the morning, just as originally planned. Of course, there would be visits to police stations and hospitals – they were definitely not getting home tomorrow – but at least there would be solutions.

They just had to wait it out for another twelve hours or so.

**

Alicia looked at the blood spots showing through the bandages on Brooke's arm. 'Do you think we need to take a look at that?'

Brooke shook her head. Her hair was plastered to her skin with sweat. 'I don't want to make it worse. At the minute it's bearable, and bearable I can live with.'

'But you've got a compound fracture, babe. It could be... *trouble* under there.'

Brooke smirked. 'And if we find this trouble how are you going to fix it? We'll just shriek at it and try to strap it up again. Nothing to gain apart from more worry. I can last out until morning.'

Alicia nuzzled against Brooke's free shoulder. 'I love you.'

'I love you... but your old school friends, now not so much. I think it's fair to say this is the last of the get-togethers.'

Alicia, cheek still resting against the fabric of Brooke's sweater, curled her lip. 'Fucking hell, Brooke – there's not enough of them left to be able to call it a get-together.'

'Sorry: I know you loved Steff and Justin.' She curved her body round so they were facing each other and planted a kiss on Alicia's forehead. 'We'll get out of this, and we'll make sure Benjamin pays.'

Alicia raised her face so the next kiss could be on the lips: just a light, polite one in company. They were well-practised in that: there were only certain bars and clubs were they felt truly comfortable doing more in public, even among family and friends. Alicia pulled away slightly, so the whisper didn't have far to travel. 'What do you think is going to happen to Hayley?'

'She's an accessory. I'd say she's going to prison.'

'Shit.' They kissed again. 'I don't know if I want that for her.'

'Not sure it's going to be in our hands.'

Alicia looked around. Hayley was leaning against the far wall, between two looped skipping ropes hung on hooks, still staring out of the patio doors. Kieran was all industry: the vicious-looking stakes almost done. Danni and Elliot were the nearest, behind them, the latter nursing the former. 'You think Danni's going to be okay?' Alicia whispered.

'I think she's got some foul poison in her that hopefully a hospital can find, identify and get rid of. But I don't know. She's white as a fucking ghost.' Brooke kissed Alicia's forehead again. 'Speaking of foul poison, is there any chance of you lighting me a cigarette.'

'Not a prayer. Seeing as you can't step outside, I reckon this might be a good time to try and quit for good.'

Brooke conceded without fuss; there was no point finding an argument where there didn't need to be one. 'I suppose if I can get through this without one I can get through anything. As it is, I think we're in for a long night.' She felt Alicia tense against her shoulder, so she swiftly added: 'but we'll be okay.'

**

Rhea was worried about Lucy, but that was to be expected: the poor cow had just seen her husband murdered. *Just murder? Is that what you're calling it, girl?* She afforded a quick glance at the patio doors, just in case the monstrous fuck had returned.

Lucy had taken to muttering under her breath. 'We were going to live for a thousand years… grow old without growing old… go and get Rozzy and then *whoosh* into the night…' The 'whoosh' was louder, making Rhea start, sat next to her on the settee.

'It's okay, sweetie. We're gonna work this thing out. You just need to relax, maybe try and sleep.' Rhea rubbed Lucy's upper arm, rhythmically, soothingly, hoping to slow everything down for her.

Kieran was done. He stacked a pile of foot-long wooden spikes against the stationary bike. He then glanced around for something else to do. Rhea knew that he had to take his own advice and somehow chill. But she understood him: he wasn't happy unless he was moving. He went to the mini-fridge, leant the axe against it, then took out a bottle of energy drink and drained a third of it in record speed.

Rhea stroked Lucy again, perhaps with a little more pressure, as if she was trying to ease Lucy into the settee so she couldn't move from her spot. Then she got up and crossed the room to Kieran. 'You worked up quite a thirst there, making your anti-vampire kit.'

'Yeah. I just wish that when we sent you to make snacks with Hayley, we also told you to bring back the garlic. I'll take whatever we can get.' He grinned. 'And I'm kinda hoping the Reverend Brooke Hughes can turn the hot tub into a vat of holy water.'

Rhea smiled. 'I'm not sure remembering a prayer or two gives her that particular power.' They looked across to the two couples on the L-shaped seating lining the wall by the foosball. They were huddled to each other, still, slowing everything down, slipping into their evening vigil. 'You got them all to relax,' she said.

'Yeah, we're getting a bit of control back.'

'You need to do the same though. There's nothing else to do now.'

'I was going to go round with drinks for everybody.'

Rhea poked him in the stomach. 'They're adults and they've seen the fridge. When they want something they'll get it. You need to take five.' There were a couple of rolled up yoga mats by the wall. 'You could have a lie down, or take a seat next to-'

She'd turned back to the settee, expecting to see Lucy there, but she was up on her feet, heading to the patio doors and Hayley. 'I think we should-'

'-yeah.' They moved in synch. They gravitated towards whichever woman was nearest, which meant Lucy for Kieran and Hayley for Rhea.

Lucy was applying pressure again, wanting the last two names. 'You were going to choose Justin, which means you were going to choose *me*. Say it now. Say it!'

Hayley immediately starting crying. Rhea hoped that as Kieran guided Lucy back to the settee that the sobbing would cease.

But it didn't. Which made Rhea think that perhaps Hayley had been crying all along. 'Girl, you've got to calm yourself down; you're not doing yourself any good.' She indicated the plastic chair that Kieran had been on. 'Come on; these tears solve nothing.'

Rhea stepped back as Hayley made to sit, but instead she straightened up and tramped towards the centre of the room, her body still hitching with the spasmodic sobs she was unable to shake. Everyone took notice: she was now in the round and had an audience on all sides.

'I know none of you love me, even though you say you do. Shit, I'm not sure you even *like* me.' She waved and shushed at the dissenting voices. 'And I don't even like myself anymore, not after everything that I've made happen. But I've come this far, and things have got too messed up to try and take it back.' She took in a gulp of breath; put a hand to her fluttering chest. 'I've already chosen Danni and Elliot. Now the other two: I choose Kieran… and Rhea.'

Lucy howled *No!* Kieran instinctively lowered her down onto the settee in a move that was almost a shove.

Rhea was the nearest to Hayley, and the most shocked. 'What? Us? *Me?*'

'Kieran once walked me home from school in the rain when I didn't have the bus fare but the girls all got on without me. And you… you've been *nice* to me this weekend, when you didn't have to be. I'd like to try and be your friend.'

Rhea didn't know what to say. She looked – she supposed pityingly – at Hayley trying to smile at her, and then turned away, to find Kieran. He was slowly walking towards them both, brow furrowed, trying to work out what all this meant.

Alicia stood up from the bench. 'Fair enough, Hayley. I guess that means we don't have to pretend anymore. Come the morning, me and Brooke will be gone and that'll be that between us.'

A light went out of Hayley's eyes. 'Sorry, but you'll not see the morning.' She took in a lungful of air then yelled: 'Benjamin!'

Now that the moment required action and not thought, Kieran was on the move. He rushed past Rhea towards Hayley. Hayley was making an announcement. 'I welcome y-' Then Kieran was there, and he clamped a big mitt across the lower half of her face, and wrapped his other arm around her shoulder and chest. She had a free hand and tried to pull away his fingers from her mouth, but he was locked on and not budging.

'Holy fuck, that was close! Stop wriggling, Hayles! I'm not letting go!'

Now they were all up, except for Danni. Elliot didn't move far from her; he still had fingertips against her shoulder. 'Shit, Kee: what are we going to do now?'

'I dunno! Quit that, Hayley!' She was alternating legs and kicking back into his shins. Now her free hand was pounding into his side.

Brooke winced as she spoke; standing up had brought her fresh pain. 'You've gotta... throw her out. She can't be in here with us now.'

'That's right!' Alicia said. She darted towards the door and then jerked back like she was on a spring.

Benjamin was at the entrance, his arms stretched out so his hands gripped the outside frame of the glass double doors. His face was fully unfolded; both circular sets of teeth throbbed forward with the pulsating flesh from inside his mouth. The tongue twirled like its own sentient being; the spines on the end almost scratching against the glass.

Could they get her out of there without crossing the threshold themselves and coming into contact with Benjamin? Kieran didn't think it was worth the risk. He picked Hayley up – her toes just brushing against the floor – and hauled her in the direction of the patio doors. 'Tell me if he moves!'

Before he could receive any update, something else happened.

Lucy was standing in front of them, and she was holding one of the wooden stakes. She jabbed it forward. Kieran didn't react fast enough. It lodged deep into Hayley's stomach. She curled up in his arms, knees rising, neck straining to bow her head. She blew out hard against his hand and a thin squeal escaped through his fingers.

'Fuck you, bitch,' Lucy muttered. 'Fuck the lot of you.'

She turned, went straight to the patio doors and pulled them open.

Alicia called out something about Benjamin.

Lucy stepped out into the night.

Benjamin suddenly flew over the wooden rail that bordered the decking. He landed in front of Lucy and reached for her face. It was the hand with the longer nails and he tore down from the forehead and into the eyes.

Lucy screamed, but then it was stifled by the thumb that forced itself into her mouth. Benjamin grabbed flesh and teeth and wrenched his hand away. The front of Lucy's face detached in a spatter of blood and bone.

Nearly forty years trying to preserve it and it was off in seconds.

Then Benjamin's unfolded mouth was all over the hole he had created and he gobbled noisily. Lucy's body slumped to the deck and Benjamin's followed, hunkered over her like an animal.

There was no helping her.

Kieran backed away, still keeping a tight hold of Hayley. Her hands now occupied themselves with the piece of wood sticking out of her gut; she alternated between gripping it and frantically shaking them around it. Blood ran down her lower half and onto the floor.

Rhea yelled: 'Put her down, Kieran!'

'I can't! I can't let her talk!'

Alicia and Brooke were there, aghast at both scenes. Elliot started to make his way over. 'What's happening?' No one answered him: they were drawn by the spectacle of either Benjamin feeding or Hayley being held upright as she bled out.

'How do we help her?' Rhea asked to no one in particular. She was looking round for a solution.

It was a voice from outside that answered her. It used to be Benjamin's voice, but it was distorted and guttural through his monstrous new mouth. 'Give her to me.'

He was standing now, Lucy a discarded red mess on the deck next to him, her blood dripping down the front of his shirt. He stood on the edge of the threshold, looking in through the open door. He extended a bloody hand, careful not to pass across the invisible line that held him back.

'Give her to me. Now.'

CHAPTER TWENTY

'We can't,' Kieran said. 'It's too risky.'

'What are you talking about?' Alicia asked. 'Just throw her to him and then we're done with her!'

Kieran still held Hayley up, one hand clasped over her mouth. Kieran shook his head; the action meant Hayley rocked slightly, causing her to moan. 'What if she speaks? What if – just before she leaves – she invites him in?'

Hayley tried to talk with her eyes and brows. *I wouldn't do that,* said the expression.

'Kieran's right,' Brooke said. 'It only takes a couple of words.' She stared at Benjamin, hovering on the threshold, arms waiting to receive Hayley, his worm tongue thrashing around.

'Then don't let go until she's outside!'

'Liss: then a part of me has to *be* outside. Where *he* can get at it.'

'Then we make him back up, or leave.' Alicia turned to Benjamin. 'Get off the deck and we'll put her outside!'

Benjamin took a couple of steps back, but nothing more. 'Give her to me, or not a single one of you will be spared.'

Brooke approached Alicia and led her away from the glass. 'What if he does go, and we put Hayley outside? All she has to do is step back in for a second and we could be in the same mess.'

'We just slam the door across!' Alicia just wanted rid of Hayley. If Benjamin had her he might just take her away and leave the rest of them alone.

Rhea was still hovering, doing an inventory of everything in the room. 'We have to decide something: she can't stay like this. We need her lying down, Kieran, and her feet raised.'

Kieran didn't comply, still unsure about the whole thing. He just knew that her struggle was lessening.

Then Elliot was there. Tentative, glancing behind him to make sure Danni wasn't moving. Once satisfied he spoke. 'We keep her. Make her comfortable if we can. Benjamin can have her once he's told me how to make Danielle better.'

Benjamin's raspy voice addressed him. 'The transference has already started. She will become like me. It is inevitable.'

Elliot jabbed a finger in Benjamin's direction and spat. 'I won't accept that! And you don't get Hayley until you tell me what to do to improve Danni's health! If I don't get results, then neither do you!'

Benjamin hissed, but didn't advance any further.

'Bring that chair over!' yelled Kieran. Alicia grabbed the plastic chair and brought it to him. He lowered Hayley onto it; she groaned as her middle creased and the stake scraped against a different internal piece of her. A fresh rivulet of blood flowed onto her thigh.

Rhea was over by the curled yoga mats at the wall. 'This will help!' Behind them, was a broad roll of grey tape. It was no doubt used to secure the edges to the floor before a session. She scooped it up and ran back. 'For her wound.' She knew it would be best to keep the stake in and tape around it.

'And for her mouth. Alicia, help us out here.' Kieran got Alicia to put one hand on Hayley's head and the other on her lower jaw, forcing her mouth shut. He wrapped both his arms around her, trying not to knock the stake as he tightened his grip and held her writhing body in position. 'Babe, put tape across her mouth. Make sure the nostrils are clear.'

Rhea ripped a length off and placed it over Hayley's lips, apologising as she did so. When Alicia was able to ease off, Kieran sent her for the skipping ropes. Together they bound Hayley to the chair. By this time there wasn't much fight left in her. Her eyes brimmed with tears and she stared imploringly at Benjamin. He continued to seethe and hiss on the edge of the boundary they'd created.

Alicia stepped back and took it all in, breathed long and deeply. 'Oh God, what are we doing here?' Rhea crouched and applied tape tightly around the wound; securing the foreign body and patching up everything else as best she could.

Kieran spoke, but to Benjamin. 'We'll push her outside, chair and all, when you tell Elliot how he can help Danni.'

His face reassembled somewhat, making his speech clearer. 'She has my blood in her. The only way this can be stopped is with a full transfusion. She will need a hospital. But this is not possible.'

Elliot started shouting; it was so out of character it startled them all. 'It is fucking possible! You let me take her and you get Hayley back!'

Brooke glanced back at Danni; she seemed catatonic. 'El, you'll never be able to walk her out of here.'

'I'm gonna take his car! Him and Hayley can be gone before the emergency services get here – I don't give a shit. But Danni will be safe and you guys rescued. That's it, Benjamin: that's the only deal. Do you want Hayley or not?'

He didn't respond, just looked at Hayley. She was beginning to sag in the chair, just the ropes holding her upright.

Rhea sidled over to Kieran. 'Are we really trying to bargain with her life? She's the one that needs the hospital most.'

'It's on him now. We can't help her here anyway. Decide, Benson!'

A silence followed, broken within a minute by Danni behind them, calling for Elliot. She was trying to stand, like a new-born mammal finding the use of its limbs. He turned and ran over to her.

Benjamin prowled along the deck, only stopping when he was as close to Kieran as he could be. 'Here is my deal. Give me Hayley and I will allow one of you to leave here, on foot, to try and get some help.'

'No chance. As soon as I step out you might rip me in half. We keep Hayley.'

'That is not acceptable.'

'You haven't got much choice.' But then neither had they, if they were serious about saving Hayley's life. Kieran drummed his fingers against the glass as he mulled it over. A compromise, maybe? 'Okay, this: you don't get Hayley straight away. Half an hour after I've gone they push her out.' He turned to the others as if the deal was done. He only looked back at Benjamin when he hadn't responded.

With eyes back on him, Benjamin spoke. 'I will allow one of you fifteen minutes to go and find help. After fifteen minutes, whoever is here will give me Hayley, I will start to make her better, and we will leave. We will take the bodies of your friends. It will help with Hayley's recovery and her transference. When your help arrives we will be gone, and you will never see us again. This is a good deal, I think.'

Kieran shook his head. 'Give Elliot the car.'

'I need the car to get us back to safety before the night is over. And to take the bodies. Help will come for you.' He chuckled. 'Not if you say there is a vampire on the loose. No. Perhaps tell them there is a fire. They say this is the quickest way to get people to assist.'

Brooke was by Kieran's shoulder, watching Benjamin. 'How can we trust you?'

Now that Benjamin's face was fully reassembled, he looked like a tired, malnourished middle-aged man. 'I have been with Hayley for two years. I wanted to honour her wish for this because I love her. But now it has gone so badly wrong I do not want her to die. This is my only objective now. I do not care about you at all. I just need Hayley.'

They all looked at her. She was fully reliant on the ropes now, having lost consciousness. It was only a weak whistling from her nose that told them she was still alive. Rhea, still monitoring the job she'd done with the tape, whispered: 'We have to do something.'

**

Over on the L-shaped bench there was a development with Danni. She was more alert than before. She succeeded in standing, new energy coursing through her, but Elliot encouraged her to stay put. She looked past him: over his shoulder, past his elbow. 'Has Benjamin come in?'

'No, of course not. You don't need to get involved – you need to rest.' His own words alerted him to the changes in her appearance. Suddenly he couldn't help but notice the shadows which had formed under her eyes, the distinct shape of her cheekbones that normally needed assistance from blush. Her shoulder felt bony under her woollen sweater. He took a step back. Christ, she looked like she'd lost twenty pounds. He didn't want to alarm her so he offered a slightly hesitant: 'How are you feeling?'

'Like I need Benjamin. And soon.'

'I don't understand.'

She looked at him like a stranger. She spoke to him like an addict. 'I need his blood. Just a little to make me feel better. If he's not coming in, then I need to go to him.' She made to walk past Elliot. He reached out and grabbed her wrist. His fingers went all the way around, and her skin was hot.

'Danni, you're not well.'

'I'll be better when I see Benjamin.' It didn't sound like her, and when she shrugged him off she stopped looking at him. She lurched her way across the room towards the others.

Kieran was crouching down to try and get a better look at Hayley's injury. The blood seemed to be coagulating and the flow slowing down thanks to Rhea's work; other than that he had no further prognosis. Sweat ran from the skin of her face onto the strip of tape that gagged her. A snot bubble came and went.

Danni staggered over. She ignored Hayley which caught them all by surprise: they assumed she was coming across to be the selfless nurse they expected of her. It meant she almost made it through the patio doors. Benjamin was sitting on the edge of the hot tub like he was in a hospital waiting room. When she approached he stood unnaturally fast, ready to receive her.

Elliot got there just in time to drag her back. She whined at him, no real words in her argument; he ignored her and pulled her back towards the pool table.

Benjamin's gaze flitted between Hayley and Danni. 'You cannot waste any more time, and neither can I. Danielle needs either my blood to assist the transference or a hospital to rid her of it. Hayley needs me to give her the strength to heal herself. I do not think either of them has an hour left in them without intervention. You do not have the luxury of waiting until morning. If you leave things like this, both will die.'

'Danni's going to be fine!' Elliot yelled.

'She has a fire inside her, blazing its way through her body, fighting my blood. She needs more of me to extinguish it, or else she burns away to nothing. She is becoming a creature of night. To allow it rather than fight it, is – of course – her best option. However, you could choose to seek help with the aid of a transfusion, if a hospital believes you.'

Kieran, now on his feet, punched the glass. 'Shut up, Benson!'

'If you want to try this, agree to the terms. One of you goes for help. Hayley comes to me. I will take her away. But decide now. Both are dying.'

Brooke walked a slow half circle around them, cradling her arm. Then she addressed the group. 'The fucker's right. We can't just sit still.'

Rhea raised an eyebrow. 'You want someone to go out there, where he is, and run for help? Have you seen your girl's face on the deck? Or the lack of it.'

Brooke shrugged. 'Lucy was never *my girl*, and Hayley neither. But I love Danni – we both do – and she's fucking *dying*.'

'Don't say that!' Elliot called. He was standing next to Danni, having urged her to sit on the pool table; he pinned her with a hand firmly on her thigh, trying not to be too forceful. Danni was looking at him like she was trying to solve a puzzle.

Rhea shook her head. 'No one's going out there: it's too risky.'

In many ways she knew it was inevitable. Kieran stepped forward. 'I'll go.'

'Babe, no.'

'Look, I'm the fastest, and I spotted that route just behind the building, remember? I can be across the field and onto the road in a minute. I might not even need to reach the next village. It's Sunday evening: there could be a car.'

'Kieran, it's too much. And you're not the fastest, especially not with a nose you can hardly breathe through.'

He ignored her comment. 'I might even find help before you have to hand over Hayley.'

Rhea's hands found her hips. 'Or you might be running around in the dark and snow, and then when he's got Hayley and your dead friends tucked away in his car, it's him that you end up flagging down. And then you become tomorrow's supper.'

'Rhea, what else can we do? Elliot isn't going to leave Danni. Brooke can't do it with her arm. Liss isn't as fast as me-'

'If someone has to go, it should be me. You know it.' She fixed him with a steely glare.

'Don't do that. You can't say no to me and then volunteer yourself. That's not how this works. Those risks you just mentioned apply to you too. You don't mean it – you just want to stop me from going.'

She softened slightly. 'Is that so terrible?'

'No.' He leaned over and gave her a light kiss. 'But I'm going anyway. I owe it to Justin.' He squeezed her hand and then stepped

155

away. His face was glum but resolute. He looked through the glass at Benjamin. 'Fifteen minutes.'

He nodded in reply, then moved to the entrance in readiness to receive Hayley. Kieran addressed the rest of them. 'I'll be quick. I'll not stop until I've found someone.' He pointed to the wall-mounted clock. It read 8.30pm. 'Fifteen minutes.'

Rhea tried one last time, as Kieran started bouncing on the spot. 'Please, take another minute to think about this. There could be something else to try.'

'No: this is it.' He winked, and then jogged across the floor of the annex. He pulled the glass double-doors open, and then was gone. Rhea went over and looked out at the empty space.

All other eyes fell on Benjamin. He didn't move, but watched Hayley intently, slumped on the chair, six yards in front of him. She was still unconscious, still bleeding, but still breathing. They all froze for a moment.

Alicia asked after Danni, who had leant back and was now lying on the pool table. Elliot responded: 'I don't know. She's so hot. And… and thin.'

She'd been out of it a little, but with a shudder at Elliot's words she came back. She propped her head up with a combination of hand and elbow. 'I can speak for myself. I'll be fine. You just need to let me see Benjamin.' She looked to the glass. 'Tell them.'

Benjamin replied without taking his eyes off Hayley. 'I have done so, but they would rather try and prevent what is already happening to you. So much optimism in the face of increasing chaos. It is the way of blinkered humanity.'

'You said it was possible,' Brooke snapped. 'We can get your poisonous shit out of Danni, and you can take Hayley away and make her… well make her into whatever it is you are.' She looked up at the clock. 'In… thirteen minutes.'

He stood closer to the threshold and his face began to open up again. 'You could just give her to me now. Thirteen minutes might be too late for her.' His voice came throatier. 'Push the chair over here.'

'Forget it,' Alicia replied, by her partner's side. 'We stick to the plan.'

Benjamin sighed: it left his distorted face like the release of dead air from an old coffin. 'Do not say I did not give you that chance.'

Then he sprung up, both feet at once, and landed on top of the

wooden rail. A second later he was away into the darkness.
   Rhea screamed what the others were thinking.
   'Kieran!'

CHAPTER TWENTY-ONE

Kieran stumbled on a couple of occasions in his haste to cross the field, so by the time he hurdled the low stone wall on the far side, his sleeves and knees were sodden. But at least now the ground was surer: he had the choice of a narrow pavement or the one lane road. He took a moment to assess and to get in some good, strong breaths. Rhea had been right: the broken nose was an impediment.

There had been cars at some point; there were flattened tracks where the tyres had been. Kieran figured that these might be safest to run on with regard to keeping his footing. Plus, should a car come along it would have no choice but to stop for him – either that or hit him. Either way he wouldn't be ignored. He started running.

As he did, he tried to align the local geography with his memory of yesterday's walk: the snowball fight, the banter, the ruin, the pub. *God, was that only yesterday?* It was tricky in the dark, particularly with the absence of buildings as markers. Still, something told him that if he kept pushing he could be at the pub in quarter of an hour having already cut off a big corner. He would give the castle ruin a miss this time.

A little further on and he slowed a touch. The field that had contained the sheep was on his left, he was sure of it. The silhouette of the distant barn marked it out. The land was empty now: the farmers clearly taking precautions and – of course – Benjamin having found something better to feed on. Kieran was about to keep going but then a thought brought him to a sliding stop.

Farmer's fields usually had access to farmhouses.

He looked out across the darkness. No flicker of light on the immediate horizon, but surely if he ploughed his way through the field, over the crest of the uneven landscape, he'd find light and life, perhaps in a valley. He could be there inside five minutes.

But what if he was wrong? What if he only found a long track that led to a more distant farm, the men perhaps having driven some way to check on their flock? He'd have lost a good chunk of time finding that out, that's what. *No: stick to the plan.* Sunday night meant people in the pub, and a working telephone.

He gave his arms and legs a rub and then started running.

He got twenty yards before he stopped again.

There was a figure up ahead.

Odd, because it wasn't walking along one of the sides but was positioned in the middle of the road. *Just trying to pick the flattest track, like me.* But the figure wasn't moving.

Kieran called out. 'Hello? Are you local? I need some help!'

The figure didn't respond, nor did it move towards him. Kieran wondered whether the road curved and this was actually some kind of memorial statue or monument on the path instead. He moved closer, hoping to get a clearer look.

Now there was movement, just a kink in an elbow and a slight turn of the hip. But still this person held their ground rather than come to meet him.

What was it Benson had said? People shy away from help, but are quick to get involved if…

'There's a fire! At Kilbride House! Do you know it?'

Now the figure moved forward, and with Kieran still walking it was only a few more seconds before clarity.

'I know it very well,' Benjamin replied. He was in his more human form, gaunt face reassembled. His clothes were streaked black with Lucy's blood.

Fuck.

Kieran stopped; wondered how he might buy himself time, fashion his next move. 'It's not been fifteen minutes. You've lied.'

'I have killed some of your friends but you are more concerned about my dishonesty?'

'But you've put Hayley at risk. They won't give her to you now.'

'Yes they will. In exchange for you.' Benjamin spread his arms and his face cracked open.

That made up Kieran's mind for him. He had to run.

He turned around and sprinted as hard as he could. He did his best to keep upright and watch his feet – one slip and it would all be over.

There was a flicker of shadow to his left.

And then Benjamin was standing in front of him again, this time between him and the house. 'Give it up, Kieran. This is not going to end well for you.'

He's fucking toying with me.

Kieran didn't know what options he had left. He went for something he hadn't tried before: he screamed for help as loud as he could.

Then Benjamin was on him and threw him to the ground.

**

Brooke risked sticking her head out and placed a foot on the decking. 'He's definitely gone.'

Alicia was behind her. 'Do we take a chance and try to get away? His car?'

'He won't have left the keys in it.' She looked around and chanced another step so that she was fully outside. She did her best not to look at Lucy's savaged corpse. 'I'm not sure. What if he's not far, but just waiting for us to move?' She glanced up at the roof.

Rhea pushed herself forward, nudging Alicia aside at the open door. 'He's gone for Kieran, I know it! I told him not to go!' She thought about the car; it was a serious option.

Elliot spoke up from the pool table. 'Kieran can't be told anything. Never has. He could still make it though. He's quick and strong.'

Rhea whipped around. 'Have you fucking forgotten Benjamin? Look at your goddamn wife!'

Alicia pulled Rhea away. 'Easy, easy.' It meant though that they all took in Danni; Brooke stepped back in for the very purpose.

She was now lying on the pool table in a foetal position, clearly feverish, sweat almost bubbling at her pores. She was also junkie-thin, her face almost skeletal. Her eyes seemed to be on a dimmer switch, alternating between being alert and powering down.

Rhea apologised, then went over to the stationary bike and shoved it over.

The resulting crash instigated a spark of life in Hayley; she sat up in her chair prison and looked for the source of the commotion. Then she took in deep, nasal breaths; the resulting oxygen almost made her eyes spin.

Alicia knelt in front of her. 'Hayley! Hayley! Are you okay? Nod if you are!'

She looked straight at her, eyes wide and focused, and made muffled noises against the tape. Alicia looked around at the others. 'If Benjamin's gone can we let her talk, for a minute?'

'A minute,' Brooke said. 'I'll keep watch for him.' She faced outwards on the threshold.

Alicia peeled back the tape, plucking at Hayley's skin. 'How are you feeling?'

Hayley took in a big gulp of air and then grimaced, the effort sending vibrations to the wound in her stomach. Then she refocused on Alicia. 'I'm sorry I didn't choose you.' Her voice was croaky and brittle.

'Forget that – it makes no difference. Rhea: grab a water from the fridge, will you?' When she came back with it, Alicia poured a little onto Hayley's puckering lips and then increased the flow when she nodded that she could take more.

Alicia spoke. 'Benjamin lies, Hayley. We think he's gone after Kieran. He went for help, Benjamin said he would wait here with us but he's gone. We were going to give him to you so he could help you, but he's gone.'

'But you didn't give me over straight away.' She looked down at the wooden stake sticking out of her middle and the gross discolouration of her sticky clothes. 'I might be *dying*.'

Brooke barked from the doorway. 'Hold your fucking horses there, Hayley! You were going to invite him in so he could kill us. Shit, you're happy for all but four of us to die!'

Hayley's face slackened. 'There's no way back from this.'

'I suppose not,' Alicia replied. 'But let's hope it's over soon.'

'Re-tape that bitch!' Brooke yelled. 'I hear something!'

Alicia pushed the tape back in place and stood. She watched Brooke at the door; she was backing away from the entrance, still looking out.

There was a small gate in the railing around the deck. It flew open, perhaps from a kick. Benjamin – face writhing in its vampire mode – stepped onto the boards. He had Kieran in a headlock and was dragging him along.

Rhea shouted and ran for the door; Brooke stuck out her good arm to hold her back.

Kieran was struggling against his captor, but weakly. His face was battered and swollen; there was enough light cast from the annex onto the deck to see the pink and purple hues of the pulverised flesh. A wound seeped on his bald head.

Benjamin brought him up to the door; Brooke backed away, almost expecting Benjamin to throw him in. Instead, he reached for one of Kieran's ears and jerked his head up, exposing his bleeding nose and mouth. 'Invite me in, or I will kill him.'

Rhea shouted Kieran's name again. Brooke told her to stay quiet, fearful that she would do what Benjamin asked.

'Fuck you, Brooke!' she responded. She rounded her to get to the back of Hayley's chair. She started pushing it towards the doorway. 'Give me Kieran and you can have Hayley!' She heaved and grunted. 'Help me with her!'

Benjamin repeated his demand: 'Invite me in, or I will kill him.'

Elliot left Danni on the pool table and stood in front of Hayley's chair, halting Rhea's progress. 'What are you doing?' she implored. 'Either help me or move.'

He's not asking for Hayley, Elliot thought. 'We can't trust him!'

'We've got to trust him! He's got Kieran! Move!'

She's not his priority any more, if she ever was. He didn't know if he should voice what he was thinking, couldn't work out if saying it out loud benefitted Benjamin in some way. 'I don't think he's going to give Kieran back! If he was happy with our so-called deal he wouldn't have chased him down in the first place.' He turned to Benjamin. 'We were going to stick to the plan but you broke it! Give us Kieran and we'll push Hayley out there.' Elliot knew now that Benjamin wouldn't allow them to get help for Danni, not anymore. It was now going to be a case of how many of them could survive until sunrise.

Danni won't last that long. He didn't know what he could do about that, but in this second he had to try and help his friend.

Benjamin didn't move, except to adjust his hold on Kieran's neck as he wriggled under his arm.

'Go on,' Elliot said. 'If she means so much to you, you'll do it, especially as she chose Kieran to be with you. With us – me, Danni and Rhea too.'

Brooke huffed. 'Thanks a fucking bunch.'

Elliot held out a hand. *Not now, Brooke.* 'Honour Hayley's wishes and we'll grant you yours. Give us Kieran. She can be with you in ten seconds.'

Benjamin's eyes narrowed and he stared at Elliot, through him almost. 'Invite me in, or I will kill him.'

'I knew it! He doesn't care about her!' Behind him, Hayley – becoming increasingly awake and aware – bucked against her restraints and then squeaked at the pain in her stomach.

Elliot looked down at her. 'Sorry.' And then he said the same to Rhea. He was, truly, because he didn't know how they were going to save Kieran.

Benjamin walked over to the hot tub, tore off the cumbersome padded lid and skimmed it away like a Frisbee. He readjusted his hold on Kieran, grabbing him by his clothes, and dunked him head first into the warm water.

Rhea screamed *No!* and pushed hard at Hayley's chair. She was getting her out onto the decking and that was that. It didn't have wheels though, and a combination of Rhea's lopsided placement of effort and Hayley's weight shifting to the front sent it toppling over. Hayley's shoulder and head smacked hard against the smooth floor. The stake loosened at her gut, and with that, more blood.

Benjamin pulled Kieran back up; he gasped for air, making a noise like a seal. Then Benjamin put him under again. 'Invite me in, Rhea, and he will not drown.'

She was about to shove Hayley and the chair again, even in their horizontal position, when Elliot wrestled her away.

But then Alicia took over, wanting rid of Hayley, wanting done with this situation. She got on her hands and knees and pushed, scraping the chair – and the side of Hayley's forehead – along the floor. The pool of blood which had formed made the floor slicker and the movement got easier, certain parts of the chair always getting lubrication from the life leaving Hayley.

Brooke shouted at her but she ignored it. Alicia wanted to vomit but she suppressed the urge. It would soon be over. Benjamin would make Hayley better and then they would both go away, forever. Hayley's head was almost at the threshold.

Kieran was back out of the water, wheezing and spluttering at the end of Benjamin's extended arm. 'You have one last chance. Invite me in.'

Brooke got on the floor next to Alicia and stayed her hands. 'Enough, You're getting too close!'

Alicia nudged her off, careful not to upset her broken arm. 'Just a bit more and then he can pull her out.' She flipped her position so that her feet were furthest forward. She planted them on the square bases of two of the chair legs and pushed. In front of them, Hayley's head bumped up the lip of the patio door floor runner.

Benjamin left Kieran hanging over the hot tub and dropped into a crouch by Hayley's head. The top of her scalp was accessible to him and he tangled his fingers in the strands. He pulled and she moved slightly, but then her position got lodged. When he tugged again, his hand came away with a handful of hair.

She winced, and rolled her eyes to try and see him.

His hands explored again: it didn't look like there was enough of her skull across the threshold for him to get purchase.

Alicia was about to give the chair another kick when Elliot slid over and stopped her. 'He just wants to take the tape off her mouth! So she will invite him in!'

Brooke concurred. 'Pretty sure I said that shit earlier.' She reached out with her good arm, found a supporting strut on Hayley's chair, and yanked it back as far as she could. Hayley's head once again bounced on the lip of the threshold.

Rhea, now freed, pushed herself up against the glass. Kieran was trying to lift himself up from the rim of the hot tub but there was no strength left in his arms. His head drooped, almost touching the water. He managed to crane it round so he could look at her. When his swollen eyes found hers, he coughed, and managed a word.

'Fire.'

Then Benjamin was up on the rim, both feet planted like he was about to jump in.

Instead he stomped on Kieran's head.

There was a crack and his neck bent in a way that shouldn't be possible.

Rhea couldn't help herself: she ran sideways for the open door.

She leapt to avoid possible contact with Hayley and hit the cold air mid-flight. Both hers and Benjamin's feet slapped against the decking at the same time: Rhea looking to dart towards her fallen man, Benjamin looking to intercept her. His face was fully open and the prickly tongue looked lively. He pounced in her direction, hands out front, ready to grab.

Rhea was going to try and sway past him when arms caught her from behind. Try as she might, she couldn't propel herself forward, and as soon as she lifted a step, her weight was dragged backwards by what felt like a dozen hands on her body.

Benjamin matched her forced retreat for speed. His long-nailed fingers reached out and snagged on her chest, tearing fabric. The fleshy mouth pulsed, flexing its shark teeth.

Her shoulder slammed against a door frame. Benjamin's mouth was so close she could smell foul breath like garbage left in the sun. The fingernails tightly scrunched the fabric of her top.

And then she was on the threshold. Hayley was close — an obstacle on the floor — and bodies tumbled backwards: Alicia, Elliot and Rhea.

An agonised cry issued from Benjamin's gaping maw. He hung by the door frame, inspecting his hand. Then he squeezed it and shook it, spraying blood onto the first slats of the decking.

Rhea — on her back, Alicia's leg caught underneath her — looked down her front at the crumpled and creased material of her sweater. Caught in the torn fabric were five fingernails, with the very tips of fingers still attached. As she stared, the fragments of flesh turned grey and crumbled to ash. The nails still held firm.

Benjamin retreated towards the hot tub. He detoured slightly, gave a roar of frustration, and sent a sharp kick to Lucy's corpse, propelling it into the rails. Then he reached out with his uninjured hand, grabbed one of Kieran's legs, and tipped him fully into the water.

He did not resurface.

Rhea started to half-cry, half-scream, as hands once again tried to keep her from going to him.

CHAPTER TWENTY-TWO

After such moments of intense hostility and stress, the ensuing calm was oddly oppressive and almost harder to take. Everyone was spent, but felt the weight of their devastating and seemingly untenable situation intently.

They weren't leaving any time soon.

They gathered in the middle of the floor, between the exercise gear and the pool table. Hayley had been removed from the chair; the captivity act seemed redundant now. She was dying, having slipped into another lull. They used more of the tape to wrap around her middle again, in an attempt to keep the bleeding to a minimum now the stake had been fully dislodged. They laid her down; Alicia stroked her hair. They kept the gag on though, not yet fully trusting her. Even though Benjamin seemed in no rush to save her, they had to assume she still felt loyalty towards him and their original plan.

What a shit show that had turned into.

Danni also lay down, now off the pool table, her head in Elliot's lap. She was painfully thin – looked almost brittle. She too was in a quiet, stuporous phase. There were no further thoughts of reaching a hospital for either of them; it was now just a question of whether or not they would last until morning.

And if they could all hold their shit together until then.

With that in mind, Elliot, Brooke and Alicia watched Rhea.

She sat with them, but was the only one engaged in an activity. She held the axe and was sharpening the wood that Kieran had already tended to, whittling them into even finer points. She was mumbling to each one, as if she was talking to him, discussing the work like they were doing it together. They'd asked a couple of times if she was okay. She'd responded coolly, and insisted she had to get on. They left her to it, for now. Alicia wondered what would happen when the girl ran out of wood.

As for Benjamin, he had disappeared from the decking. He'd taken Lucy's remains with him, but as far as they knew Kieran was still floating in the hot tub. No one went out to check, not even Rhea. And just because Benjamin wasn't in visible range, it didn't mean they were foolish enough to go exploring. They knew now – if they didn't know before – that they couldn't trust anything he said.

The upshot of it all was that they were stuck. And waiting... for something.

Brooke got up and went over to the settee. With one arm she pulled off all the cushions and coverings and tossed them in turn towards the group. 'Might as well be comfortable.'

Alicia rescued a couple of them and pushed them under Hayley. She also picked out cushions for her and Brooke. Elliot grabbed one and propped his elbow on it. It seemed ridiculous, but he felt tired. He wondered if he allowed himself to close his eyes would he actually fall asleep. In the midst of all this murder and mayhem, might he switch off completely? It was farcical, but it would... be so welcome.

No. Didn't he have to stay awake for Danni? He didn't know how to help her, if he even *could* help her, but failing at his watch was unthinkable.

The real reason entered his head like a hot, twisted wire: *I need to be here with her if she dies.* He banished the thought, but it would not leave – not entirely. He brushed his fingers across the hot, taut skin of her cheek.

Alicia slid herself over to him. 'We're going to take turns being on watch. I said I was happy to go first.'

'What? You mean sleeping? I can't do that while she's... like this.'

'Everyone needs some rest, even if it's just for an hour.' She looked down at Danni in his lap. 'I think she'll be okay for now, El, but you look knackered.'

'I can't...'

'Look, what if we have to act fast as soon as the sun comes up and you're so exhausted that you can't help her?'

Brooke chipped in. 'What if we have to respond *before* that? I think Benjamin will try something just before sunrise, if not earlier. He won't want us getting out of this. We all need to be sharp for when that happens.'

The discussion went round a couple more times, this time including Rhea, and a rota was devised. Alicia was keeping the initial watch, but then Elliot wanted to be woken first change. He didn't vocalise it, but they all knew it was then going to be his intention to stay awake for the duration of the night. He would feel like he was betraying Danni if he didn't sit up for her.

But before that, sleep. Danni and Hayley were already unconscious. Brooke and Elliot placed cushions under their heads and lay back. Before doing the same, Rhea handed Alicia one of her smooth and sharp wooden spikes. 'Stake through the fucking heart,' she said, and pointed to the patio doors.

It was just a wall of darkness and the outline of the hot tub – nothing else. 'Yeah,' Alicia replied. 'If I see Benjamin I'll skewer the bastard.'

Rhea nodded approvingly, and then settled down on her own cushion.

When she thought they were all close to sleep, Alicia got up and started what she imagined would be the first of many laps around the room. She was going to aim for two hundred then wake Elliot. By that time she hoped she'd be so exhausted she'd fall asleep immediately, and then with any luck they'd be able to leave her until daylight brought her round naturally. Times such as these made you reassess your ambitions. That's all she wanted for herself and Brooke in the future: to once again be woken by the sun.

She started walking.

**

Alicia was halfway through lap 181 when she turned round the foosball table on the other side of the room and – on the return leg – saw Rhea standing by the cushions. She walked back, saving her whisper until she was in range. 'You don't need to be awake. Elliot's next.'

Rhea rolled her head on her shoulders and tugged her clothes straight. 'But I'm up, and he's in a coma, so we might as well leave him.'

They looked down at the lightly snoring figure. Danni had rolled off him and he hadn't noticed. Her breath was a little more ragged, and she was thinner still – her clothes drooped around her. It wouldn't help Elliot to see her like that. Alicia took a closer step to Hayley: also still breathing, somehow. 'Okay,' she said.

Alicia had succeeded in her watch, and the realisation brought with it a wave of relief and fatigue she didn't know she was capable of feeling. 'Wake Elliot next. Wake all of us if there are any developments.'

'Got it.'

There was no enthusiasm in Rhea's tone. *Why would there be?* Alicia thought. She got down next to Brooke and tried to not let that worry her. She thought about early morning sunlight streaming through, shielding her eyes, blinking away sleep. Yes – that was now the sum total of her life's ambition. She put her head down and worked on making the dream a reality.

Rhea stood and watched them all dispassionately for a good ten minutes.

She hadn't slept at all through Alicia's shift, but was thinking and plotting about how she wanted the rest of the night to go. When she'd thought the moment was right she'd got up and taken over. Now she had a window of time to herself in which to execute her plan.

Revenge.

There was no way she was going to just sit the night out, allowing Benjamin to slope off at some point in the morning around 6am.

He was going to pay for what he'd done to Kieran. She looked at the hot tub. She had no desire to go in there and fish him out. She knew he was dead, and with that, knew he was no longer there. What remained was a carcass, a shell. She had no sentiment towards a bag of flesh and bones. No. She kept Kieran in her head, and she'd never be able to face him fully up there until she had avenged him.

The others would probably be surprised at the depth of feeling she had for him; they were, after all, the couple who had been together for the shortest amount of time. But what did time matter? There was no stopwatch to measure love. And your Personal Best could come sooner than you ever thought.

Benjamin was going to pay for taking Kieran from her.

When she was sure the rest of them were settled, she moved around the annex, gathering all the things she thought she would need.

**

Back on her cushion, organising her arsenal, she noticed movement from across the floor. It was Danni. She had wriggled free of Elliot without waking him and was now moving gingerly on her hands and knees towards the patio door.

Rhea considered calling out, but thought better of it. Not because she didn't want to wake the others, but because she was curious about what Danni might do, and didn't want Elliot to intervene. She got up and moved closer to her, but not too close. Danni didn't acknowledge her but crawled on towards the door, all angles and joints, not noticing the sticky splodges of Hayley's blood that were leaving imprints on her hands and clothes. Once she reached her destination she raised herself up on her knees and reached for the door handle. She pressed down on the mechanism and – despite having very little strength left in those spindly arms – slid the door open.

Cold air came in and the room temperature changed. Rhea looked at the sleepers to see if it made any difference to their slumber; no one stirred.

Danni was back into her crawl pose. She shuffled forward, so that half of her body was over the threshold.

Rhea didn't rush to pull Danni in as she might have done earlier. Instead, she picked up a couple of stakes and watched the darkness around the deck railing. If this brought Benjamin out of hiding, then it might also be her moment.

Nothing from the night. Rhea's eyes fell back on Danni. She was sniffing the icy boards like an animal. Then she stopped and started to pick at something. Rhea edged over for a closer look.

There were spots of blood, perhaps on the verge of freezing, dotted on the thin and compacted wintry layer that covered the deck entrance. What was left of Lucy's blood amounted to a gathering of slush to the right of the door - like someone had dropped and kicked a supersized cherry ice cone – but this was not the same. These were scarlet buttons. Danni was tracking them down, picking them off and eating them.

Rhea remembered Benjamin shaking his hand in frustration when his fingertips and nails came off. She watched Danni ingest a little more of him.

When she was done, she reversed back in. Now she was more interested in the stains on her hands, those she had picked up from the floor inside. She licked her fingers and palms clean, and then sought out more of Hayley's drying blood, dragging her fingers across the hard floor, making tacky pools for her to devour. She lapped at them like a cat.

Rhea let it happen, deciding that she would only intervene if Danni tried to get blood from Hayley herself. The injured woman still slept, as did the others.

Danni made her way back across the floor, towards the group. Rhea walked parallel to her, tracking her. When Danni reached Elliot she stopped and lowered herself down onto the cushion, getting ready to adopt a sleeping position. Before she did fully, she – for the very first time in this bizarre episode – locked eyes on Rhea. She offered her a timid smile and added: 'Now I feel better.'

'Right. That's good.' She didn't know what else to say.

Danni's smile got a little wider, and stayed on her face as she placed her head on the cushion and closed her eyes.

Rhea watched her – watched them all – for a few minutes more and then walked over to the open door. From a standing position she could see the outline of Kieran's back in the hot tub, flotsam from the wreck of this weekend. Again, she pushed sentimentality away. *It's not him anymore. I don't need to concern myself with that thing.* Kieran stayed with her in her heart, but now she had to occupy herself with the living.

And the living dead. She scanned the darkness for her adversary.

To the left were the lights from the driveway and the silhouettes of their cars. Directly in front were shadowy shrubs and to her right a tall, imposing phalanx of trees. There was no sign of Benjamin.

That doesn't mean anything. The annex had a flat roof, and Rhea believed that he was up there, just waiting to see if any of them dared venture out from the sanctuary of the building.

There would be none of that. She would face Benjamin, yes, but on her terms.

She went back to her stock of weapons and got herself ready. She would stash things all around – in pool table pockets, under the settee, propped against the stationary bike – any place where she might need assistance in the heat of a fight.

171

Benjamin was going to pay.

CHAPTER TWENTY-THREE

The park was still one of their favourite places. Even though Oliver was eleven and had started high school, he wasn't too cool to enjoy a climb on the castle-shaped frame or take his turn on the helter-skelter slide. Of course, if you asked him he'd say he was only doing it to help keep his brother and sister entertained; Dad needed help managing Harry and Grace after all. He was just doing the brotherly thing.

Elliot let the boy think that. It didn't matter, because his kids were all having a lovely time in the sunshine. The simplest moments were the best, because you could repeat them as many times as you wanted.

'Faster, Daddy!' Harry was giving orders from the swing seat in front of Elliot. He obliged and gave his youngest a firmer shove. The boy offered a *wheeee!* at the zenith of his arc. Across the playground, Oliver was gently spinning the roundabout, with Grace lying back on it, giggling.

He was pleased he'd promised them ice cream after – rather than before – the playground, otherwise he might have some upset tummies to contend with. Another ten minutes and they'd seek out the *Frederick's Ices* van.

The timing was perfect. Just as he was rounding them up, he heard the tinkling music and the sound of an approaching vehicle. Harry clapped with excitement and Grace skipped. Oliver retrieved the football they'd brought with them, kicked it forward and chased after it.

Elliot bought them all their favourites, including a mint choc chip for himself. It was a good moment.

The car wasn't too far away and the kids were in good spirits along the short walk. 'Will mum be home when we get back?' Oliver asked.

Elliot checked the time. 3 o'clock. 'Yeah, I think so.' She was having lunch with her brother, but they were meeting up pretty close to the house so there was every chance she'd beat them home. In the car, the kids discussed the afternoon, and decided on the best moments they could share with Danni.

When he pulled onto the drive, Danni's car was already there. She had yet to enter their semi-detached house; she and her brother were leaning against the side of the Kia, chatting and taking in the sun. Elliot parked carefully, making sure there was space for all the doors to open.

As he killed the engine, an uneasy feeling came over him.

The kids flung open the doors and tipped out onto the driveway.

Danni doesn't have a brother.

'Uncle Benjamin! Uncle Benjamin!'

The gentleman next to Danni crouched and opened up his arms. The children ran to him and he wrapped them in an embrace. It almost didn't seem possible to get arms around all three but he somehow managed it. Elliot noticed long fingernails on the left hand.

When Benjamin stood up, he took Grace with him, cradled in the crook of his right arm. The other two went to Danni and she kissed them both on the cheek. She looked radiant, healthy. Elliot couldn't remember for the life of him why she might present otherwise.

'Shall we head inside?' she asked. When they came together on the drive she had a kiss for him too.

'You okay?' he asked her.

'Of course. Why wouldn't I be?'

Because there is a monster on our driveway. 'I dunno. Weird feeling.'

She smirked at him and opened the front door. 'Are you going to invite Benjamin in or what?' She disappeared into the hallway.

Oliver and Harry came next, nudging and tickling each other as they moved, Oliver trying to look like he was above such things but enjoying it as much as his younger brother. 'Pack it in, Harry!' but he laughed along with him. As they both took to the step in front of the door, Oliver asked of Elliot the same thing as Danni. 'Can Uncle Ben come in for a bit, Dad?'

'*Benjamin*,' said the man holding Elliot's daughter.

174

Oliver didn't say anything else but disappeared into the darkness of the hall with his brother.

Now it was just Elliot, Benjamin and little Gracie.

The tall, slender man in the spectacles smiled, then spoke in a low, deep voice. 'I think it is time for you to invite me in, Elliot.'

Elliot felt sick to his stomach. Mint choc chip churned around in there, threatening to reappear. 'I… I don't want to.'

'And why might that be?'

'Because you're not the kids' uncle – you're someone else.'

Gracie looked shocked at this, scrutinised closely the man who held her, but then gave him a squeeze. Benjamin accepted it and grinned at Elliot over the top of the little girl's head. 'If I am not their uncle, who do you think I am?'

'You're a monster, and if I invite you in, you'll kill us.' But who was *us*? Not Danni and the kids. Correction: yes, Danni, but also others. Friends. *What's going on?*

Benjamin pursed his lips at the accusation, then took in Grace's face. She mirrored his expression; they both looked very disappointed with Elliot.

'Put my daughter down.' Elliot made to walk towards them but for some reason his feet wouldn't move. He stared down at them. They were stuck in snow. Which was impossible because it was a bright sunny day. Also impossible was the fact that it was night-time around his shins and ankles. *None of this can be real.*

'It is real enough, Elliot. Let me show you.' He tickled Gracie's stomach with his left hand, but then one of the long nails got caught in her t-shirt and she yelped. Benjamin ignored the distress and pushed the nail in further. She started crying and bucked against his arm.

'Stop that!' yelled Elliot. His feet were still stuck and he could not cross the couple of metres needed to rescue his daughter. 'It's okay, baby; don't worry, you're not really hurt!' Blood, like an ink spot, welled up in the cotton.

'Invite me in, Elliot.'

He ignored Benjamin and tried to connect with his daughter's face. 'This isn't real, baby! I know what this is: I'm dreaming, miles away from home. You're safe at your friend's, you're safe!'

Her cries began to subside, and Benjamin also consoled her. 'Your daddy is right: this isn't really happening. We aren't really here…' He then took to gazing around their surroundings: the high hedge separating them from next door, the large bay window, the brick arch over the door. 'We are not here at your house... at 27 Sycamore Avenue.' He looked around again. 'It is very pleasant here. I imagine you feel so safe, growing up in the bosom of your loving family.' Grace had stopped crying completely; Benjamin jiggled her on his arm and smiled at her. 'Not real right now...'

Then Benjamin looked up at Elliot, his eyes completely black like pools of tar. 'But if you do not invite me into Kilbride House, this will be real some time very soon. I will visit 27 Sycamore Avenue in the dead of night and I shall feast on your children.'

Elliot's heart throbbed in his chest, then seemed to detach itself and find lodging in his throat. 'You can't...'

'I can, Elliot, and I will. One of them will let me in and then you won't be able to stop me. Just like now.'

He rammed his hand into Gracie's stomach and ripped a piece of her away. Blood and intestine splattered against his chest.

Gracie was conscious for barely a second of it.

Unfortunately, Elliot – screaming – had to watch it all, watch the vampire gorge itself on his daughter's organs.

**

Elliot's head shot up a little too fast, so that the images in his vision seemed to lag behind where his eyes looked. He felt frantic, but quickly placed himself in the Kilbride House annex and not on his driveway at Sycamore Avenue. He sat up, again too hasty. It was the motion of a man who felt instinctively that he had overslept and somehow had to catch up with time. It put a pulse in his forehead and made his stomach churn.

But not with mint choc chip.

His first response was to check on Danni next to him. He put a hand on her chest and felt the rise and fall; he could also hear the rhythm of her breathing. His second response was to check his watch. It was 3am. He'd been asleep for hours.

But not 3pm. Not at home.

That wasn't as reassuring as it should have been. He had no doubt that Benjamin had just been in his head. He remembered Hayley's explanation of how he had found the phones and car keys.

He knows where we live.

The others were prostrate humps in the gloom. 'We should wake up!' he said, a loud voice in the silence. 'Benjamin's close. He-' Elliot stopped, not sure whether it was wise to say it.

If I don't invite him in he will kill my children.

Brooke's head answered the call, rising up off her cushion, blinking, snorting. 'What is it? My turn?'

'It should be my turn. I slept too long.'

And Benjamin came to me in my sleep and took from me.

It was then that Elliot realised Rhea wasn't there.

He scanned the annex and saw her at the far end, behind the foosball table, on the bench seating.

Brooke knelt and looked in the same direction. 'Why didn't you wake us? We were supposed to take shifts.'

'I wasn't tired,' Rhea replied, busying herself with something on the bench. 'You guys needed the rest.' It was left at that. Alicia sat up and said hey.

Somehow, the moment had passed in which to discuss what had happened in Elliot's dream. And more interestingly, what he wanted to do about it.

Let him in and die, or don't let him in and kill my children?

Brooke took charge. Now that the healthy were all awake, it seemed prudent to check on the injured.

Elliot lay down again next to Danni, and smoothed a hand over her cheek. It felt more substantial than before...

Alicia and Brooke looked Hayley over. She was still alive; that was probably as good as it got. Alicia tugged at the tape on her lips. Brooke was about to protest when Alicia grabbed a water bottle. 'Just a little. If the wound doesn't kill her she'll end up dying of thirst.'

'Okay, but be careful.'

The prickly pain caused by the tape's removal brought Hayley round a little. Parched lips welcomed the water; she closed her eyes as she took the cool liquid in, like it was a reverential moment.

'Are you hurting?' Alicia asked.

'Numb,' she muttered, shivering, her face twitching. 'Cold.' She looked at Alicia, but not fully focused; her eyes flitted, not quite locking with hers. 'Benjamin?'

Alicia glanced at the windows. 'Somewhere. We haven't seen him for hours. I think you need to forget about him, Hayles.'

She closed her eyes at this; Alicia thought she detected a tiny shake of the head.

Brook pointed to the curling length of tape hanging from Hayley's cheek. For now, Alicia ignored her. She'd seen too many of her friends die today and here might be another. The least they could do was let her potential last breath be drawn freely.

Elliot's voice drew their attention. He was repeating Danni's name as a question. Alicia feared the worst, until Danni sat up from the floor and said: 'I feel fine. Honestly.'

And she looked fine, or at least better. There was colour in her cheeks, and flesh in them too: a fullness that had been missing, what, four hours ago? She almost looked back to her usual self, apart from a tiredness around the eyes, a shadowy underscore that cast a little doubt over her claim to be as right as rain.

But it was positive, and they'd take that with both hands, current situation considered. Elliot rubbed his fingers over her upper arms and planted kisses on her cheek. Danni told him not to fuss, but did so blithely.

Rhea walked back over, and those on the floor paused. She had a stake in her hand and waved it nonchalantly in Danni's direction. 'She looks better because she drank some more of Benjamin's blood, and then Hayley's. She's becoming like him.'

There were calls from the three of them for her to explain. She summarised what she'd witnessed: Danni's double feed. As Rhea spoke, Danni listened intently, as if this was all news to her. She looked over at Hayley, acknowledging her friend's condition for the first time. 'Oh my God – how bad is she?'

Elliot stood, scathing in his reaction to Rhea. 'And you didn't stop her? You just let that happen?'

Rhea sniffed. 'She was shrivelling away into nothing. You were content to wait until morning. By then I didn't think there'd be anything of her left. I thought it was worth letting it play out.'

'Letting it play out? It's not a game!'

There was a snarl on Rhea's face. 'Kieran's face down in the hot tub: I fucking know it's not a game! Either way, waiting until eight o'clock in the morning, or whenever it gets light up here, wasn't going to be an option: not for Hayley, not for Danni.'

Danni raised a hand from the floor. 'Please can we stop fighting? Hayley needs our help, not me.' She moved across to her on her hands and knees. 'I think I'm going to be fine, but, shit – look at her!' She took up one of Hayley's hands in both of hers. Her friend murmured.

Rhea continued. 'Yeah, well sure, I think you would have died if you didn't take in your… sustenance, and you're looking good for now, but I bet in about an hour you're going to need some more. Either that or you've already taken in what you need and any time now your face is going to flip inside out and you'll try to suck the life out of us. Like I said, none of us are making the morning at this rate.'

The choice popped into Elliot's head again: *Let him in and die, or don't let him in and kill my children.*

Danni's voice snapped him out of it. 'Can we just do something for her?'

Brooke shook her head, but at Rhea, not Danni. 'That's all just guesswork.' But she didn't sound her usual belligerent and confident self; instead it was a comment seeking validation. No one was able to give it. She stood as well, holding her broken arm.

Alicia was crouched by Danni and Hayley. 'So what now?'

Rhea shrugged. 'I say we keep the tape off Hayley's mouth and let her either die with dignity or do what she thinks she needs to do to survive.' She flipped the stake over in her hand, holding it like a dagger. 'I'm ready if it's the latter.'

Another thought arrived fully-formed for Elliot to conjure with. *Of course, there's a third option: let him in and just kill the fucker.* He remembered the dream: Gracie being eaten by a monster. A dream that Benjamin gave him and threatened to make real. *He can't be trusted to do as he says he will; we've been there before.*

Brooke and Rhea were bickering.

'You're crazy,' muttered Brooke. 'Missing a few screws up here.' She tapped a finger against her temple.

'And you're missing something from your pocket.' Rhea walked back towards the foosball table, leaving her cryptic sign-off line hanging in the air.

Brooke patted her pockets down with her good hand. 'I'm not even sure I've… oh, shit: I know.' She nudged past Elliot and trotted after Rhea.

She saw the younger woman's stock-pile of weapons first: numerous needle-like stakes on one of the long bench cushions. Then – on the other one positioned against the far wall – a pile of pulled-out cushion stuffing, and wood shavings from the stock of logs she'd whittled down further after Kieran's efforts.

Rhea flicked the wheel on Brooke's lighter and dropped it onto her mini-bonfire.

It went up with a whoosh. The flames immediately licked the wooden panel of the wall, sketching out the shadow of a fire silhouette and moving on; up, up, leaving charcoal-coloured blisters in its wake. It devoured the rest of the seat padding, fanning out rapidly. *Shit - we're not putting that out,* Brooke thought, stepping back into the foosball table.

Rhea crossed in front of it, not to try and quash it but to grab the tail of the other long cushion on the bench that her weapons rested on. She pulled it away from the flames, down the length of the other part of the L. 'Fire brings people. That means he'll have to do something now.'

Brook followed her. '*We'll* have to fucking do something! We were safe in here but now you're burning it down!'

The cushion slid off the bench, losing a few pieces of cargo. Rhea stooped and loaded it up again, then proceeded to drag it across the annex.

Alicia met them halfway across the room, Elliot and Danni close behind. They stared at the blazing wall at the far side of the building. Elliot was aghast. 'What have you done?' In his head though, he knew: *the third option.*

'Kick-started the end. If you want to help, pick up something pointy. We're about to have the fight of our lives.' She wafted her stake back in Hayley's direction.

Alicia remembered the tape she'd loosened; she trotted back over. Hayley was in a foetal position but she was conscious. She twisted her neck so that her face was towards the ceiling. Her eyes closed, she whispered in a cracked and hoarse voice just as Alicia dropped to a knee and reached for the tape: 'Benjamin, please come in.'

Having missed the moment, Alicia took the edge of the tape between thumb and forefinger and removed it fully from Hayley's cheek. It didn't matter now. She looked at the patio doors and the darkness beyond.

There was a thud: a shadow landed on the decking.

Brooke grabbed Alicia's shoulder and pulled her up. 'Come on: you need to grab a weapon.'

Alicia turned to see that they all held pointed stakes; Brooke's was tucked under her arm – along with a spare – only having one hand to pull Alicia away. They backed towards the centre of the room, away from Hayley, towards the fire, eyes on the patio doors.

A hand from the outside found the handle and slid it across.

A cold blast of air came in, and with it, Benjamin.

He stood tall, angular, grey clothes creased and smeared with blood. His face was intact but streaked with gore. His hair was plastered to his head with the moisture from melted snow. His glasses steamed up a little and he had to take them off to give them a wipe. The action looked ludicrous given the situation. He was checking them over when he spoke, twirling them for inspection with fingertips that had grown back. 'Thank you for inviting me in. I am happy to be back in your company. However, I think it is time to bring the weekend's proceedings to a conclusion.' He glanced down at Hayley, still curled up on the floor, but conscious. 'It will be over soon, I promise.'

Then he looked up at the others and smiled.

CHAPTER TWENTY-FOUR

They didn't form a defensive line but an uncertain huddle. Elliot was urging Danni to stand behind him. Alicia and Brooke seemed intent on trying to protect each other and kept exchanging places. The fire cracked and spat behind them, causing them to flinch. Only Rhea stood firm at the nearest point of a rough diamond.

Benjamin smirked at their weapons. He kept eyes on them as he took a knee by Hayley. 'Those small sticks will not be adequate.' He stroked her cheek but without looking at her. She murmured to him and he responded with a soothing hush, his gaze still on the would-be aggressors. He spoke to them again. 'I have faced harder challenges than you could ever pose. I have been here for over 100 years. I fought in the second Balkan war and killed deadlier people than you when I was merely human. Then, when I lay dying in a forest in Tutrakan, what I thought was a wolf started to feed on me. Of course, it was something *more* than a wolf. That was the only fight I ever lost.'

'Bullshit,' Brooke said. 'If you lay dying then some fucker put you there. Get ready for that again.'

'Tough talk from someone with a broken arm. An arm that I snapped like a twig.' He stood and they all took a step back. He looked past them. 'However, I am curious about why you have set fire to the building. Did you expect me to panic and try to put it out?'

'People will come,' Elliot said. 'You'll be outnumbered. You're going to lose.'

'Yes, they will come, I imagine within ten minutes or so. That's more time than I need.'

Rhea pointed to Hayley. 'She's dying. What are you going to do for her?'

Hayley responded to the reference and tried to adjust her position. She winced as she pushed up onto one elbow, puffed out her cheeks and blinked as she tried to steady her head on her shoulders. 'Benjamin…'

This time he did look at her, just held out a hand in the direction of the others. 'Yes, my love?'

'Save us all…' She licked at her dry lips. 'Four or five: it shouldn't matter.' She gritted her teeth against a wave of pain before adding. 'Turn us all. No more killing.'

He crouched again and ran his fingers over her hair. 'Not long now. Do not exert yourself.'

'Give her your blood,' Alicia said. 'Stop her pain.'

'And start the transference?' he asked, still stroking her head. 'Just as she wants me to do with each of you? To make all of you *Vampyri*?'

'Fuck that,' Brooke responded.

'Indeed. Because it would prove difficult at this moment, with the building burning and time ticking by. She needs my blood, and then some of your human blood. Who would like to volunteer? All the other bodies are frozen.'

'Kieran's not,' Alicia replied.

'No way,' Rhea muttered. She was still poised, stake in each hand, eyes firmly on Benjamin, following his every move. 'No one touches that body.'

Benjamin laughed at them. 'So you see the problem!' He spoke softly to Hayley. 'No, not all of them.'

'Not *any* of them.' Rhea said. 'Not any of us. Not even Danni. Tell Hayley, honestly this time.'

'I am not sure what you mean.'

'You were never going to give her what she wanted. I realised that as soon as you killed Kieran.'

'You do not know what I am thinking. On the other hand, Elliot is thinking about me paying his children a home visit.'

Elliot thrust his stake outwards. 'Shut up!'

'Ell?' Danni enquired behind him.

Benjamin answered. 'Elliot has not told you that I visited him in his sleep and we struck bargains over your offspring.'

More demands for clarification, and although Danni's was the most urgent, all the group were now invested. Elliot shouted to be heard. 'He tried to make me give you all up! He's messing with our heads! Don't listen to him!'

'The kids!' Danni implored.

'They're fine!'

'For now,' Benjamin said.

There was a loud crack behind them, followed by a creak and a crash. The whole back of the room was engulfed in flame and a part of the ceiling fell in. Instinct pulled them away from the fire, but that meant being closer to Benjamin and Hayley. It felt like they were seconds from a necessary skirmish.

Alicia spoke up, pointing down at Hayley. 'You've not even looked at her wound! Help her! You have to help her!'

Benjamin hissed up at her, but then checked himself. His face quivered but did not open up. 'Okay,' he said. 'We just about have time for the truth before I end this. And if you will stop waving your sticks around, I think this might be something you all want to hear.' He crouched and took Hayley's hand. 'I am sorry this has happened to you. I did not think I would have to protect you from one of your so-called friends. But you are dying and I do not want to start the transference with you, so this is the end.'

Hayley moaned before replying. 'Why... why don't you want me?'

'I don't want *any* of you, not as *Vampyri*. You talked so much about your love for these people, I knew that if you were going to stay as my day companion for the rest of your natural life, you would have to give them up. I brought you here to say goodbye to them. It was always my intention to kill them and then for us to move away, back to Europe.'

'Motherfucker!' Brooke barked.

Hayley whined. 'But we were going to be together, forever...'

'No, my love. Not as *Vampyri*. It just does not work. If I were to take you through the transference, yes, you would be changed, and we would be drawn to each other more than ever. But this only lasts for a time. *Vampyri* in each other's company feel intense emotions. First it is love and passion, but then – within days – it changes to hate and rage, the worst kind of lust, and a desire to drink the other's blood. We would be driven uncontrollably by an urge to kill each other. We are a nomadic species. We cannot live together, work together, *be* together. That is our great weakness. For instance, I know of three other *Vampyri* in Cluj but we have to keep our distance, have our daytime companions complete detailed reconnaissance so our paths do not cross. You did not realise it at the time but that is what you were doing for me in those early days, and doing it perfectly. So all this, here at the house? I just needed to make you my permanent, committed companion, and that meant losing those you loved.'

Hayley didn't have words; she was crying, and each weak tear hurt, in every conceivable manner. The others were also processing what they had just heard, each in their own way.

It had all been a lie. Everyone was to die.

Arms braced once more with needle-pointed weapons outstretched.

'I am sorry,' Benjamin said, standing. 'But it is over.' He stared across to the others, the fire raging behind them, their shadows licking his feet. 'And now you know the truth, it is time to end this.'

Elliot shouted over the roar of the blaze. 'So you're just going to let her die?'

'I will not make her *Vampyri* and she can no longer be my companion.'

'What about Danni?'

'She is not yet *Vampyri*, and in a moment she will be nothing.' The threat drew the couple closer together. Everyone tensed.

Except Benjamin. He strolled a small semi-circle in front of them until he came to lean against the stationary bike. He smirked at another stash of stakes propped up there. 'Of course, now you do know everything, I suddenly have an inclination to offer you this. Would one of *you* like to take up the role of day companion? Be my familiar?' He sauntered back towards the settee. 'It cannot be Danielle – she has started the transference. But if you can put the emotions of this aside, I can give you a life of privilege and adventure. I have accumulated considerable wealth. You will see such sights! And the occasional drink from my fingertip will prolong your life without changing it beyond measure. It is a good offer.'

The foosball table collapsed behind them, gobbled up by the fire. The flames were reaching towards the pool table, and had cut off any potential exit via the other door. Smoke billowed towards them, searching for the open patio door.

Their only way out was through Benjamin. They hovered in a

tentative formation, stakes pointing forward. They would have to charge him. Imminently.

Then something changed.

'I'll take it,' Rhea said, dropping her weapons. The others were instantly interrogative, not quite sure what she meant. She clarified. 'Day companion. Fuck it: I'll do it. Kieran's dead; I've got nothing else to hold me back.'

Brooke was boiling over. 'Are you fucking insane?' She punched Rhea on the shoulder with the hand that held the stake. Rhea rocked forward, moving her away from the group and closer to Benjamin.

She turned to them, all glaring at her incredulously. 'What? I hardly know you people and I owe you nothing. You've been shit with me since Kieran died.' She looked at Benjamin. 'I'm willing to do it. I'll drive you out of here, if that's what you need.'

'You bitch!' Alicia yelled. 'You lit the fire and told us to fight! Now you've shit out on us?'

'I didn't know there'd be another way. Now there's on offer on the table.' She stepped closer to Benjamin. 'Are you serious or is this another bullshit lie, because…' she showed him her empty hands.

'No, I am serious.' He ignored Hayley's timid whimpers from the floor. 'Of course, just as you worry if you can trust me, I have the same concerns. You need to prove yourself.'

He darted sideways. The others jumped back, felt the heat on their backs and then tipped the other way, almost instigating the start of the fight. There was still just enough distance between them to prevent it, and Benjamin retreated seconds after he'd advanced.

He'd only moved to scoop up one of the stakes behind the stationary bike. He offered it to Rhea. 'I have found you to be quite impressive this weekend, and you might make an excellent companion… Now kill one of them.'

Rhea took it, and nodded.

Then she spun on her toes, but not towards the four holding out their quivering stakes, but in Hayley's direction. She dropped to her knees and slammed the needle-sharp wooden splint deep into the stricken woman's chest.

The other women screamed but all Hayley could manage was something akin to a weak belch, followed by a bubbling expulsion of blood and spittle. Her eyeballs rolled to the side and then there was nothing else: that was all it took to finish her.

Rhea turned to look up at Benjamin. He still held out the hand with which he had handed over the stake. 'I suppose I did not specify whom.'

'Listen,' Rhea said, panting. 'I'm in this to stay alive. I can't take *them*. You're the fucking vampire – you do it.'

'You fucking bitch!' screamed Alicia.

Benjamin laughed. 'I can see you are going to keep me, as is the saying, on my toes!'

Then he turned to face the other four and dipped his shoulders. His jaw split and his face unfurled itself, revealing the vicious teeth and the eel-like, spiky tongue. Now redundant, his glasses fell to the floor.

Elliot pulled Danni away, but where could he push her to? It was roasting hot behind them; the blue felt on the pool table crisped up and caught fire. The far side of the room couldn't be seen for all the smoke; somewhere in the depths of it, whatever remained of that half of the structure groaned. He felt his own skin tighten and burn, and breathing was becoming increasingly difficult. Benjamin was their only path. He stood before them, arms outstretched. Behind him, the cowardly Rhea scuttled away from Hayley's body towards the stripped settee and perhaps the safety of the decking.

Alicia and Brooke were jabbing their stakes towards Benjamin, but without enough conviction. Benjamin caught Alicia's weapon hand and squeezed hard. The fingers cracked and snapped, and the wood underneath them splintered in a mini-explosion. Alicia howled. Brooke ran forward but was swatted away by Benjamin's other fist. He still held Alicia and he yanked her closer. The two devastating rows of saw-like teeth were mere inches from her face, but she couldn't get away. His cold saliva spattered against her cheek.

And then he let out a terrifying shriek himself, and his convulsing brow seemed to swallow up his eyes. He let go of Alicia's hand and she fell backwards into Brooke's legs.

There was something sticking out of Benjamin's neck, like a silver-grey collar.

Rhea's face loomed behind his shoulder, eyes wide, teeth bared. She roared and wrenched the axe head out of Benjamin's flesh.

Deep red arterial blood spurted out like a burst pipe. He'd barely got a hand to it when Rhea was following through with another mighty swing. This one caught him just under the ear, the blur of the axe head disappearing behind the distended flap of his expanded face. He bit down instinctively, but something had been dislodged in his fluid physiology and he sliced through his own cheek with his frothing fangs.

Elliot ran forward and rammed his stake under Benjamin's breastbone. The spiky tongue shot towards him but its radar was off and it missed his face by some distance. He stepped away and reached out for Danni.

Benjamin grabbed the stake and ripped it out, along with another spray of blood. He turned with it, no doubt intent on forcing it through Rhea's face.

He lunged at her but was uncoordinated; she sidestepped him easily.

The axe swung again, this time connecting with the other side his neck. His misshaped skull rocked back. He was almost beheaded, like a tree ready to fall. There was now a fanned spray of blood like a sprinkler. Rhea growled at him. 'You on your toes yet, fucker?' Benjamin gargled something incoherent.

She took the axe in both hands and held it at head height, the gore-smeared head of it out in front. Then she jabbed it hard into Benjamin's mouth, dislodging a number of teeth.

In an instinctive, impulsive reaction, the vampire's maw closed around the axe head, as if it was accepting food. Benjamin's face tried to rebuild itself around the hunk of metal. It looked like he had no conscious control over it; his hand reached up and pawed at his jaw.

Rhea wrestled with the handle, manipulating Benjamin's head as she did so. Bizarrely, his face was not going to let go. Alicia and Elliot both came around and clapped hands on it and helped her pull. Brooke, still behind Benjamin, locked her good arm around his skinny middle and pulled the other way. Danni then wrapped her arms around Brooke and lent her momentum to the fight.

They all heaved at the same time. There was a tear and a pop. Brooke and Danni fell back with Benjamin. The other three fell back with the axe held above them.

Still enveloping the heavy blade was Benjamin's malformed head, like they'd impaled it on a pole as a warning to others. It splattered them as they lay underneath it. Rhea nodded to her right and they understood: they tossed it to the side.

They peeled themselves off each other and stood up. Brooke and

Danni did the same and hurried towards them. The fire was almost on them; there was a wall of intense heat and smoke pushing their backs.

Alicia got to the patio doors and gulped in cool air. The rest followed and they all bundled out onto the decking. Rhea was last. She saw Benjamin's spectacles on the floor; she crushed them hard under her foot. It wasn't enough. She needed more. She screamed and stamped again, and again. Kieran deserved better. She reached down and picked up the axe, heavy with Benjamin's monstrous, lifeless head. She hadn't time for insults or recriminations. She just swore at it and hurled it into the blaze. Then the fire blew towards her and she almost felt its embrace.

She ran out into the night air.

Straight into a vicious slap across the face.

CHAPTER TWENTY-FIVE

'You killed Hayley, you bitch!' Alicia's hand was stinging but she gave it to Rhea again.

Rhea recoiled, but took it without retaliation. She pointed towards the parked cars. 'We should get safe.' As if to punctuate the point, half of the annex collapsed behind her, sending a giant plume of fire and smoke into the night.

They pushed through the gate and then fought through some low shrubbery to get to the relative safety of the gravel. It was clear though from how they gathered that there was a divide: the two couples on one side of it, nearest the vehicles, and Rhea on her own with her back to the blaze.

'Why did you do it?' Elliot asked, wiping sweat from his brow with his sleeve.

Rhea pointed over her shoulder. 'What? Hayley? Wasn't it obvious? I saw a chance for him to drop his guard and I took it.'

'But you killed her!' Alicia repeated.

'Honey, she was ten minutes from being dead anyway – we couldn't have saved her.'

Brook shook her head. 'You don't know that.'

'That piece of shit was letting her die; he knew there was no hope for her. And let's not forget it was one of you that punctured her gut in the first place.'

Alicia was spitting. 'Don't you dare put the blame anywhere else!'

Rhea couldn't believe it. How could they not see that she'd done exactly as she had to in order to get them out of there? Distracted him, rescued the axe from its hiding place under the settee, took his motherfucking head off.

She cocked her head and pointed to the sky. 'Listen.' In the distance, the thin wail of sirens. Help was coming – probably all three of the emergency services. *She* did that; how could they not be grateful?

Instead it was spite. Brooke jabbed a finger at her. 'Just stay the fuck away from us, killer. You're going to prison for this.'

'What? I saved your arses!'

Elliot got in the middle and mediated. 'Come on – let's not be too hasty. The important thing is that we're safe and help is coming. Brooke, you just need to concentrate on that arm, and we've all got lungs full of smoke that'll need attention. When the police ask we obviously can't say vampire, but we do need to put all of this on Benjamin. *All* of this! Hayley brought a psycho with her, and he tried to kill us all.' He walked across to the last of the parked cars, Kieran's Audi. There were still frozen bodies behind it. 'It was him, just him.'

Rhea walked in his direction, giving the others a wide berth. It meant she was able to see Danni for the first time; she'd been quiet since they'd left the annex.

That was because she was more interested in her clothing. They were all covered, in varying degrees, with Benjamin's blood. However, Danni wasn't picking at it with disgust. Instead she was finding the dampest swatches and squeezing them into her cupped palm.

Rhea trotted over and managed to slap Danni's hand away before she put it to her lips. Her look was one of disappointment rather than rage.

Alicia had enough of that for everyone. 'Will you just fucking stop?' She ran over and gave Rhea a shove.

Rhea took the momentum and went with it, turning it into a jog. *Fuck 'em*, she thought. *Sorry, Kieran.* As she passed Elliot going the other way towards Danni, she offered: 'She wouldn't have made it 'til morning, you know that, right?'

He gave a little nod. 'I know.'

'And she can't do any more of that shit.'

'I'll help her.' He reached Danni and grabbed both her hands.

Rhea had to get out of there. She knew the tyres on Kieran's car were done, and because of that she'd struggle to get the Audi off the drive, let alone out of the country. *And then there's the tricky multi-point turn to pull off in order to avoid the dead bodies.* She spied Benjamin's

Volvo, where he'd reversed it near the other side of the house. Could he have left the keys in there? It was possible. Arrogance, hubris – he might have thought he was in complete control and there was no danger of anyone taking his car without him eating them first. She ran towards it.

No such luck. He'd taken the precaution after all. The keys were currently melting in the pocket of his grey slacks. Not that it really mattered. *Because I'm still taking it, you headless, barbequed, bloodsucking freak.* She fished out the vegetable peeler from her pocket and jabbed it at the underside of the steering column. She knew how to hotwire a car, particularly one as old as this.

By the other parked cars, Elliot was trying to get through to Danni. 'You're doing great. Good, at least.' He grinned.

She gave him nothing back, but looked longingly at the stains on her clothes and tried to pull her wrists away from his hands. Her body temperature was rising again.

The sirens were getting louder but still not on top of them. The other two linked arms and stared at Rhea in the Volvo. Brooke was just about to shout something when the car jolted forward.

Rhea drove it ten metres, then stopped. She looked in the rear view mirror, to see if any of the others might call her back. They stood, impassive, just catching their collective breaths. Elliot was holding Danni's hands, keeping her still.

She got out of the car, but not to address them again. Rhea Bennett was not someone who pleaded. Instead she took a couple of steps across to where the plastic bag of electronic hardware still dangled. Danni's poker was on the ground. Rhea tore it from the frozen grass then used it to tear a large hole in the base of the bag. A cascade of phones, keys and snow followed. And the ignition cylinder from Brooke's VW. Rhea crouched and easier located her Samsung: the lime green case gave it away. She rammed the poker in the earth and went back to the car. The others hadn't moved from their positions.

Rhea shoved it back into first and accelerated away, throwing up gravel and snow.

She got to the edge of the property and turned left onto the road, just as a cavalcade of fire engines and ambulances approached from the right.

She put Kilbride House behind her as quickly as she could.

NO ONE IS LEAVING

EPILOGUE

They'd been at the Queen Elizabeth University Hospital in Glasgow for three days. Elliot had had to call in some favours back home to keep the children looked after; thankfully friends and family were more than happy to help. He was actually able to be discharged today, but Danni not so. He was going to stay in Scotland for a while longer, hopefully till she was better.

They weren't 100% sure what was wrong with her. They were running dozens of tests. So far they knew it was an issue with her blood. She'd already had one transfusion and was being scheduled for another. In layman's terms, they'd said to him they had to take the bad stuff out and put the good stuff in. He just prayed it would be enough.

He was sitting in the hospital café, waiting for Brooke and Alicia to join him. They were going home today; there was to be coffee, cake and goodbyes. The two women were currently in the queue with their cafeteria trays. Once they were sufficiently laden and the items paid for, they joined him.

Brooke skilfully handled her loaded tray, despite having one arm fully cocooned in a cast. It looked like Alicia or somebody had already graffitied it with a rude drawing. Alicia sat down first, placed her items, and then relieved Brooke of hers. 'Team work makes the dream work,' she said, prompting Brooke to roll her eyes. Once they were both seated, they grinned at him.

'How's Danni?' Alicia asked.

'Getting there, I think. Let's see what the next few days hold.'

Brooke whispered. 'Have they got a name for it?' She didn't add: *other than vampirism?*

'They're probably making one up as we speak. They're... cleaning her blood up, and she's responding, so...' He shrugged.

'So fingers crossed,' Alicia said. She reached across and patted his hand. She kept it there for a few seconds longer and added: 'Have

194

you had that detective inspector, Campbell, round again this morning?'

'No, just yesterday...'

'Hmmm... Perhaps it's because they know you're staying for a while. Us, we've had another grilling to send us on our way.'

'You kept it to what we agreed?'

In the couple of minutes between Rhea's departure and them being attended to by the vital and efficient emergency service crews, they'd concocted a loose story. They'd watched Rhea go, and agreed they'd have no choice but to mention her to the authorities as she would have been spotted leaving. In the end they decided they would offer only her first name, and say she had been scared and panicked, driving off without thinking about any of the others. It made her a slight villain, a coward, but not a culprit. Not a killer. That was Benjamin. In the pursuit of his remaining prey he had set fire to the annex, and then foolishly got himself caught in the blaze.

Not a culprit. Not a killer. Alicia still found that a sore point. She couldn't shake the image burnt into her brain of Rhea ferociously forcing a stake into her friend's chest.

Already dying friend, Elliot had reminded her more than once across the last few days.

'They're becoming more focused on Benjamin,' Brooke said. 'They're buying the idea that we found out more about him because his backstory was more interesting.' They had shared with the police his surname, his connection to Hayley, and what they remembered about his job in Edinburgh and his origins in Romania.

'Did they push you on why you thought he did it?' Elliot asked.

'We towed the party line of: *how the hell should we know? We're not insane psychopaths.* It seemed to work.'

Elliot nodded slowly. 'I imagine they're not going to leave us alone for a good while yet.' He took a sip of coffee as they all considered what that might mean. No one really felt like eating cake.

When Elliot put his mug down, he leaned in towards them. 'Listen, I want to make something clear to you both. Whatever we think about what Rhea did, I know now that Danni couldn't have waited until the sun came up for us to find our phones and call for help. She had... an episode in the ambulance.'

He explained that once the two of them had got into the back with the paramedics, Danni had tried to ingest Benjamin's blood again. She fought against them when they prevented her, to the point where Elliot had to intervene, and not on the side of his wife. He managed to strip her of the bloodiest clothes and they got her strapped to the bed. By the time they reached the hospital forty minutes later, she looked like she'd lost ten pounds. By the time she was in the ICU she looked like the shell of a human. It took fresh blood to bring her back.

Elliot sighed and rubbed the back of his head. 'It was still dark when they stabilised her. Rhea made that possible.' When he looked up there were tears in his eyes. 'Had we waited 'til sunrise she would have died. I think we all would have died.'

Alicia was breaking up a flapjack with her fingers, a little too forcefully. 'Don't worry: I won't mention her and Hayley in the same breath.'

They each returned to their drinks and their thoughts.

A moment later they were sitting to attention: across the café, the detective inspector they'd spoken to previously was approaching, accompanied by a uniformed female constable. The detective wore a creased, brown suit and a loose tie at his flabby neck.

He grinned when he reached the table. 'Our Kilbride House survivors! How's it going?'

Brooke sneered. 'Same as it was a couple of hours ago.'

'Right enough, I guess there's not much gonna change inside a coupla hours in the hospital. In policing though, that's a long time. How about yourself, Mr Tilson? How are you and the wife?'

'I'm fine. Danni's stable. Hopefully she'll be okay.'

'Well, isn't that the best news? I hope she makes a full recovery.'

Elliot thanked him and returned to his drink. Alicia picked things up. 'So has something happened in the last couple of hours?'

The question prompted the detective to pull up a chair and sit. His constable stood behind him. 'Do you know, it has! We've got some information to share about your friend, Rhea.' He pulled a crumpled piece of paper out of his inside jacket pocket at the same time as Brooke pointed out that they weren't really friends. Campbell nodded but didn't really entertain it.

'First though, I need to admit to holding a little bit of something back from you all.' The three of them looked at each other, and tried hard not to appear nervous. Time to try the cake and flapjack: that's what relaxed people would do.

The detective smoothed out his piece of paper on the table. 'We actually found this yesterday. In the recycling box outside the house. I'm surprised none of you remembered it.'

Elliot recognised it immediately. It was a copy of the guest list Justin had placed on the dining table on the first night. *Christ, when am I supposed to grieve for him? He was my oldest friend...*

'*Alumni and Arseholes.* Very amusing. I guess Benjamin Bălan counts as one of the arseholes. What about Rhea Bennett?' He pointed to her name on the paper. 'There it is, her surname, plain as day. And none of you remembered it?'

'It's... pretty ordinary.' Alicia offered.

'Tell me about it. I'm a Campbell, remember? They're two a penny up here.' He smiled again. His constable remained neutral in her expression. 'Okay,' Campbell continued. 'You didn't remember her name. We kept hold of that for a wee while just in case it came back to you. So, let's play a game of what else you don't know.'

Elliot started to tidy up his crockery. 'I don't really have time for games; I need to get back to Danni.'

'Of course. So I'll make this quick. Do you actually have any idea who Rhea Bennett is?'

They shook their heads.

Campbell encouraged the constable to be ready to take notes. Then he pushed them again. 'She was at the house as the plus-one of Kieran Mooney? What did they say about her background? Did they say how they met?'

Alicia suggested tentatively: 'She was working as a waitress?'

Campbell smirked. 'What? In a cocktail bar? Like in that old *Human League* song?'

Elliot sucked his teeth. 'We, erm... we sang a couple of verses and choruses of that around the dining table.'

'And you still believed them after all that? Okay... do you know what? I'm beginning to think you don't know anything more than what you've told us.'

Brooke shrugged. 'We... we don't.'

'So let me tell you what I do know. She is the daughter of Colonel Felix Bennett of the Royal Marines. She served herself too, for five years, signed up as soon as they let women in. It's unclear in what capacity though; a number of her postings are *classified*.' Campbell's eyes widened as if he was a teacher engaging children in a mystery story. When no one pulled the thread he'd dangled, he added another. 'We've also traced Rhea Bennett's whereabouts. Sort of. We don't know exactly *where* she is, but we know where she's gone. Since she drove away from Kilbride House in the wee hours of Monday morning she's been on three aeroplanes. The last one touched down in Cluj-Napoca. Now what do you suppose we should make of that?'

They each in their different ways said that they had no clue.

'Of course, Bălan was Romanian, and the man who allegedly killed the victims at Kilbride. Does this mean she was in on it, do you think? Is Bennett an *Arsehole* too?'

'No,' said Elliot. 'There's absolutely no way. She fought him as hard as any of us.'

'But then she ran away scared? This ex-royal marine?'

'I... I can't say what went through her mind at the end.'

'No, I suppose not. How can we every really know anyone, right?'

'I just know she's definitely not in Romania because she was somehow like him. Or with him.' Elliot thought he knew exactly why she was there. What was it Benjamin had said? *I know of three other Vampyri in Cluj.*

'So let me just check I've got this straight. You met this woman on Friday, were in her company for two days, didn't remember her name but categorically know she's not like Bălan?'

Alicia interjected. 'It was a hard two days. We *know*.'

The constable's pen stopped scribbling and she spoke for the first time; monotone, almost disinterested. 'Maybe she's not like Bălan because he's actually innocent and she's the killer.'

Their denials were vociferous.

Campbell placated them. 'Hennessey here is just throwing ideas around. Your statements are strong; they line up so nicely. We think we have the picture, or at least most of the pieces. I suppose we just need Rhea Bennett.'

'So you're going to Romania?' Brooke asked.

'Oh no – our budgets don't stretch that far. We'll file our reports, put the information through the right channels... but I imagine we'll just wait until she comes back from her... *holiday*. Yeah, let's call it a holiday.' He pushed his chair back and stood. 'No doubt we'll be in touch, but if anything else comes to mind that you think is important, do let us know.'

They agreed, were cordial, shook hands and everyone was wished well.

Once the detective had left, they continued to converse in whispers. 'What the fuck is she playing at?' Brooke asked.

'If we're lucky,' Elliot replied. 'We'll never find out. For us, this is done. I need to go and see Danni.' He stood up and held out his arms for a hug. Alicia met him first, and then Brooke – careful with her cast.

'The police'll be back, you know.'

'That doesn't matter,' he replied. 'We've done nothing wrong, and other than not giving her full name we've been completely honest. We've just got to get on with our lives.'

Brooke kissed him on the cheek. 'Give our love to Danni. I hope she's okay.'

He nodded, and Alicia hugged him again.

**

They left the café together, but parted in the hall.

Back on the ward, Elliot was pleased to see Danni sitting up in bed. There was some colour in her cheeks, more vitality in her presence. She was smiling at her phone. When she saw him she tilted the handset in his direction. 'It's the kids; Gracie has sent a dance and Harry has been destroying that drum kit he got at Christmas. They're doing great.'

Elliot found her foot under the covers and gave it a squeeze. 'And so are you.'

She smiled again but this time her face looked a little strained. Closer inspection revealed the smudge of shadows under her eyes and her lips were paler than usual. 'Not yet. But I think I will be.' Then she added, a little mischievously. 'Good, at least.'

He grinned. 'Adequate.'

'Mediocre.'

'Satisfactory.' His hand had now tracked her contours to her waist.

'Average.'

'Stuck in the middle...' They said the last two words together. 'With you.'

He kissed her, and then encouraged her to shuffle over. Elliot climbed up onto the bed and together they watched the videos their children had sent them.

THE END

Translated from the edition of the newspaper România liberă *published on February 20ᵗʰ 2023:*

HEADLESS BODY FOUND IN CLUJ

The headless body of an unidentified man was discovered yesterday in the Zorilor district of Cluj-Napoca. Police have said they are following leads but have yet to release any key information, including any knowledge of the deceased. All that is known is that he was a well-dressed man, and the identification papers found upon his person were alleged to be falsified.

The body was discovered in a dumpster just off Strada Meteor. The head has yet to be recovered. Police are urging residents not to panic and see this as a gangland-style slaying or an example of criminal enterprise gone wrong.

They do not anticipate any repeat of what they are describing as a 'disturbing yet wholly unique incident'…

ABOUT THE AUTHOR

Stephen Barnard has been writing fiction (and non-fiction cricket exploits) for a number of years. The success of his short story collection 'A Very Bad Year' encouraged him to push further. He now has over 15 published works, mainly in the horror/suspense genre. When he's not writing he teaches, reads, snoozes and binge-watches horror films.

Printed in Great Britain
by Amazon